On Silver Shores

by V.T. Hoang

D1736131

For my therapist–

This is what I did instead of seeing you. My bad.

TABLE OF CONTENTS

Content warnings available at the end of the book.

CHAPTER ONE

Carver was one hundred sixty-four years old—much too young to die. But then again, that had never stopped him from trying to throw himself into death's embrace. This time seemed promising enough, as he bled onto damp concrete. A dark sky hung overhead. Thunder rumbled distantly. Raindrops fell on him and diluted the crimson streams flowing from the hole in his chest.

One of his lungs had collapsed. The other was full of blood. He could normally hold his breath for forty-five minutes—maybe fifteen with blood loss—so breathing wasn't as big an issue as the poison metal in his chest. It burned like someone had lit a fire between his ribs, and it prevented him from healing. Maybe he really would die here.

No, he'd never be that lucky.

He glanced to his side where his attacker lay unmoving. The giant wolf looked out of place, lying dead on a green lawn in the suburbs. Her gray fur was soaked. Blood still seeped from where Carver's knife was lodged in her neck. Her gun lay in the grass by her hind legs. She'd shot him while still in humanoid form, and then transitioned into a wolf after he'd knocked the weapon from her hands. Her claws had taken a decent chunk out of his leg.

All the houses around them were dark and quiet. The low, distant rumble of thunder sounded overhead, followed by a flash of light and another boom.

"The storm should have concealed the gunshot."

Thomas' deep voice floated through the air before he crouched down. The rain didn't touch him. His white button-down was dry, and the dark trousers held up by black suspenders didn't have a drop of water on them. Silvery lines cut through his umber skin along his forearms. Soft streaks of gray twisted through his beard and in the short, black curls atop his head. Gentle, brown eyes peered down at Carver.

"I did tell you not to go alone, love," Thomas said softly. "You get shot far too much."

Carver pointedly stared up at the sky, away from his husband.

"Oh, are you going to pout now about this entirely predictable and preventable state of affairs?"

Carver's indignant grunt made blood well from his mouth.

Thomas' eyes flicked up before he disappeared from view at the next flash of lightning. As thunder boomed and then faded, the click of high heels over wet pavement joined the patter of the rain.

"Oh, dear. What have we here?"

The smoky voice wrapped in an Imperial accent reminded Carver of whiskey and fire and sin—all things the Professor often indulged in. He peered up at her. A black trench coat hung from her shoulders. Red stilettos covered her dainty feet. A matching red dress hugged

2

every curve of her figure. She didn't look older than twenty-five, like most preternaturals. In truth, she was forty-one times Carver's age. The rain had soaked her short, black hair, so it fell over her right eye. Her irises were almost gold — a light amber that wasn't natural. Carver could never stare at them too long. There was something incredibly ancient about her eyes, as if they had witnessed the rise and downfall of empires. They probably had.

His boss always knew how to make an entrance. They'd only been working together for six months now, but she had already made an impression so profound that just looking at her filled him with equal parts exasperation and relief. It was unexpected really. He hadn't felt much of anything for the better part of a century, yet this enigmatic woman had inspired a sort of aggravated, begrudging fondness in him. Perhaps he should have been more respectful. She was one of the oldest creatures walking the earth. He must have seemed an infant to her, and yet she went through life with an almost childlike delight. She was probably amused by this whole situation.

"Would you like a hand, dear boy?" she asked with her usual cheer.

"Grgh," Carver gurgled, which roughly meant 'What the fuck do you think?'

"So sassy," the Professor muttered and bent over him.

He mentally braced himself when she pressed her hand against the hole in his chest. Two fingers slid into the wound, and an involuntary convulsion compressed his throat. He wanted to scream, but the only thing that escaped him was blood. It dribbled out of his mouth as fresh pain spread through his chest.

"Easy," the Professor said gently.

She dug deeper and deeper until she grasped the twisted metal lodged in his lung.

The burn of the bullet, paired with the pressure of her fingers, made Carver's vision blacken. She was careful in easing the metal from him. The moment it left his body, iciness filled his chest, easing the pressure in it. Rain soaked into the wound. His collapsed lung healed in an instant. The shredded flesh of his chest mended together with the water's aid. Carver found the strength to turn onto his side and cough out the blood from his lungs.

"Feel better?" the Professor asked, even though she knew the answer. "You're lucky it's raining. I hate having to break open fire hydrants for you."

"I appreciate your help," he grumbled unappreciatively.

"Yes, well, I was having a lovely evening with my partners at a soiree when you called." She glanced at the dead lycanthrope. "It seems you didn't really need me anyway."

Carver arched a brow. "I was shot."

"Oh, did you not want to die?"

He paused a moment, considering the question, and then shrugged. She had him there.

"Sometimes I don't know when you're joking," she muttered with a sigh.

That made two of them.

She pulled him to his feet when he finished coughing up blood. He shuffled toward the wolf and crouched to inspect her body. In this form, she rivaled him in length at over six feet, and she was probably twice his weight in muscle alone. He pulled his knife from her neck and wiped the blade on his pants before sliding it into the holster at his hip. The blood that welled in the open wound dyed her fur bright red.

"This is the one that escaped the prison transport, isn't it?" the Professor said as she stepped around the wolf.

Carver nodded. "She was incorrectly tagged as a vampire. Sonic restraints did nothing, and she got out."

He coughed. Blood welled up his throat and burned through his nose. His hands shook as he wiped at his face and stood on unsteady feet.

"I need to get back to the Court," he muttered, thinking of all the paperwork he'd have to fill out for this incident. "I didn't get anything out of the wolf before we fought."

The Professor looked him over. "My dear, please know I mean this with the utmost respect, but you look like a drowned rat. You're going to go home and rest. I will go to the Court and complete your paperwork."

He grimaced, annoyed at being dismissed so readily. "I'm fine now. The rain—"

"Is insufficient. I know how hungry you are, dear. You are not your best, and you will not be until you feed." She waved a hand dismissively at him. "Go rest. That is an order."

Once again, Carver coughed up blood, his traitorous body

struggling to heal completely.

"Fine," he bit out.

"And do clean yourself up," the Professor said and peeled the bloody lapel of his duster from his shirt. "I think this outfit might be done for."

He glanced down at himself. Dirt and blood covered his rain-soaked clothes. He lifted his hands. The blue and gold webbing between his fingers had extended up to the top knuckles from prolonged contact with water. A waxy sheen coated his umber skin. The lightened line around his ring finger made his stomach drop. His wedding band must have fallen off in the fight, but he couldn't say when. If it was anywhere nearby, the cleaning crew would find it. And if they didn't... Well, maybe that was for the best.

When he looked up at the Professor, Thomas stood a few paces behind her, staring at Carver's hand.

"That's going to sting," Thomas commented with a tilt of his head. "Impressive line on that finger, too."

The Professor followed Carver's gaze to look back over her shoulder. Her eyes narrowed before she returned her attention to him.

"What are you looking at?" she asked.

Carver shook his head and ran a hand over his eyes. Thomas was gone when he could see again.

"Nothing, just tired," he mumbled.

He turned without another word and headed down the sidewalk. His chest throbbed a bit, but his skin was still sucking in water. A

6

bath would do some good.

His automobile was where he'd left it in front of a beige ranch-style house. The nondescript black hatchback had a blocky body with a spare tire on the back. It was just two years old and already had 50,000 miles on it from his biannual visits up north. His sister kept telling him to fly out, but she also hated air travel.

He climbed into his automobile and started it up. The headlights flicked on—though he didn't need them. His eyes were designed to see into the dark depths of the ocean. Unfortunately, human cops would be wary of an auto driving through a rainy night without its headlights on, and looking as he did now, Carver would end the night with another bullet in him if he were pulled over.

"You ever going to tell her about me?" Thomas asked from the passenger seat.

Carver jumped at his husband's sudden appearance and then let out a breath through his teeth.

"It's none of her business," he muttered. "Can I just drive in peace?"

Thomas waved a hand dismissively, but didn't say anything else. He just stared out the rain-spattered window. Carver pulled away from the curb.

The streets of Vespera Bay were a maze of winding roads through uneven hills. Most of the houses were reminiscent of the colonial era, all smooth columns and boxy shapes. Honestly, they reminded him of his old home in Havitzford back in the 1700s. He'd built it with his own hands for his husband and sister. Maybe it was still standing.

His apartment complex was a rectangular mass of brick and bronze fixings. A rusted walkway led up to the second level apartments. Each door was maroon. An overhang shielded them from the rain, but puddles still amassed on uneven sections of the walkway. The first floor looked much the same. Venetian blinds hid everything beyond them in the little windows beside the doors. Across from the building was an autoport, with numbers over the spaces corresponding to the apartments.

Carver parked in space 103 and got out. His hands were shaking while he pulled his keys from his pants pocket. There was always a slight tremor in his limbs, but it got worse whenever he was starving. How long had it been since he'd last fed? Two months? The recommended frequency of feeding for sirens was at least once a week. But he didn't feel the drive anymore. The primal lust, that delicious urge to gorge on pleasure, had been absent since 1811. The irony of it wasn't lost on him. He was a siren, yet had spent more of his years than not disinterested in sex.

His apartment was on the first floor. He struggled to get his key into the lock from the shaking in his hands. The hunger was reaching a point where it wouldn't be ignored. If he didn't feed soon, his instincts would take over, and he'd ravage the nearest man in sight. That was unacceptable, even if the person likely wouldn't have protested. A siren's allure was near impossible to resist. Even so, rape wasn't on Carver's list of sins. He preferred to keep it that way.

Hardwood floors and sepia walls formed his apartment's interior. It was wide and open, with a kitchen in one corner and a dining area beside it. A chocolate leather couch sat on the opposite side of the room. The door near the dining area led to the bedroom. It wasn't much, but it was home.

"Mrao."

He looked down at a black cat. She wound between his ankles while he stepped in and closed the door after himself.

"Hi, Mouna," he murmured. "Sorry for being late. Are you hungry?"

Mouna was a tiny thing, barely eight pounds, with bright green eyes. She mewled at him and rubbed her head into his ankle. He smiled and headed to the fridge. A half-empty can of cat food sat on the top shelf. Mouna paced at his feet while he took out a plate and emptied the can onto it. She sniffed it for a while when he set it on the floor, but eventually took a bite.

He headed for the bathroom next to the living area. It was impeccably clean, as he liked to keep it. There wasn't even a toothpaste glob in the sink. The floor tiles were a pristine white. Unblemished, olive green paint colored the walls. A phone hung above the toilet.

The mirror hanging over the sink showed the mess of tight curls atop his head. Just a century ago, he'd had to hide his natural blue hair, highlighted with bright splashes of blond. The world had changed significantly in that time, for the better in some ways. It wasn't so long ago that his dark skin would have been regarded with outright hostility, rather than the insidious hostility of the modern age. The Republic's racial notions were so odd—had been for several centuries. At least no one called him a mulatto anymore.

Pain abruptly shot from his ring finger to his shoulder. He rubbed the pale line around the digit with a curse. The pulses would be worse tomorrow. With any luck, they wouldn't distract him from work, but eventually, in a few weeks maybe, he'd have to cut off the finger. If he didn't, his nervous system would keep increasing the pain until he wouldn't be able to function.

Thomas appeared in the bathroom entryway. He leaned on the doorframe with his arms crossed.

"The ring got pulled off in the fight with the wolf," he said. "You could go back to look for it, unless you're set on cutting off that finger."

Carver ignored the comment and peeled his clothes off, leaving them in a heap on the floor. The waxy film on his skin shimmered. It was an automatic reaction to water, meant to decrease drag in the ocean. The film withered in the air, but never fully went away.

He stepped into the tub before turning on the showerhead. The spray was cold, as he preferred. Hot water for his kind was usually dangerous. Sirens preferred temperatures sub 70 degrees, which was why Vespera Bay was a convenient place to live. It rarely got above 80.

His shower was brief, intended only to scrub the dirt and blood off him, and then he switched over to the bath faucet and clicked the drain stopper in. A mason jar with sea salt sat on a corner of the tub. He poured a fair amount in the water before sitting down. Saltwater baths never felt like enough compared to the ocean's embrace, but they were better than nothing.

Thunder shook through the floor and walls. The rainy season was starting up again. There were always a handful of thunderstorms every year, none quite so powerful or long as the ones on the southern coast, but the west in general had fairer weather. Earthquakes were far more dangerous here.

Carver ran his webbed hands through the water. The edges of his long fingers had taken a soft blue color that matched the thin membranes between them. Gold flecks spotted the webbing. His toes, long by human standards, also had webbing between them. Submerged long enough, they'd elongate into proper fins.

His banding pattern was the same blue and gold as his mother. The colors streaked across his limbs and the sides of his torso where scales lay just beneath the skin. Spines a deep blue, almost black, decorated the backs of his arms and lined the center of his back. They had barbs at the ends of them with paralytic venom, meant to stall prey long enough to consume it. The fangs retracted into his gums were designed for tearing flesh from bone. He kept his nails trimmed, but left alone, they grew into claws.

A siren's strength didn't lie solely in their predatorial attributes, however. No, they were feared for their allure. Everything about them, from their lean physiques to their perfectly symmetrical faces to the music of their voices, was designed to attract. Pleasure of the flesh was their real sustenance, not the meat itself.

Thomas sat beside the tub with a heavy sigh. The gold band around his left ring finger shimmered in the dim overhead lights. The muscle of many years of labor corded along his forearms and strained against the fabric of his shirt. Calluses from swinging hammers to hot metal covered his palms.

"You need to feed soon," he remarked. "I'm sorry it can't be me."

Carver took a deep breath. The Court provided consorts for their siren employees. He had been resisting going, but with the gunshot wound, he would probably have to soon, lest he risk losing his control. The first couple times he'd fed after his mate died had felt like a betrayal. He'd vomited afterward. Time had lessened the revulsion, but had done little in returning Carver's appetite. It would have been easier if he'd died with his mate like most sirens.

Pain shot up his arm from his ring finger again, and he held his breath until the ache subsided. He hadn't taken off his ring for longer than a few seconds in the hundred twenty-five years he'd had it. But maybe this was for the best. He couldn't carry Thomas with him forever, as much as his body wanted it.

"Don't apologize," he whispered against his better judgement.

Engaging with the hallucination of his dead mate was cautioned against by every psychiatrist he'd had. If he were honest with himself, he felt lonelier when Thomas wasn't here—well, as *here* as here could be for a figment of his decaying imagination.

Thomas glanced askance at him. "I never wanted you to suffer for me like this. If I'd known it would have ended this way—"

"I would have married you anyway," Carver whispered. "I would have married you a million times over and died as many deaths."

Thomas didn't respond.

A moment later, a tinny chime rang through the apartment. He leaned over the edge of the tub and reached up to the phone above the toilet. The cord was exceptionally long, so he didn't need to leave the tub to hold the receiver to his ear.

"Carver," he answered with a sigh.

"Good evening." The deep, Imperial-accented voice of the Professor's husband sounded no less smooth through the phone as it did in person.

"Hello, Damian," Carver greeted with forced politeness. He was tired and feeling antisocial, but his manners wouldn't let him show it.

"My wife informed me that you were shot earlier," Damian explained, even though Carver knew exactly why he'd gotten a call.

Damian was the best doctor in the Republic—maybe in the world. At several thousand years old, he'd certainly had time to perfect his craft.

Carver glanced down at the pale, starburst scar over his pectoral where the bullet had torn through him. It had healed over already. The bath was only for comfort at this point. As a siren, Carver's vitality was tied intimately with water—perhaps even more than sex.

"I think I'm all right," he said. "I'm soaking in water right now."

"Good. Did you add salt to your bath?" Damian's clinical tone was oddly soothing.

"Yes." Carver ran his hand over the water absently. It rose to meet him gently like an old friend.

"Do you have any shortness of breath or dizziness?"

"No."

"Chest pain?"

"No."

"Irregular heartbeats?"

"No."

Carver kept answering all of Damian's questions until the Professor said something indistinct through the phone.

"I'd feel more comfortable if I could examine him in person," Damian muttered, and then after a pause: "What do you mean he's fine? He was *shot*."

"I am fine, Damian," Carver said, trying to sound reassuring and not irritated. "I'll let you know if anything is wrong."

Damian sighed. "Call me if you experience any unusual symptoms."

"Wilco." Carver hung up and set the phone back in its cradle on the wall.

A minute had barely passed before it rang again. He sighed and pulled the phone to his ear.

"Is Damian coming over anyway?" he asked, confused as to why he was being pestered.

The Professor's chuckle crackled through the receiver.

"No, much to his dismay," she said, which prompted grumbling from Damian in the background. "I'm actually calling for business reasons."

Carver ran a hand over his face, wanting nothing more than to fall asleep in his tub and forget about the world for a while.

"Yeah, sure," he mumbled. "What's up?"

"The Superiors were impressed that you found the wolf tonight." The Professor drew out some of her words, as if she were contemplating something. "They're less thrilled that she's dead, and you got nothing out of her about the Garsuk."

Carver sighed, anticipating this. The Garsuk were a group of extremist lycanthropes who believed in the eradication of all interracial unions. Being half-human himself, Carver was on their kill list, but it wasn't just human unions they hated. They opposed any mixing of the races—vampires, sirens, fae, wolves, demons, shifters, or otherwise. A faction in the West had been hunting interracial preterns for a couple years, but they were too splintered to be much of a threat. Recent evidence suggested an organized unit had sprung up in a nearby city. The wolf Carver had killed was allegedly part of that unit, and now he'd never be able to confirm it one way or the other.

"I'm calling in an analyst," the Professor continued. "Hopefully, he can help us get another lead with what we have."

Carver frowned, disliking the idea of working with someone new. He got along with the Professor well enough, but he still preferred solitude.

"What analyst?" he asked.

"Jian used to be a senior member of the Court," the Professor explained, "but don't be fooled by the 'senior' part. He's a decade or so younger than you."

Carver probably should have held his tongue, but the Professor had always encouraged him to speak his mind. So he said, "I don't know if it's a good idea to bring an analyst in. We already have a lot to work with, and he may just slow us down by trying to find out things we already know."

"Not this analyst." The Professor sounded confident, which was more reassuring than Carver cared to admit. "He was a commander in the Red Army. He understands practicality."

The Red Army was known for being as skillful as they were ruthless on the battlefield. Analysts worked at a desk. What a dramatic change in career.

"Why did he go from commander to analyst?" Carver asked, expecting anything from crippling injuries to PTSD.

"It's not my story to tell." The Professor paused a long moment, as if in thought. "Jian acts open and friendly, but he's harder to read than an oral language. So, naturally, I'm sure you two will get along swimmingly."

Carver elected to ignore that comment. "How can he help us?"

"His specialty is hunting people. If anyone can locate the Garsuk, it's him."

Thunder rumbled over the receiver.

"He hates this time of year," the Professor added softly.

Carver glanced at the rain-spattered window beside the showerhead. "Is he averse to water?"

"Well, he is a demon. Prolonged inundation in water would kill him, but that's not the only reason he hates the rainy season." The Professor sighed. "Never mind. You'll meet him yourself tomorrow."

"All right, then. I'll—" The pulse that seized Carver's arm was the strongest yet. He clutched his ring finger, tempted to rip the offending

16

appendage off right then.

"Fuck!" he hissed.

"Well, that's not a nice word." The Professor spoke lightly, but there was a note of real concern in her tone. "What's wrong?"

He breathed through the pain until it ebbed. "I lost my wedding band in the fight earlier. My nervous system is upset by the absence."

"Will you have to lose your finger?"

The softness of her voice irked him. People always looked on him with pity when they discovered his condition, like he really was as fractured as he felt—one splintered half of a whole, doomed to incompletion.

"Probably," he muttered and glared down at his finger.

"I'll ask the clean-up crew to look for the ring at the scene, but if they don't find it—"

"I'll be fine with one less finger."

His work was necessary as the only thing keeping him sane. If the Professor refused him now, he'd just move on to the next job, but he would have preferred not to. This one was the best he'd had in years.

The Professor let out a long breath, sending a puff of static through the receiver. "We will discuss continuing your work with me tomorrow."

That sounded like a threat, but before Carver could say as much, she added, "It's not a punishment, Carver, and when I say 'discussion,' I mean just that. I am honestly wondering if you are fit to continue working with the Court. You are always starving. You are always in pain. You are never going to recover."

Carver stared at the pale line on his finger, a deep ache as familiar as his shadow settling in his chest. Most sirens who survived their mate's death killed themselves within a couple days if they weren't cognitively crippled by the experience. He was arguably one of the lucky ones. His nervous system had endured the violent ripping of its other half to death's hand, and he'd come out the other side with only a tremor, chronic nerve pain, and an appetite that was somehow both insatiable and absent. That was the price of survival—to be a 'lucky one.'

He wasn't lucky at all.

"Do what's right for yourself, Carver," the Professor murmured.

He didn't respond—didn't know how when an old grief constricted around his neck and stole his breath.

The line clicked out of connection.

He leaned back, compressing his spines against the tub. He was supposed to be dead now. From the moment he'd said his vows to a human with a tenth of his lifespan, he'd been prepared to die an early death. But then it hadn't happened. And a century later, his choice had cursed him as an incurable illness.

The Professor was right. There was no recovery for him, just coping.

"Don't lose this job, love," Thomas said, but when Carver turned to look at him, there was only the empty bathroom.

CHAPTER TWO

Jian dropped his plate as thunder shook his house. Shards flew across the russet tile floor in a spray of blue ceramic. Rain struck the window over the sink. Light flashed across the glass just before a boom rattled the house again.

Logically, there was no reason to be afraid of thunder. It was only the sound lightning made, and regardless, Jian didn't fear being struck by a hundred million volts—as if it could do anything to him. No, the thunder, that booming roar, was what made his skin seem to shrink over his bones. It vibrated through his body until nothing else filled his ears. The fading rolls always brought screams with it until he wished the thunder would return to drown them out.

Another flash of light preceded a boom that shook the house's walls. A groan escaped his throat as he hunched over. The strands of dark hair that had escaped their tie fell in his eyes. His breaths came raggedly. Cold flashes shot through his body.

There was nothing different about his kitchen. Granite countertops, cream-colored walls, a pan of simmering vegetables on the stovetop—they hadn't changed. But maybe it was another illusion. Maybe the walls were really blood-spattered concrete. Maybe the vegetables were burning flesh.

No, that wasn't it.

Thunder boomed again. He focused on breathing, counting the beats he spent inhaling and exhaling. His nails dug into his forearm until his skin gave. With any luck, the wounds wouldn't scar. There were already so many scars in his skin, each with their own painful history. Most were covered by black tattoos. The newest scars broke the lines of ink that made a winding serpent up his shoulders. Cords of muscle along his arms flexed as he bit his nails deeper. The pain was easy to focus on. It was real and here—not an echo of the past.

Blood dripped down his arms.

The next bout of thunder made him jump away from the counter and pace through his kitchen. He pressed his hands over his ears, but it couldn't block out the screaming. The rumbles in the floor and through the walls crawled under his skin like parasites burrowing into him.

He jolted when his messenger buzzed in his pocket and pulled it out. It was little more than a black, metal rectangle with a thin screen above a keypad. A message projected over the top. The number tag on it belonged to the Professor.

You still out of commission?

His hands shook as he typed a reply. *No. What do you need?*

Technical support.

Send me a report.

I will. Cheers.

His messenger buzzed with a notification of an incoming package as thunder crashed again. Work was a welcome distraction. The Professor never came to him these days unless she was desperate, which meant a challenge for him.

He hurried to the small port in the wall beside his fridge. It had a long pipe with an opening at the base for a package to come out. A minute passed before a russet, cylindrical container emerged from the pipe with a soft pop. The Professor had insisted on creating a direct pneumatic tube to his house almost fifty years ago, and then that had expanded into a system that also connected to the High Court and all its smaller offices in the city. It hadn't seen much use since he returned from the war.

Thunder boomed overhead, and he froze for a moment to look around and remind himself that his surroundings were real. A glass coffee table in front of a bookcase. The worn leather couch that he'd had for years. His daughter's picture beneath a cracked window. The shards of the plate he'd just dropped on the floor.

He took the container to the couch and rubbed his arm. The friction generated enough heat to heal the skin. The little crescent marks in his forearms fleshed over until there was no trace of them.

The container hissed softly when he twisted the top off. A bundle of papers were rolled up inside, and he pried them out. The front page had CLASSIFIED in red, bold letters. At the top read: *Report Compiled by Dr. Idylla*. The Professor's winding, elegant script filled the pages.

Thunder crashed louder than it had before. The air seemed to vanish. Jian stood and sucked in a breath, then another…and another.

The room spun. He sat down again and held his head in his hands.

The phone hanging on the wall by his kitchen sink rang, making him jump. He padded over to it, but hesitated before picking it up.

"Jian," he answered, phone trembling against his ear.

"I almost forgot," the Professor said. "There's a storm going on right now."

"I didn't forget about it."

"Well, I know *you* didn't, darling. That's why I called." An indistinct voice said something in the background. "He's fine, Damian. Stop fussing over him."

Jian let out a slow breath. "Do you have company over?"

"No, my husband just won't stop being a doctor for two minutes. He's drilling my apprentice over the phone." The voice spoke again. "He's an able-bodied man, Damian. Let him rest."

"You have a new apprentice?"

"That I do. Detective Ernest Declan Carver. His name is more outdated than me."

"Impossible." Jian let go of his arm. His nails had punctured his skin again.

"Careful there. Don't say anything you'll regret." The Professor's tone was hard, but didn't have any real bite to it.

He made a sound that would have been a chuckle if it hadn't been so strangled. "You're seven thousand years old, Professor."

She groaned in distaste. "You make me sound ancient."

"You are." Jian relaxed with the familiarity of the conversation.

"Yes, but you don't have to point it out."

A flash of light preceded the loudest boom of thunder yet. Jian hunched over and squeezed his eyes shut, feeling as if he would vomit any second.

"*Ne hanet, ika,*" the Professor said softly. "*Kwr ta o shar nahan eru.*"

Jian had heard the Professor speak her native tongue before. It had an unusual cadence that had a calming, almost lulling effect when she spoke. He'd yet to hear another language like it.

"I'm fine," he mumbled.

"You're not fine." Her voice was gentle, but not pitying. "You're on the verge of a panic attack. I can hear it."

Thunder rumbled, softer than the last bout.

"The storm is passing," he said and forced himself to breathe through his nose.

"There was nothing you could do, *ika,*" the Professor reminded him—as if he didn't know, as if he didn't spend his waking hours with the knowledge pressing on him heavier than any weight could.

"That's what haunts me," he murmured, voice almost a rasp.

Thunder crashed when she asked, "Do you have any questions about the case?"

She was probably trying to distract him, which was welcome.

He rubbed his face. "I haven't had a chance to look over it yet."

"No matter. Here's the gist." She paused a moment, presumably to gather her thoughts. "We have reason to believe there's an organized Garsuk chapter in Astoria, but we keep killing our leads. So I think it's time we changed tactics, namely bringing in an expert."

Jian's brows rose. "I'm your expert?"

"I know your bounty hunter days are long past, but I wouldn't trust anyone else." Before he could reply, she added, "No, I'm not trying to recruit you to the Court again. This is strictly contract work."

Jian skimmed through the report in his hand. There were maps of Garsuk activity and some speculative notes from the Professor, but ultimately nothing substantial to go on. He'd need more to reveal the pattern, which probably wouldn't be hard. Wolves were the easiest race to track down, especially the Garsuk. If the paper trail didn't give them away, the trail of bodies did. There was something odd in the report, however, that had nothing to do with tracking wolf movements through cities.

"You've been betrayed," he said, seeing no other option.

The Professor didn't reply immediately. "How do you figure that?"

Thunder rumbled distantly. Jian tensed, but he forced himself to focus on the work more than the screaming in his head.

"It's stated in your report," he explained with only a slight tremor to his voice, "that a prisoner last month was logged as a wolf when she was first brought into the High Court. In the prison transfer order, her race is listed as vampire. So the guards didn't take the proper restraint measures, and she escaped as soon as the transport took off. If I recall correctly—and I do—transfer orders come directly from the Court's records database, which can only be changed by administrators. A change would be logged in the record unless someone circumvented the programming."

The Professor hummed tersely. "How do you know it's not just a program error?"

"The program doesn't make mistakes. I designed it."

She chuckled. "Well, besides you, there are only a couple people in the High Court who could tinker with the program."

The Garsuk had been rebuilding over the years, becoming less splintered factions and more cohesive. It wasn't inconceivable to think they had infiltrated the High Court. Still, the spy couldn't have been just anyone. They needed programming knowledge and, more importantly, the security clearance to access it. Someone had been playing the long con.

"It's a short list," he reasoned. "There are the archivist manager, the chief analyst, and the entirety of the tech department who could do this."

"Forget the tech department. I had Palus vet them, and none of them have strong ties to the Garsuk. The archivist manager and chief analyst do have connections."

Jian mentally rifled through what he knew of the archivist manager and chief analyst. Both were fullblood wolves. The archivist was slightly older at six hundred thirty, and she had several family members who were either current Garsuk or deceased Garsuk. The analyst was four hundred ninety, with a son who'd married into a known Garsuk pack. He didn't have any other evident connections.

The archivist was a solitary woman, preferring the company of the written word to people. She'd grown up in a Garsuk pack, if Jian remembered correctly, but had escaped and estranged herself from her family. It was possible that her family had finally caught up to her again.

By comparison, the analyst didn't have any personal connection to the Gars in his history. That his son had bound himself to a Gar wasn't necessarily an indictment on his parenting. Still, it took a special kind of bigot to cavort with genocidal terrorists. The son had to share Garsuk beliefs, and that might have been indicative of the beliefs he'd been raised with. Radicalization was much easier when the target already had some radical ideas.

Jian had trouble believing the archivist, who'd risked her life to leave a traumatic and dangerous situation, had returned to it. More likely, the analyst had some prejudicial thinking to begin with and passed it on to his son, who'd then taken the final step into violent extremism.

"Pretty sure it's the analyst," he said after a moment.

The Professor hummed tersely. "Just like that?"

"Doubting me now?"

"The best spies know the people they work with as well as their enemies, but it's been a couple years since we had you back."

"So what's our next step?" he prompted, eager to stop any discussion of his skills as a spy.

The Professor took a moment to respond. "I'll have the chief analyst brought down to the interrogation rooms tomorrow morning."

The next crash of thunder was soft enough that Jian could bear it. He breathed deeply.

"I can come in tomorrow morning to assist you," he offered, "if you need it."

"That would be wonderful," the Professor said.

Thunder drifted faintly through the receiver.

"I do believe the storm has come to me now," she continued softly. "Will you be all right, Jian? I'd hate to leave you in distress."

"I'll be all right," he said, only half-believing it.

'All right' had developed a different meaning to him in the last two years. It could mean anything from 'dissociating for hours' to 'only had two panic attacks today.'

The Professor whispered something in her native language, presumably not to him. A moment later, she said louder, "Take care of yourself, love."

Jian hung up and set his phone on the table. He glanced back at the door to the kitchen, wondering if he could hold down any food now.

Thunder rumbled and faded into the soft patter of rain, which was almost as bad. His stomach turned. He'd just have to give dinner to his neighbor again.

◊◊◊

The Professor came to Carver's apartment in the morning. He made himself presentable in a different duster, sans blood, and a navy blue button-down. The black jeans he'd paired with it were unusual for him since he usually wore slacks to work. The Professor said as much when he climbed into her automobile, but he only muttered that he'd ruined his last clean pair the night before, which prompted her to tease him about wearing nice clothes in a job that often required getting dirty.

Carver didn't like driving with the Professor. Her relentless teasing aside, she had a black sports auto that she insisted on zipping through Vespera at twenty to thirty miles per hour over the speed limit. The interior was all black leather and always smelled of pine and old earth—much like the Professor herself. He clutched the sides of his seat as she tore through the suburban, hilly streets far too quickly.

Thomas' reflection in the rearview mirror showed him sitting in the backseat. He stared out the window with a small smile.

"Can you imagine telling my father that automobiles could go this fast?" he remarked.

The Professor pulled something out of her jacket pocket, taking Carver's attention.

"Here," she said.

His heart skipped when he recognized the thin, gold band in her hand. He took it reluctantly and slid it over his finger. The throbbing in his hand dissipated almost instantly, and he resented the relief it brought.

"The clean-up crew couldn't find it," the Professor explained, "so I went looking for it myself."

He wasn't sure if he wanted to thank her or follow through with cutting off his finger. The wedding ring felt like a shackle now, and he would rather not have a finger than think of anything his mate had gifted him as restraining.

"You could chuck it out the window," Thomas suggested with a chuckle.

"I've been thinking," the Professor continued when Carver didn't speak. "You've handled yourself admirably well, given the circumstances, and I'm reluctant to pull you out of the Peacekeeper program."

Carver watched the houses fly by the window, something like determination burning in his chest.

"I really was prepared to cut off my finger," he said, "if that was what it took."

"I know you were." She glanced away from the windscreen to look him over. "You're strong, Carver, and in the ways that matter. I just don't want to see you tear yourself apart trying to do your work while managing your condition. Your health matters, too."

He would tear himself apart over anything if it was ultimately beneficial. The method of breaking his back didn't matter much, but the result did.

Thomas laughed. "Do you think she knows she's talking to the greatest martyr since Saipos?"

"I'll manage myself," Carver said stiffly, as much a promise to her as himself.

She glanced at him again and then nodded. "I'll hold you to it."

They fell silent, and Thomas thankfully didn't have anything else to add.

The Court was a large, spiraling building near the coast. The ocean stretched past the horizon behind it. In the interest of surviving earthquakes, it wasn't taller than ten stories, but massive nonetheless. Glass lined the outside, displaying people walking through the circular halls around the perimeter of each floor. The walls between the windows were white. A glass dome fit over the top where the Superiors resided.

As the head of the Interracial Court System, the High Court acted as the primary judicial power in all preternatural matters. The ICS was something of its own sovereign entity, in a way. It could challenge other preternatural governments, and while it tried to be a neutral party in world affairs, it also followed its own code of ethics and would intervene in the event of violations. The humans had a close equivalent with the Federation of Allied Nations, albeit the ICS was often more willing to use force to prevent or stop things like genocide and universal rights' violations.

The Professor pulled up to the iron gates in the wall encompassing the High Court and its parking lot. As she rolled down her window, Carver's arms and legs tingled, and a dull ache throbbed at the base of his skull. It was a familiar feeling. The neuropathy that persisted through his body made him numb on the best of days. The worst left his skin and bones ablaze, and it only got worse the longer he starved.

"Do you need breakfast?" the Professor asked, as if sensing his thoughts.

She pulled a white card from a pocket of her jacket and swiped it in front of a console beside the gate.

He cast a withering look at her. "I don't think I'll be able to feed for another day or so. The…desperation…hasn't set in."

She glanced at him sidelong. The gate slid open, and she drove into the parking lot. They stopped in a space near the front entrance that had "Special Persons" painted on it.

"You're not being a martyr again, are you?" she asked as they climbed out of the automobile. "You know you can take the first hour of work with the consorts, if you need it."

He grimaced. "I can't quite stomach feeding yet. Besides, I don't think this is an issue I can solve within an hour."

Her brows rose. "You need more than an hour of wild sex? Isn't three hours a week the recommendation?"

Maybe for normal sirens.

"I haven't fed in two months," he pointed out. "That's quite a few hours to make up."

Something reminiscent of sympathy crossed her face. "You hate every moment of it, don't you?"

He did. The consorts were kindly people, but his body only wanted his mate.

Her messenger beeped before he could reply.

"A moment," she mumbled and stepped away.

Carver leaned against the automobile and pulled his messenger out, figuring he could send a message of his own. The chat thread he pulled was at the top of his favorites list. He typed out a short: *Are you okay?*

There was no response, and there hadn't been in several weeks.

He sighed. Saoirse was probably on a deep undercover mission or something, but she usually found time to respond to him at least once a week.

He pocketed his messenger, feeling like a nagging parent. His sister was an adult and a better soldier than him. She could handle herself. Still, it was nice to talk with her every once in a while, and besides that, he was her older brother. Worrying about her was as innate as breathing.

"This isn't like her," Thomas commented, appearing beside Carver. "She's always been diligent about keeping in touch."

Carver closed his eyes and tried not to think of the anxiety in his gut or the tingling in his limbs. His senses drifted to the clouds. He didn't have an affinity for water that allowed him to control it like female sirens, but he always felt a connection to it. The water suspended in the air over him seemed to hum, some parts louder than others. They shifted and twisted and turned with the flow of the air. Another storm was coming.

"Carver," the Professor said, interrupting his thoughts.

He opened his eyes to see her standing directly in front of him. Her ability to move rapidly and silently never failed to unnerve him. He'd never been able to hear her coming, which wasn't characteristic of the fae she claimed to be part of. Fae couldn't cross vast distances in seconds or make entirely silent footfalls.

"I have to meet with the Superiors," she said, heedless of his alarm at her abrupt appearance. "Call the chief analyst down for interrogation, and I'll leave Jian in your hands for now."

He narrowed his eyes. "I hope you mean that figuratively," he muttered, suspecting she had ulterior motives. She always had ulterior motives.

"Maybe." She shrugged. "Jian has never been one to engage in meaningless sex, but he always finds ways to surprise me."

Carver was so tired. "What do the Superiors need you for?"

The Professor waved a hand. "It's some bullshit political nonsense that I need to weigh in on. Shouldn't take more than a couple minutes."

Carver bit back a question about why she, a Peacekeeper, was needed for a direct audience. The Superiors, especially the older ones, treated her almost reverently. They were supposed to be the leaders of the international community, the most wise and powerful of the preternaturals, but Carver had seen the almost worshipful way they regarded the Professor. She was probably older than all of them, too.

He sometimes suspected that she'd chosen him to be her apprentice only because his tenuous attachment to life ensured he'd neither revere nor fear her.

"I'll meet you and Jian for the interrogation," she continued. "Shouldn't be gone long enough to hear that you've jumped his bones."

"Jumped his…" Carver's brows lowered. "Professor, I have self-control."

Her lips twitched. "I don't doubt you, but he'd make a mess of you, given the chance."

Carver blinked. Rarely had anyone implied that he would be on the receiving end of things, and the few who had were all humans who didn't know the nature of sirens. The Professor definitely knew the nature of sirens.

"What do you mean he'd make a mess of me?" he asked, honestly perplexed by her assertion.

"Demons don't submit to sirens." Her smile was borderline a smirk. "They're emboldened by the allure. Jian is kindly, but he's no exception."

Thomas stepped out from behind her, staring at the front steps of the Court.

"You could use someone like that," he commented. "You always liked some pain with your pleasure."

Carver let out a long-suffering sigh. "I have no intention of seducing a colleague."

The Professor glanced over her shoulder, following Carver's gaze, and then mumbled, "Noted."

Before Carver could reply, she added, "See you in a bit, dear."

She disappeared, leaving only a whirl of dead leaves where she'd stood. Carver trotted up the marble front steps of the Court. He took his gloves off and stuffed them into a pocket of his duster as he stepped through the revolving door into the lobby.

Sandstone floors and vanilla walls formed the interior. Morning sunlight filtered through the windows lining one wall, casting warm light through the space. The help desk at the back had four clerks manning it. Lines of people stood in front of it. Every so often a clerk would stamp something and send the person they were helping away to continue their business. Most of the people in line were probably friends and family of the convicts held in the underground jail, looking to visit or pay bail.

A man stood off to the side of the help desk, chatting with one of the clerks. His black hair was tied back into a low ponytail. He wore a

34

leather jacket and baggy jeans. The combination should have obscured his form, but it only made his shoulders seem broader and hips slimmer. A hint of ink in his skin peeked out from the ends of his sleeves.

Carver stopped in his tracks as tingles rushed through him.

Well, fuck me, he thought tiredly.

Then just because his brain was a piece of shit, it added, *Please.*

He took a deep breath and reminded himself that this was neither the time nor place to be thinking about his primal needs. Somewhere in the rational part of his mind, Carver noted the man's attire was too informal for ICS staff, but he didn't seem like a civilian. The straight-backed way he stood and his muscular build indicated some kind of military training.

"—good to hear your kids are doing well," the man was saying, his voice becoming clear as Carver drew closer. "I was worried Michael would never grow into his chin."

The clerk laughed. She was a stout woman with wild, red hair and green eyes—Angie, if Carver remembered her name correctly.

"We were certainly surprised when he hit a growth spurt," she said with a smile. "His proportions righted themselves."

The man offered a small smile that showed teeth. Carver's heart inexplicably skipped a beat.

"Sorry to interrupt, Angie," he said as pleasantly as he could, "but the Professor is meeting with the Superiors. Is the chief analyst ready?"

Angie nodded, her face schooling into a serious expression. "I'll have him brought down, detective," she said immediately. "Shouldn't be more than a couple minutes."

The man looked Carver over. "A detective working with the Professor?" he mused, seemingly more to himself than anyone else. "Would you be Detective Carver?"

Carver didn't respond immediately, not from being surprised to hear his name on a stranger's lips, but because his name spoken with *that* voice made heat bloom in his chest. That siren-emboldened desire, the need to consume—to *take*—pulsed through him unbidden. He must have been closer to the end of his rope than he'd realized.

"You are?" he prompted, his voice lower than it normally was.

"Your analyst." The man offered a hand. "Jian."

When Carver shook the extended hand, that tingling sensation returned full force. He held his breath until he could let go.

"Carver," he mumbled, almost forgetting to give his name.

Upon closer inspection, gold ringed Jian's pupils, but the rest of his irises were brown. A couple strands of his hair had escaped their tie and hung around his face. Carver had the urge to sweep it back, but kept his hands firmly at his sides. Seducing a colleague was highly unprofessional and rude.

"The Professor spoke of you briefly," Jian said, "but she didn't mention you were a siren."

Carver tensed, hoping the hunger wasn't plain on his face. "How did you figure that out?"

"You're uncommonly tall, and your hair seems to naturally be that colorful. It matches your eyes." Jian had a small smile. "I'm guessing blue and yellow are your scale colors."

Relief rushed through Carver. Noticing biological traits was better than noticing hunger.

"Perceptive of you," he remarked and clasped his hands behind his back to resist the temptation of letting them wander.

"That's my job." Jian's eyes traveled over Carver much too deliberately for comfort. "A male siren. How did you manage that?"

It wasn't the first time Carver had been asked that, and he doubted it would be the last. He settled for the simplest explanation. "My human father contributed the Y chromosome."

"Remarkable." Jian spoke the one word almost breathlessly.

Carver couldn't determine if Jian thought of him as a genetic abnormality or a genetic miracle. Either way, he wanted to show this demon just how much of a siren he was.

Gods preserve him. Maybe he should have headed straight for the consorts.

His messenger buzzed, truncating his increasingly inappropriate thoughts. He pulled it from his pants' pocket.

The Professor had sent: *Taking a little longer.*

"Something wrong, detective?" Jian asked.

Carver pocketed his messenger with a grimace. "The Professor says she's going to take a while, so we have some time to kill."

"As per usual." Jian headed toward the front doors. "Probably enough time to get some coffee. Care to walk with me to the cafe across the street?"

Carver swallowed against the way his need seemed to roil in him with the thought of being alone with this demon.

"Yes, coffee would be nice," he said stiffly.

He stepped forward, and Jian matched his pace as they headed out.

Carver brushed his thumb over the gold ring on his left hand, hoping it would quell the ache in his gut.

It didn't.

◊◊◊

The rain came down in thick sheets. Occidental Reach wasn't as rainy as Balfour, but at this time of year, it could compete. It would hopefully wash away some of Saoirse's scent as she walked through the streets. Her wounds weren't healing, despite how much water poured over her. There was decay metal somewhere in her wounds. She hugged her jacket closer, trying to conceal the plethora of deep lacerations running in parallel lines across her chest and back. Her tank top was entirely soaked with water and blood.

Her blue dreads were tied high on her head. Water dripped steadily from them down her face and neck. The blue and gold scales that she and her brother had inherited from their mother glittered through her umber skin from water exposure. There weren't people around in this downpour to stumble on her. That was probably for the best. She just needed to get to her brother, and he'd patch her up, as he had when they were still Inquisitors together.

Why did Meallán have to live so far south? Vespera was still several dozen miles out. He couldn't have kept his shitty detective job in Palitz? The main ICS hub out there was so much smaller and closer.

No, he had to run off to the High Court and be apprenticed to the fucking Professor. Saoirse had half a mind to drag him up to Balfour to live with her again, just so she could keep an eye on him. The Peacekeepers were a decidedly better job than the Inquisitors, but not by much—not for the High Court.

Pain shot through her left eye, as it did periodically. The surrounding colonial-style houses blurred and then seemed to double and then triple. Their images overlayed each other until she was dizzy with it. She gripped the metal fence enclosing a house's yard to hold herself steady as she forced herself to breathe through the pain. She'd survived injuries that should have been fatal because of her left eye, but it had been hurting more than when she first got it.

The Gars had cornered her out in Asterna. She was normally better about checking for ambushes, but she hadn't expected to see Maeva of all people with them. The fae bitch herself had probably been hired by the Atlantean Ministry to track down and kill Saoirse. Maeva was almost certainly leading the Gar contingent now. They'd already chased Saoirse all the way down the western coast and wrecked her auto a few miles back. She probably would have died if not for her left eye mending the worst injuries. There would be more Gars coming. Maeva wasn't known for giving up.

The overlapping images didn't let up. Saoirse sank to her knees as she clutched her head. It seemed to be splitting from the inside out, like something was trapped in her skull and wanted freedom. Well, maybe that was true. The woman who'd offered her salvation had said that the gift wouldn't last forever. Saoirse needed to get to her brother. He was in danger, and she didn't have much left in her to keep going. She'd lost so much blood — more than she probably should have been able to survive without the eye sustaining her.

Zero degrees equaled zero. Fifteen degrees equaled point-two-seven-nine. Thirty degrees equaled point-five. Forty-five degrees equaled point-seven-zero-seven. Sixty degrees equaled point-eight —

Another pulse of pain through her head made her hunch over. She couldn't even focus on her sine degrees to distract herself. Fire seemed to sear through her skull, blocking all other thought until it subsided a minute later. She gasped in a breath against the ache in her broken ribs as soon as she could inhale again.

How much time did she have left? Days? Hours? Minutes?

She had to keep going.

Her legs seemed to scream in protest when she pulled herself to standing, but she made herself walk. The overlaying images of the buildings became singular again as she moved. Her eye throbbed, sending pangs of pain with each step. An auto was parked on the curb of the street. It was just a plain, black sedan. That was inconspicuous enough for her.

A stream of rain amassed at the end of her fingertips as she approached the auto. The water slipped into the lock of the driver's door, and it clicked open. She slid in. Water streamed under the dashboard, and her eyes closed as she focused on how it moved through the internal structures, mindful of the circuitry. Most autos made in the twentieth century could just have the ignition switch manually turned to activate the coil without the use of a key. This one was no different.

The chug of the battery starting went a few times before the engine came to life. Saoirse closed the auto door and backed the car out onto the street. She'd only gotten a few minutes down the way before a woman appeared in the passenger's seat. Maeva's black hair was tied in a neat braid over her shoulder. Her high cheekbones and tawny skin were characteristic of the fae. She had bright green eyes that still haunted Saoirse even after a century of dealing with her. A gray suit covered her lean figure.

"Fuck off," Saoirse muttered and rubbed her eyes. "I'm going to die anyway. At least let me die in peace."

Maeva sighed and smoothed out the wrinkles on her pants, as if she were actually sitting down. Fucking fae. They could make illusions that seemed real down to body temperature. But Maeva could have been anywhere within a few miles, projecting her image from safety.

"Look, I know you have to be heading somewhere," she said. "You wouldn't fight this hard otherwise. Going to see your brother?"

Saoirse started the windshield wipers going. "He's dead. You killed him a century ago, remember?"

"My intel would suggest otherwise."

"Sounds like shit intel. No siren survives the death of their mate."

"Biology's weird." Maeva pulled a cigarette and lighter from an inner pocket of her blazer. "And your brother is a cockroach."

Saoirse's chuckle was humorless. "Cockroaches fighting cockroaches. It's a wonder I haven't killed you yet."

"Well, you can certainly try again." Maeva lit her cigarette before pocketing her lighter. "Look, it's nothing against you. The Ministry pays me so much money, just ludicrous amounts of money."

"Is that supposed to make me feel better about you killing me?"

Maeva took a drag before speaking. "No, just don't want you thinking I hold anything against you or your brother. Won't hunt your loved ones or anything like that after you're both gone."

"My brother's already dead."

"Sure, sure." Maeva sighed out smoke. "How did you get out of custody anyway?"

Saoirse resisted the urge to tense. She had been restrained by Maeva's Gars, waiting for the end, when that woman—whatever she was—offered a bargain. Saoirse could never forget her eyes. They were amber like the setting sun, and just looking into them had been impossible. There was something ancient in her gaze, like she'd witnessed the universe come alive with light at the synthesis of the first photons.

She'd claimed that the left eye she'd gifted could aid Saoirse in surviving any injury. That had been true thus far. Saoirse had even ripped the eye out when the pain had gotten to be too much, but it regrew instantly.

The woman with amber eyes insisted Saoirse get to Vespera. Meallán was going to die otherwise. The woman didn't explain why or how, but Saoirse knew it was true in the same way she knew the earth orbited the sun. Her brother needed her.

"If your brother is actually dead," Maeva said when silence met her, "I have no reason to keep you alive."

Saoirse almost laughed at the threat. "You think I'd want him to come waltzing in to save me? Even if he were alive, I wouldn't do that to him."

"Then where are you going?"

Saoirse gave a wry smile. "I'm just taking a road trip, Mae-Mae. Need there be another reason?"

Maeva's chuckle was more a huff. "I've always loved your sense of humor. All right. Have it your way."

Her form disappeared as she dropped her illusion.

There were only a few seconds before a large shadow emerged from the rain and slammed into the side of the auto. A spray of glass hit Saoirse before the auto turned over. The world spun at dizzying speed. Pain shot up her leg with the unyielding crunch of metal that filled the air, but she couldn't see what had bent. Her head slammed against the window when the auto came to an abrupt halt.

Ringing filled her ears. Pain burst through her skull. She blinked until her eyes focused to see the world upside down. Rain slid up the windshield and pooled on the street above. She reached up to unbuckle her seatbelt. Something sharp burrowed into her leg, stopping her from falling. Her glance up revealed that the driver's side door had broken and folded around her shin.

Massive, black paws stepped in front of the windshield, heading for her side of the auto. She cursed, held her breath, and wrenched her leg free. The pain was blinding, but she collapsed to the top of the auto. Her leg bent at an impossible angle. Those paws outside morphed into hands and feet as it walked, and then the lycan stood on two humanoid legs.

The broken auto door opened to show a naked man holding the crumpled base of it. His black hair, the same color his fur had been, was soaked with the rain. A holster around his bicep—the band an elastic that could probably expand to the circumference of a wolf's forelimb—had a black hilt emerging from it. He drew a dagger of entirely black metal.

Saoirse didn't have time to react before he yanked her out of the auto by her arm and sank the blade into her side. A hiss escaped her, and her left eye seemed to heat until it burned in her skull. The rain spun into thin, sharp ribbons as she blindly swung a hand over her. The man growled and staggered back as blood sprayed out around them.

She lifted her eyes to see his arm missing and deep cuts in his abdomen. He dropped to the ground, twitching and gasping.

There were probably more Gars around. She needed to move.

A cry left her as she wrenched her broken leg back into some semblance of straightness. Water coalesced around the break and froze into a makeshift splint of ice. She forced herself to rise. The man's severed hand, still clutching the black hilt of a broken blade, lay on the rain-soaked pavement. She glanced down at her side. Just under her ribs, the sliver of the broken dagger emerged from her. She must have cut through the metal with her water. The entire blade was still in her. Her fingers wrapped around what was protruding of it.

Don't.

The thought seemed to slam into her—both hers and not. The blade was decay metal, and she would bleed out if she removed it without immediate medical attention. Not even her eye could spare her from that kind of blood loss. She didn't know how she knew that, but she did. The blade had to stay in.

She ignored the pain and hobbled forward on her broken leg. Blood trailed on the road behind her, washing away in the rain as she went. Another auto was parked on the street, and she used a thin stream of water to unlock it before climbing in. Getting the ignition going was no different than the other auto. She peeled off as soon as the engine rumbled to life. Her eyes scanned the streets, looking for any other wolves in the rain. The pain in her broken leg started to fade under growing numbness. She might lose it altogether if she bled enough.

It was still a long way to Vespera.

CHAPTER THREE

Jian didn't know what to make of Detective Ernest Declan Carver. Male sirens were virtually unheard of. Since fullblood sirens were all female, there were only ever X chromosomes being circulated amongst them, and in interracial unions, the chance of a Y chromosome surviving in-utero was so low that it was nothing short of miraculous that Carver had been born male. There was only a 1 in 2.8 million chance a siren could be male, and even then, most had both female and male anatomy.

Jian was thankful that the Professor didn't say anything when she found him and Carver in the Court lobby with identical cups of coffee in their hands. She was prone to teasing, and Jian was trying to have a pleasant conversation bereft of any sexual tension. He thought he was succeeding, focusing on what Carver was saying and not the lips that moved with each word. Treating their chat like a job where he was trying to get information helped him concentrate.

The Professor interrupted to lead them down into the jail under the Court. It was massive—a maze of concrete hallways and holding cells. There were five sections. One was for lycanthropes and had decay metal plating that stopped them from shifting. The vampire section had sonic cannons between its bars that would trigger upon direct contact. Sirens were kept with decay metal restraints and dry, hot air to deter from manipulating water. The demon cells had a sprinkler system that would douse convicts if they got too rowdy. And fae had to be kept in sound-absorbent, warded rooms with a gag at all times, so they couldn't speak curses or make illusions.

Jian bit his fingers into his forearms as he stepped through narrow, concrete corridors behind the Professor and Carver. The last time he'd been in a place like this, he'd left with fewer teeth and fingernails. There was some comfort with the Professor in his line of sight. The amber of her eyes and the unnatural grace of her movements might always mean safety to him now, even when they unnerved everyone else. She'd pulled him out of real and proverbial disasters more times than he cared to count.

The click of her heels echoing off the walls eased some of the tension building in his shoulders as they walked. But there was a restlessness in his bones this time of year that even she couldn't alleviate entirely. His stress demanded release—to unleash fury and sate itself in blood. He was overdue a hunt.

"On my way down," the Professor said as they walked, "Palus messaged me that they caught a report of an auto wreck in Occidental Reach involving a wolf. Two DNA profiles from blood taken on scene—the wolf's and a siren. Wolf was a known Gar. No ties to anyone on this coast. Siren wasn't registered in any ICS database. Wolf was found with a broken decay blade that had siren blood on it. Forensics think she was stabbed and cut through the blade, but it's not on the scene. They also think she walked away from the situation with the blade, which shouldn't be possible if she was stabbed."

Jian's brows pinched together. "A siren who could survive a decay blade who's not in the system and having scuffs with Gars? That's no normal person."

"It doesn't seem like coincidence that this is happening while we're investigating Gar attacks this far south."

"You think she's involved with them somehow? A target beyond just being mixed blood?"

"Only time and investigation will tell. Right now, anything I say is just conjecture."

Carver sighed and chewed his bottom lip. Jian forced himself not to think about how the soft flesh would yield to his teeth.

"Maybe our guy here will have something to say about it," Carver suggested. "Whoever this siren is, she survived having a decay blade in her. People like that don't elude the ICS unless they're really trying."

"What are you thinking?" the Professor prompted with a glance at him over her shoulder.

He shrugged. "Could be an Atlantean defector—young, too, if the ICS hasn't catalogued her yet. I can speak from personal experience that the Ministry doesn't have any qualms hiring mercenaries or even Gars to hunt enemies of the state on land. Doesn't always work in their favor."

The Professor's face fell. "You'd know that better than me."

She stopped in front of a door at the end of the corridor. "You willing to take point on this, Jian?" she asked. "You're more…personable…than Carver or me."

Jian cocked a brow. "I'm flattered, but forgive me if I'm a bit skeptical about that logic, given one of you is part of a race whose charm is a central aspect of their life and the other is some kind of primordial being."

"Must you always jab at my age?" she grumbled.

"Absolutely." Jian handed her his coffee and stepped past her to the interrogation room door. "Very well. I'll take point. I assume you two will just stand in a corner menacingly "

"Of course." The Professor sipped his coffee with a smile.

Carver rolled his eyes. "We'll be available if you need assistance, Jian," he offered with a withering glance at the Professor.

Jian wouldn't need the assistance, but he appreciated the gesture all the same.

The interrogation rooms at the Court were all the same—a concrete cube with bare walls and a cast iron table in the center. Their suspect sat at the table, his hands clasped over it. He looked mid-thirties like any other preternatural sub-seven hundred, with dense black hair cut short on his head and a hint of stubble on his jaw. Coal black eyes lifted from the table to Jian when he stepped in.

Chief Analyst Balam Espina was approaching five hundred. He had just one son from his previous marriage and two ex-wives who didn't care for his current one. His attitude toward mixed race people had always been vaguely hostile. Wolves were particularly susceptible to losing phenotypic expression in their offspring from mixed pairings, and many of them feared interbreeding would end with the gradual extinction of their race. Balam was no exception.

"So she pulled you," he said as he leaned back in his chair. "Thought you gave up this life to commit genocide."

Jian strolled toward the empty chair across the table, as if he couldn't be rushed. "War's over," he said. "Got to make a living somehow."

Carver closed the door after he and the Professor stepped in. Jian glanced back at them, and the Professor's gaze connected with his, as if she'd meant for him to look directly at her. He ignored how his gut coiled just at the eye contact. Her stare held too much behind it—too much history and too much power.

"Let's get to it, shall we?" Jian prompted when he returned his attention to Balam. "Do you know why you're here?"

Balam glared at the Professor. "Because that one thinks I had something to do with the Gar attacks."

Jian looked Balam over, noting the tension around his eyes and the awkward stiffness in his shoulders. Uncertainty. As much as Balam seemed annoyed, he was nervous about what would happen in this room, and for good reason. The Professor technically wasn't beholden to the Superiors—or any authority, for that matter. She could cut Balam open right here and wouldn't see a single consequence for it.

"I don't recommend antagonizing her," Jian said with a tired sigh. "I'll follow the rules. She'll make up new ones that involve your entrails."

Balam narrowed his eyes at Jian. "Just what do you want from me?"

"Honesty would be a start. We've got Gar attacks all along the west coast and a decay blade in an unregistered siren who just...walked it off."

Balam's fingers curled in his lap ever so slightly at the mention of the siren, and Jian's mouth virtually watered at the subtle show of discomfort.

"And I've been doing my part to hunt the Garsuk down like everyone else at the Court," Balam muttered.

"I'm sure." Jian resisted the urge to lick his lips. "Your son, though, married into them. When was the last time you spoke with him?"

"It's been years." The flex of Balam's jaw gave away his rising panic.

"I asked for honesty, Balam." Jian dragged his tongue over the sharp points trying to extend from his gums at the display of weakness in front of him. "Here's what I think happened. Your son got into things deeper than he wanted, so you tried to pull him out. But it was too late, wasn't it? He'd made promises, done things he couldn't take back. You had to send us looking in the wrong direction, perhaps with a failed prison transport."

Balam was unnaturally still, every muscle down his neck and shoulders stiff.

Jian did lick his lips then. The thrill of the hunt sang in his blood, strong as it would have been if he were stalking prey through the forest.

"What did your son do, Balam?" he asked with forced evenness.

Silence fell, heavy as that moment when the prey knew it had no chance of escape. Jian forced his fangs to stay retracted, despite how they ached.

"It was supposed to be his last job," Balam whispered finally, so quiet that Jian almost missed the words.

"What was?" Jian pressed. His heart pounded in his throat.

Balam swallowed. "His mother-in-law ordered him to assassinate some siren traveling from Asterna to Vespera. He panicked. Didn't want to kill anyone, so I got one of their own, the one Carver killed, to escape custody. She was a fighter, better suited to the task, and would have taken the job from my son."

"But the detective got to her first," Jian deduced. "So your son was still on the hook."

Balam clenched and unclenched his fists repeatedly. "They would have killed him if he didn't comply."

Jian forced his breaths to even as his cardinal fire purred with satisfaction. "And where's your son now?"

"I don't know. The pack moved, and I... I haven't heard from him again."

The brokenness in Balam's voice nearly drew an excited growl from Jian's chest.

"What about the siren?" Jian pressed. "Why do they want her?"

Balam swallowed. "I'm not sure. There was something about her eyes being worth money."

Jian stared a moment, noting every tense line in Balam's face, before he was sure he'd gotten all the information he could.

"Are you satisfied?" Jian asked with a glance back at the Professor. She arched a brow as a corner of her lips curled up. "Are you?"

He knew his bloodlust had to be clear in his eyes, and when he smiled, he doubtlessly flashed the tips of his half-extended fangs. "I'm satisfied."

"Then let's get going." She headed for the door.

Jian's eyes shot to Carver when he didn't move to follow. The scent of the sea burst through the room, something both earthen and oceanic like the shore at high tide. Jian couldn't stop the low rumble that started in his chest. Carver's eyes went wide. His lips were parted slightly, almost inviting. Every rise and fall of his chest made the cords of muscle along his neck flex, as if with the temptation to have teeth and tongue upon them.

The urge to close the distance between them coiled in Jian's gut. His cardinal fire burned hot against the back of his sternum, demanding to subdue this other predator—with fangs and claws or tongue and fingertips. Desire thrummed through him, both carnal and violent at once. His prey drive had never been sexual in nature, but this siren drew something out of him that demanded pleasure of the flesh in all its meanings.

The Professor tutted, breaking the unspoken tension.

"Now, boys," she said. "You'll have plenty of time for that later." She left without another word.

Jian stood and shoved his hands in his pockets against the itch to put them on the siren swallowing his attention.

"After you, detective," he said, his voice almost hoarse with the effort to hold back a growl.

Carver hesitated before stepping out. Jian swallowed his urge to jump on the back exposed to him as he followed. He'd have plenty of time to work out whatever this feeling was when he got home.

But his eyes involuntarily tracked every sway in Carver's hips, and he knew this problem wasn't going to go away that easily.

◊◊◊

Carver didn't understand how he could have been so very, very wrong about his initial impression of someone. Jian had seemed innocuous enough, if a bit measured in his responses. Maybe Carver should have known that those measured, careful words hid something that could only be described as beastly. The look in Jian's eyes, with pupils blown wide and the gold ring around them almost glowing, had been nothing short of predatory. His smile had displayed a row of fangs over his normal teeth, not yet distended enough to be harmful, but the promise of violence was in the expression all the same.

And the delight…

Carver had felt it waft off Jian with every question that broke Balam down a little more. There was a distinctly sadistic hunger in the roll of Jian's shoulders and the curl of his lips while he took Balam's pretenses apart as easily as those fangs would rend flesh from bone. And in an instant, all the Professor's taunting comments about demons had become legitimate warnings.

Carver hadn't been prepared for the heat that'd rushed through his limbs when Jian looked back at him. It chased away the permanent

54

ache in his nerves that he'd learned to ignore like background noise. The scent of his own pheromones hit him as strongly as they once had as an unmated siren, and he couldn't tell if the electric pulses running through him were fear or need. Warmth built at the apex of his thighs when a growl, low and soft, rumbled from Jian's chest. Some part of him wanted to draw every savage sound he could from this demon. Another part of him feared he'd be consumed if he got too close.

The conflicting feelings only increased when he turned his back to Jian while they left the room. He half-expected to be shoved face first into the wall and either eviscerated or pleasured. Maybe both. But Jian did no such thing, just walked. His footsteps didn't make a sound as he trailed behind Carver and the Professor out of the Court. It was almost like a threat—a reminder that he could attack without letting his prey sense him before it was too late.

The heat didn't subside by the time they came outside amidst rain that now fell in thick sheets.

Jian pulled the hood of his jacket up as they descended the front steps of the Court. "Where to now?" he asked, deep voice slithering down Carver's spine.

The Professor glanced back at him. "Just out in the rain, so you two can cool down. Are you all right?"

Jian's eyes flashed gold for a moment. "I'm overdue for a proper hunt."

Her lips twitched. "There are other ways to sate the bloodlust."

"Like interrogating a man?"

"Amongst other things."

Jian grunted, and a puff of smoke blew out of his nose. "Was this another one of your tests?"

"I was just trying to give you an opportunity to do something you like. The rest was…a bonus." She glanced at Carver sidelong. "If either of you were anyone else, I might be worried about having you work in close quarters, but you're the most controlled men I know— perhaps to your own detriment."

Carver might have believed that if he didn't feel decidedly out of control at present. He didn't think he would act on the impulse to cling to Jian and see if those fangs were as sharp as they looked, but the vividness of the idea also didn't inspire confidence. He'd almost forgotten how overwhelming attraction—if he could call it that— could be. Every fiber of his being was heated with need that teetered on the edge of painful.

And he wanted it to be painful. How long had it been since he'd spread his legs while someone bruised him?

"You're on the edge, sweetheart." Thomas' voice cut through the blood pounding in Carver's ears. "You should go before you do something you'll regret."

Carver failed not to glance behind him, but no one was there.

"I need to go," he rasped as he took a deep breath.

"Are you all right, detective?" Jian asked with brows pinched together.

Carver shook his head and headed back into the Court without explaining himself. He dimly heard the Professor tell Jian not to follow.

The consorts were on the second floor, just two levels down, but the short trip to the offices felt like an eternity. Pulses of electricity started to shoot painfully through Carver's limbs. His vision shifted in and out of focus. Every sense was heightened to uncomfortable levels. Even the shift of his shirt on his skin burned.

He burst into the lobby of the consort department. Blue walls meant to calm the occupants did little for him. The other sirens sat in chairs lining the perimeter. They gave him curious looks. The pheromones spilling off him were hard to ignore.

"By the Goddess," Amara, the consort manager, muttered when Carver stepped up to the front desk.

She stood almost to his height. Her slim build was characteristic of a siren, as was the perfect symmetry of her face. Green curls spilled over her head, framing her scowl.

"Please tell me Miguel is available," Carver said, keenly aware of the shivers wracking his body.

"You can't keep doing this, detective," she grumbled. "My men can't work for at least three days after your visits…not that they complain about it."

Heat seared up Carver's spine, making his bones burn. "When you find a cure for Severance Syndrome, you let me know, and I'll get right on it."

He clamped his mouth shut as soon as the words were out, but it was too late now.

The other sirens' eyes widened. Some clapped their hands over their mouths.

Carver didn't care for their pity and muttered, "Is Miguel available?"

"Room eight," Amara said stiffly. "You can pay after your session."

"Thank you."

"Just treat him well."

Carver rushed into the hall adjacent to the front desk. Doors were interspersed over the walls on either side. Room eight was almost at the end. He knocked. There were muffled footsteps, and the door opened. A man stood in jeans that hung low on his hips. He didn't have a shirt, showing off an expanse of muscle and tan skin. His dark, wavy hair fell heavily to one side of his face. He stared at Carver with warm eyes, a wry smile on his lips.

"To what do I owe the pleasure?" Miguel drawled.

Carver grabbed the consort's face and pressed their lips together. The kiss sent fire through his blood. He stepped into the room, pushing Miguel back, and shut the door behind him with his foot. Despite his need, he restrained himself, moving slowly until he was certain he had wholehearted reciprocation.

Miguel leaned into the kiss. His hands threaded through Carver's hair and drawing him closer. Carver shoved a hand into Miguel's pants, eliciting a moan that vibrated down to his core.

"You are so much trouble," Miguel rasped when Carver nipped a line down his neck and his chest. It wasn't enough.

He took Miguel's cock in his hand, moving steadily. The fire in Carver's blood increased. He needed more. Miguel's head snapped back.

More.

Teeth scraped warm flesh.

More.

Trembling legs and shallow breaths.

More.

Carver bit down.

A cry escaped Miguel's throat as the heat of his release peaked. It burst from him, searing through where they touched in delicious waves that increased in intensity with every crest. Carver relished in all of it, easing his pain even as it brought a swell of nausea. The twist of his stomach seemed tighter than normal, but he didn't resent it. He didn't deserve to have his pain mollified.

Miguel slumped against the wall, clutching Carver's shoulders for support. "Let me guess," he said breathlessly. "You're not done."

Carver withheld a repulsed shudder at the prospect of the hours he'd need to sate himself. "Safeword?"

"Red. Now please keep going."

Carver dropped to his knees and ignored the painful clench in his gut.

CHAPTER FOUR

Miguel slept soundly while Carver dressed. They'd gone for over four hours, and wolf or no, Miguel's stamina couldn't withstand a siren. Fresh life hummed through Carver's skin, chasing away the ache in his nerves. His hands didn't shake while he buttoned his pants and pulled on his shirt. The scent of sex and sea salt hung heavy in the room, but that was the only trace of himself that Carver would allow. He'd tidied the bedsheets and made sure Miguel lay comfortably under them.

His duster rested in a heap on the floor where Miguel had tossed it. Carver pulled it on and hugged it close to himself. Revulsion churned in his gut, threatening to upheave what little was in his stomach. He rarely vomited after feeding anymore, but it did still happen on occasion.

"Meallán."

The sound of his given name made him freeze at the door of the room. He reluctantly looked over his shoulder to see Thomas standing behind him. The pity in his husband's eyes made the nausea worse.

"It seemed worse this time," Thomas remarked softly. "You

were…attracted."

Carver's brows furrowed. "To Miguel?"

Thomas shook his head. "To Jian. You wanted him."

A pit seemed to open in Carver's gut, but he ignored it and pushed open the door. This wasn't a conversation he wanted to have.

When he went out into the consort department's lobby, there was a whole new set of sirens waiting in the chairs through the room. Most of his kind only needed to spend an hour or so with a consort, not four.

Amara sat behind the reception desk, clicking away on her typewriter. She barely glanced up at him when he approached her.

"Don't bother," she muttered. "The Professor came in earlier and paid for the overtime."

He grimaced, hating anyone paying for his issues. It made him feel truly crippled, like he needed someone to look after him.

"Miguel's sleeping, I assume?" Amara prompted absently, her eyes fixed on her typewriter.

Carver sighed at the irritation in her voice. "Yeah, I made sure he's comfortable."

She nodded curtly. "I appreciate it."

Carver pulled his messenger from his pants pocket and started for the door, prepared to check in with the Professor. Amara's voice made him pause.

"I'm sorry."

He glanced back at her. She was still staring at her typewriter, but her fingers had stopped over the keys.

"I didn't...know." Her voice was small, but not gentle. "You never said anything. I thought you were just irresponsible with your feeding habits."

Carver's lips thinned to a line. There was something so much worse about another siren offering sympathy. The other races could empathize with the death of a loved one, but only other sirens really understood what it was to lose a bonded mate. It went beyond grief.

"I don't really like to bring it up," he mumbled honestly.

Amara took a breath. "Well, anything we can provide for you, just let me know. I..." She took another breath. "My sister survived the death of her mate. She stopped eating or sleeping...or doing anything. I had to watch her wither away until she joined her wife in Aheru."

Carver swallowed past a lump in his throat. Amara rarely showed such vulnerability, and that she was now threatened to undo years of repressed grief.

"I'm sorry for your loss," he managed to force out.

"That should be my line." She returned her attention to her typewriter, evidently exhausting her sympathy quota for now. "Have a good rest of your day, Detective Carver. I'll keep a floating appointment open for you in two months."

He bowed his head slightly in thanks and continued out. The Professor was waiting in the hall, just outside the door. She leaned against the wall with her arms folded over her chest. Those eerie, amber eyes of hers settled on him.

"How are you feeling, dear?" she asked with an even tone that betrayed none of her thoughts.

He could have answered numerous ways—angry, repulsed, sad, guilty, resentful. Instead, what came out was: "Not much different from usual."

She stood from the wall. "Well, while you were busy, I took the liberty of recruiting Jian for something more long-term. Is that going to be a problem?"

"Unlikely," Thomas muttered abruptly.

When Carver glanced at his husband out of the corner of his eye, Thomas shrugged and titled his head back and forth.

"You were holding it together well until the interrogation," he pointed out. "You even got coffee and had a civil conversation. If you weren't so starved, you probably would have conducted yourself just fine. The danger of working with him is minimal. Don't be a coward."

Carver grimaced. "I think I'll be fine. I'm not sure what happened with Jian, but it was fueled by my starvation."

The Professor nodded. "I expected as much. For the rest of today, I'd like you to rest."

His immediate reaction was to argue, assuming that she was pulling him from work because of today's lapse, but he stopped himself. Her posture was that of someone about to deliver hard news. She seemed worried, hard lines between her brows and around her mouth.

"In an official capacity, I can't ask this of you," she said slowly, as if picking her words carefully, "but I would like you to talk to Damian about what you experienced with Jian today. You were fine when I left you this morning, and you were decidedly not fine after the interrogation."

Carver's lips pressed to a line.

"Don't you dare refuse," Thomas said firmly. "Jian made you feel things."

Carver couldn't disagree. Jian had inspired something in him that almost seemed to trick his physiology, kicking his broken nerves into working order again—if only for a couple minutes. Damian knew more than anyone about the different races' anatomy. If anyone could explain what had happened, it was him.

"All right," Carver agreed reluctantly. "I'll call him when I get home."

The Professor nodded. "Good."

He narrowed his eyes at her. "Is what happened with Jian why I'm being asked to back off from work?"

"It's a factor, but not the main one. Jian will be working with you on researching the Gars while I figure out who this siren on the run is, but I don't want to create an unworkable situation for you if you can't handle being around Jian."

He narrowed his eyes. "And what if it is too much to handle?"

"Then we figure something else out." She patted his shoulder. "C'mon. There's nothing else to be done about it now. Let's get you home."

When she headed down the hall, he shuffled after her. Thomas was thankfully quiet.

She drove him to his apartment without much else to say, and he lacked any desire to talk. His stomach was still turning after feeding.

He probably should have fed from two consorts, but he only ever got a couple hours before his body decided that it had enough to continue functioning and rejected energy again. It wasn't healthy, the equivalent of fueling an automobile just to get to the next gas station. What was he supposed to do about it, though?

Would it be the same with Jian?

Carver jumped into his bathtub as soon as he got home. He seemed to be spending an increasing amount of time in it as the years went on. As it was, he only soaked in the water to calm whatever nerves were still firing from feeding. His skin didn't feel right on his body, too sensitive and too alive, and it only got worse when he thought of how the gold in Jian's eyes lit as soon as they met his gaze. How could he feel both unsettled and wanting at the same time?

Thomas appeared at the tub's edge to sit on it, heedless of the water droplets that'd splashed over. He couldn't get wet anyway.

"Laying here and wondering isn't going to give you answers," he said as he rested a hand on the phone in the wall.

He'd always been pushy. That hadn't changed after he'd died. And Carver had never been able to refuse him.

The phone rang for a long time when Carver finally worked up the will to dial, but then Damian's baritone came through.

"Carver?" He sounded out of breath. "Are you all right? Any complications with your chest injury?"

"No, it has nothing to do with my chest," Carver said quickly. "Are you all right? If this is a bad time, I can call back later."

There was the sound of rustling and clanking for a long moment, and then Damian said, "No, no. There was a bit of a situation at the hospital, but it's being handled. I just got off duty. What's going on?"

Carver chewed his lip a moment, trying to figure out how to phrase his next words. "Your wife urged me to talk to you because I felt attraction, or…something like attraction."

In the following quiet, he could almost feel Damian's surprise.

"When was this?" Damian asked, voice getting slightly higher in pitch.

"Earlier today." Carver chewed his lip some more. "I wasn't…hungry enough…to feel desire, but there was this demon. Something about him… I don't know. I've never experienced anything like it."

"A demon?" Damian almost sounded amused, a smile in his voice. "You haven't encountered many demons, have you?"

Carver frowned. Just what was so special about demons?

"So it's him," Thomas deduced with a tilt of his head, "not you."

"I highly doubt something has changed with how your symptoms have been presenting for the past century," Damian continued. "More likely, you were reactive to this demon's cardinal fire."

The increasing speed of Damian's words, likely a sign of excitement, betrayed an academic fascination.

"Cardinal fire?" Carver echoed, unfamiliar with the term.

"A demon's heart holds their affinity for fire. They call this their cardinal fire, and by all accounts, it also fuels their bloodlust." Damian paused a moment, and when he spoke again, his tone was the one he used when giving lectures to interns. "Some can have pretty extreme aggression issues. Their cardinal fire compels them to hunt, which they don't have much need for in modern civilization. Increased compulsion to violent behavior caused by resisting the call to hunt is actually a common problem, just to give you an idea of how difficult demons can have it."

Carver wouldn't have believed Jian could be anything but polite until today. He knew better now.

"Especially strong demons," Damian continued, "can have a psychological impact on others just from proximity. Humans and fae generally feel deep terror just in the presence of these demons. Vampires, wolves, and sirens can feel territorial or challenged. You're a siren, with greater empathic capabilities than most, so you probably experience this strongly. Essentially, other races' self-preservation instinct is activated just by sensing a demon's cardinal fire, generating a fight or flight response against the subconsciously perceived threat."

Carver wasn't sure how to feel about that. He didn't have much self-preservation anymore, but evidently, a demon could reinvigorate that discarded instinct.

"You're a siren out of water," Damian remarked, seemingly more to himself than Carver. "Your primary defense isn't going to be your spines or claws or fangs—not on land. It's going to be your allure. I'm willing to bet that whatever demon you met is very strong, and he triggered a defensive response."

Carver chuckled humorlessly. "If you can't fight it, seduce it?"

Maybe he had underestimated the Professor's warning about demons. Jian seemed kindly, but most people did until their veneer came off. Carver didn't know what lurked beneath it. He wasn't sure he wanted to find out.

"I wonder if this could be a form of therapy for you," Damian speculated aloud, not acknowledging Carver's words at all. "That would certainly be an unorthodox treatment to Severance Syndrome, but it could work. Controlled triggering of hormones isn't so much different from treating depression with SSRIs. The oxytocin might be addictive, though. That could backfire. Would that matter in a siren? They thrive on oxytocin."

He kept talking, straying further into expertise that Carver knew nothing about. There was something about hormonal cycles and positive feedback loops.

"Damian," Carver finally interrupted after a solid minute. "I just want to know what this means for continuing to work with this demon. Should I worry? Do I take precautions?"

"Worry? I don't think so," Damian said. "No, if anything, you might want to indulge in it—see what happens. If you're starting to experience attraction, it might be worth it to test the limits of it. Worst-case scenario, nothing changes."

"I thought the worst-case scenario is that a demon eats me."

"I highly doubt that any employee of the ICS, especially a strong demon, wouldn't have extensive training in controlling their urges. We've had sirens and demons work in close quarters for centuries without incident. More than that, the Professor would never let you get hurt."

Carver sat with the idea for a moment. Demon exposure therapy seemed a far-fetched idea, but then, he couldn't deny its effectiveness. He'd gone from no appetite to nearly losing control over it in less than an hour. But Jian probably wouldn't appreciate being a guinea pig — certainly not a sexual one — for this experiment. Carver didn't even know how he personally felt about it.

Even if he could be fixed and return to what he'd been physiologically, that wouldn't solve the deeper emotional trauma that'd come with a century of living with Severance Syndrome. He probably needed normal therapy for that, but nothing the shrinks said really mattered. A hundred years without proper dopamine or serotonin production couldn't be rectified by talking. And the pills prescribed to him often left him too cognitively impaired to do his job.

His eyes lifted to Thomas. The pills also stopped these hallucinations, and as much as he hated his attachment to the illusion of his husband, he didn't want it to disappear entirely.

He sighed and shoved a hand through his hair. This wasn't what he wanted to be thinking about right now.

"Thanks, Damian," he mumbled. "I think that answers all my questions for now."

"All right, but let me know if you have any more," Damian said.

Carver probably would if he actually followed through on testing the extent of Jian's effect on him.

"Will do," he mumbled. "Have a good evening."

When Damian mumbled a goodbye, Carver put the phone back in its cradle and then leaned back in the tub. He rubbed his eyes.

"Don't," he grumbled before Thomas could say anything.

"Just...let me think."

Thomas thankfully didn't speak.

What would this experiment with Jian even look like? Should Carver try to act on his attraction or just take note of his physiological responses? Would Jian reciprocate if he tried to show interest?

Those gold-ringed irises flashed through Carver's mind unbidden, sparking a building heat in his chest. If this was supposed to be a response to a perceived threat, why did it feel like attraction? For a siren, he supposed, the line between desire and survival was blurry. Being as adverse to sex as he currently was didn't bode well for him. Most of his kind responded to the sexual interest of others with some level of arousal, whether or not they found the person attractive. That Jian was objectively handsome probably complicated whatever biological systems still worked in Carver.

"It's not a crime, Meallán," Thomas said gently. "This is good that you find someone else attractive."

Carver looked up at his husband. Refusing to respond seemed like a futile endeavor most of the time. What was the point really? Thomas wasn't going anywhere. He hadn't for a century.

Carver released a long breath before mumbling, "It's uncomfortable."

"What is?" Thomas asked with knitted brows. "Desire?"

Carver's eyes flicked down his body where heat had built between his thighs. He'd been largely impotent for a century, so he was relieved when he remained flaccid. Today was weird enough without his body doing more things it hadn't in a long time. But some part of that region felt something.

Demons don't submit to sirens. They're emboldened by the allure.

The Professor's words rang through his head. He hadn't let anyone take control of a sexual situation since his mate, and the idea scared him. So why did the thought of Jian over him make heat pool low in his belly?

"It feels wrong," Carver mumbled, "like it shouldn't be happening."

Thomas had a small smile. "But it is. You could heal this part of you."

Carver didn't know if he believed that, but he let his fingers wander between his legs, ignoring his limp cock and dipping into the folds beneath it.

Siren genetics weren't meant to accommodate a Y chromosome, so like most males of his kind, Carver still had a functioning vagina. His testes occupied the space where ovaries would have been in a female. He didn't have a uterus. His cervix had just enough tissue that he needed triannual pap smears. At least there was no chance of him getting pregnant without a womb, and since his testes only produced hormones, he couldn't get anyone else pregnant.

Some male sirens chose to undergo surgery to make them appear more typical of the sex they presented as. Carver had chosen to remain intact, mostly because he wasn't emotionally attached to his genitalia. What did it matter really? The organs he did have functioned well enough for his purposes, and he didn't care if they were associated with a different gender. Most sirens didn't even have gender as a concept, at least not how most other races thought about it, because they were all female.

He was a little warmer than usual when he slipped a finger inside himself—increased blood flow. That was indicative of being aroused, which wasn't possible so soon after feeding...until today. Was it really just his body's instinctual response to a demon? Could it have been anything else?

He pulled his finger out and sank into the tub until his head was completely submerged, obscuring his view of Thomas. The sound of his own heartbeat echoed in the water. It was slightly faster than the usual twenty beats per minute, and he didn't know if that was more of his body's response to Jian or his growing anxiety about it.

He sighed into the water, spilling bubbles out from his lips. There was nothing he could do about his physiology now—maybe never if Jian decided not to work with him after all.

He didn't know whether or not to be disappointed by that thought.

CHAPTER FIVE

The week passed with a woeful lack of information. Looking through the genealogy records of wolf packs in the Republic didn't give Jian much to work with. The wolf pack that Balam's son ran in was more like a mercenary group than a family, as most Gar packs were these days. They'd frequently taken hit jobs and other unsavory work, but tracking their movements had proven difficult. They were good at concealing their clients and even better at hiding their migration through the Republic.

That was why Jian found himself walking through the Vespera Bay Aquarium, surrounded by copious amounts of water. Some instinct in him recognized that being submerged in any one of these aquarium tanks would kill him almost instantly. His contact liked that about this place. It made him uncomfortable, and he couldn't get violent lest he risk destroying the glass on the tanks and flooding himself to death.

The aquarium didn't see many people on Thursday mornings. There were only a few walking the upper floor bridge. A two-tiered otter enclosure rested beside massive windows overlooking the ocean. It was the first clear day all week, and the sun reflected brightly on the gentle rises and falls of the water's surface. Morning light filled the hall below and rested on a pair of life-size orca models suspended from the ceiling.

Jian glanced at Carver askance as they walked down the bridge together. The detective had kept a decidedly polite distance for all the time they'd worked together. They didn't talk about what had happened in the interrogation room or even acknowledge that it'd happened, and Jian wasn't willing to push it just yet. Carver seemed the type to hide behind his professionalism when put under pressure. Getting him to open up was going to take some time and coaxing— maybe some flirting, too. Jian was patient.

"Who is this person we're meeting?" Detective Carver asked abruptly.

"She's an old contact of mine," Jian explained as they headed for the darkened end of the bridge. "Most paranoid person I know. She always asks to meet me here."

Carver looked down at him. "Because of the amount of water?"

"Just being around this much water, especially this close to the ocean, weakens me. She considers meeting here a precaution, even if I've never threatened her."

"Being near the ocean weakens you?" Carver's brows furrowed. "Why live and work on the coast at all?"

"Having power isn't always an advantage," Jian answered vaguely, not yet willing to divulge the truth of his habitation near the ocean.

His reasons weren't so different from why his family and so many other pureblooded demons lived in coastal areas. The ocean dulled the urge to hunt, to feel flesh give under fang and claw. It might have also weakened a demon's ability to control fire and to heal, but that seemed a small trade-off for sanity. If not for the ocean being right next door, Jian suspected he would have gone for Carver's throat when they first met.

Carver thankfully didn't ask for an explanation of Jian's cryptic response as they strolled into the dimly lit jellyfish exhibit. Jellies of all sizes and colors seemed to glow in their tanks that sat interspersed along the walls—like windows into an aquatic realm. The ethereal glow might have been aided by the lights at the base of their tanks, highlighting them against dark backgrounds. Curling, delicate tendrils undulated in the water. They almost seemed weightless—little domes drifting through space.

Carver's eyes lingered on the jellyfish as he passed. Eventually, he wandered toward a tank filled with translucent, white ones. Some were smaller than a hand and some were almost two feet wide. *Moon jellyfish* was written on the placard beneath the tank.

"My mother loved these," Carver remarked when Jian came up beside him. "They change color depending on what they eat. She liked the purple ones most. Sometimes we'd take trips just to see them."

His voice was soft, almost like he was revealing a secret.

"Were you close with your mother?" Jian asked, always ready to take the opportunity to learn more about someone.

"She was my closest friend growing up." A small smile touched

Carver's lips. "But I wasn't hers. She and my father were always wrapped in each other. I used to dream of finding love like that. Well...I suppose I did."

Jian couldn't imagine loving someone quite literally to death, or what it meant to lose that. Normally, he'd try to offer sympathy, but he'd seen Carver close himself off to any display of concern from the Professor. Jian doubted his efforts would be welcome.

"Do you visit the ocean often?" he asked.

Carver chuckled humorlessly. "Only if I had a death wish." He paused a moment, and then muttered something that sounded vaguely like, "Maybe I should visit."

Jian's brows furrowed. "A death wish?"

The sirens' home was the ocean. Most got severely depressed or anxious if they spent too much time away.

"The Atlantean Ministry considers male sirens abominations," Carver explained. "They tried to kill me, forced me to flee the ocean. I'm forbidden from returning, as per my terms of asylum with the ICS."

Jian didn't know what to say, so he just mumbled, "I'm sorry."

Carver shrugged. "It is what it is."

"How old were you when you were exiled?"

"It was...1763, I believe. I would've been fifteen."

A child then. The Ministry certainly had never been known for their compassion, but hunting a child was low even for them.

"Is being here hard?" Jian asked. "This is as close to the ocean as you can get now, I guess."

Carver stared at Jian a moment before returning his eyes to the jellyfish. "It almost feels like standing on the doorstep of my home. I can't cross the threshold, but I can look through the window. It doesn't feel bad, just a bit nostalgic."

He glanced at the large, orange sea nettles down the walkway. His eyes slowly made their way back to the moon jellyfish.

"I think I like it actually," he said after a beat.

Jian smiled. "Then I'll have to bring you again."

Carver arched a brow. "Aren't you uncomfortable here?"

"My comfort doesn't mean much to me, and you get to enjoy something."

Carver blinked. "You shouldn't suffer for my fleeting fascination."

Jian shrugged and started down the hall. "Is it suffering if I enjoy my company's enjoyment?"

"I...suppose not." Carver caught up to him in two steps on those long legs. "I also enjoy my company's enjoyment and wouldn't it be better if we did something we both enjoyed?"

Jian's lips twitched as he looked up at Carver. "Inviting me to find out, detective?"

The slightest pink shone on Carver's cheeks through his dark skin. "That's not... I didn't mean it that way."

"I know. Forgive my teasing."

Jian turned down an intersecting hallway before he could say something else to fluster Carver. It was rapidly becoming one of his favorite things to do—breaking through that carefully constructed stoicism to elicit the emotion beneath.

The next room was massive. The largest tank Jian had ever seen filled one wall, standing over ten feet in height and nearly twenty feet wide. He could only guess the depth of it from looking inside. It seemed endless. A school of small fish spun around the bottom. Hammerhead sharks roamed around the top. Children crowded around a turtle that hovered near the glass, peering back at them like they were the ones on display. The water shimmered with the light streaming in from the top, casting zigzagging patterns on the sand at the bottom.

Jian took a moment just to stare at it, coming to a stop near the glass. He was weakest in this room more than any other at the aquarium, and it always stole his breath with just how terrifying and beautiful it was. Only the ocean itself had ever made him feel more fragile and insignificant.

He looked up at Carver to see him watching the turtle with a smile.

"She gets curious about them," he explained, as if answering a question Jian had yet to ask. "They move oddly, not like how things move in water, and she cannot reach them. It entertains her now that she knows they're not a threat."

Jian glanced at the small children bouncing on their heels and prodding the glass wherever the turtle drifted.

"Did you encounter many turtles in the ocean?" Jian asked.

"Oh, all the time." Carver's smile grew when the turtle followed a child's hand up and down. "The oldest I met was nearing two hundred, according to my mother. Had a bit of an attitude, but she looked after herself. Nearly fought a bull shark one time. I did feel compelled to intervene in that one. Most sharks are docile, but bull sharks can be mean sons of bitches when they want."

Jian chuckled. "I don't know if I've ever heard someone call sharks docile."

Carver looked down at him. "I felt similarly when the Professor warned me about you in the same breath as she praised you."

Jian was unsurprised that the Professor had given Carver a warning. She had known him for almost half his life at this point and seen the worst of him. A warning was certainly deserved.

"You don't seem to have heeded her words," Jian remarked. "Willing to roll the dice with me?"

The muscles of Carver's jaw flexed for a moment as he looked back to the turtle. "May I be blunt with you, Jian?"

"I would prefer it."

Carver took a breath. "Just being in your presence often feels like rolling the dice. I don't know what this is that we seem to feel near each other. I've spent more than half my life at this point unable to experience the drive to prey on someone, much less someone I just met."

Jian's chest heated at the admission, knowing that he elicited a desire to prey—to seduce. The beast in him stirred with the urge to beat a creature of grace like this at their own game.

"Do you want to prey on me, detective?" Jian murmured, voice pitching lower than normal.

Carver's eyes narrowed. "I could ask you the same."

The response could have been construed as deflection, but Jian knew better. Carver was too direct for that. He meant it as a challenge—a test of the limits of their decorum and restraint. Would Jian continue his pretense as a friendly professional or put that aside in favor of candor?

He couldn't help his smile as he started for the benches resting opposite the massive tank.

"You have nothing to fear from me," he said honestly, "not unless you ask for it."

Carver's step faltered when he moved to follow, and he took another few to even his stride. Jian had mind enough not to let his smile grow with the satisfaction at causing such a reaction from someone so controlled. If Carver wanted to see what lurked in the heart of a demon, Jian wouldn't deny him. That was only courteous.

Their contact sat in a little alcove on the far side of the room. Bo was a small woman—barely five feet, with a slight frame. Her dark hair was tied up in a messy bun. Eyes a light gray, almost like the reflection off steel, scanned the room in measured sweeps. She had the youthful face of a sub-three hundred pretern, making her look like a college student. It was deceiving. Everything about her was meant to be unassuming. She blended in, never let her enemies see even a hint of her true power. That was what made her a good spymaster.

She barely glanced at him when he sat beside her.

"Jian," she greeted tersely, flashing the tips of a pair of fangs as she spoke. "I was under the impression you were coming alone."

He glanced at Carver and nodded to the space on the bench beside him. Carver sat after a brief hesitation.

80

"This is Detective Carver," Jian introduced. "He's the Professor's apprentice and my colleague on this case. You should be the least afraid of him. He's the honest one between us."

She arched a brow and gave Carver a cursory glance. "Not a difficult bar to overcome."

Jian sighed. "You wound me as always."

"It's well-deserved."

She squinted, which might have seemed like a glare, but Jian knew she was just trying to see in the room's dim lighting. Most vampires had terrible vision, and ones with stronger blood like Bo were especially bad without any other race's genetics to offset the vampiric deficit.

"You're a siren, aren't you?" she said to Carver. "I heard there was a male siren at the High Court, but I didn't think it was true. Do you have any affinity for water?"

Carver hesitated before shaking his head. "I heal just fine in water, but I can't control it."

She glanced at Jian. "Unfortunate. This one could afford to be doused every once in a while."

"I would prefer to remain un-doused," Jian muttered. "It's a decidedly unpleasant experience."

"I suppose you of all people would know."

There were so many implications wrapped in that one sentence that Jian wasn't sure if he should have felt guilty, angry, or sad. He somehow managed to be all three.

"Who have you been talking to?" he asked, barely keeping his voice even.

"Let's just say that I know there was no love lost for your...people...in the war."

Jian's jaw clenched when he caught her meaning. The war had forced him to make many sacrifices, and he resented the implication that any of them were easy.

"I'd advise you to keep that information to yourself," he said stiffly. "Not for my sake, but for yours."

"I know the game." She waved a hand dismissively. "Besides, I wouldn't be stupid enough to anger your daughter."

He rubbed the back of his neck, feigning embarrassment that he wasn't as scary as his daughter. It was to his benefit that people underestimated him.

"There's a reason she's back home running things, and I'm here," he offered with a smile.

Bo narrowed her eyes. "I don't trust you either. You may not bare your teeth as readily as she does, but you bite all the same."

She pulled a manila envelope from inside her jacket and held it out.

"Here," she said. "Everything I could gather about your pack."

When Jian took the envelope, she continued. "Tread lightly with this one. They've got ties with the Atlantean Ministry."

Jian slid the envelope into an inner pocket of his jacket. "How do you know they're affiliated? The Ministry's usually good about covering their dirty work."

"One of my people caught them with a known Ministry agent a

few days ago. Maybe the Ministry is desperate and getting careless."

The Atlantean Ministry ran the oceanic siren cities. As a theocracy, their laws were all governed in accordance with the scriptures of their Goddess, which were largely xenophobic and intolerant of flaws. Siren castes were demarcated by genetic "superiority." It was just another way to enforce blood purity while trying to justify it as science.

That a siren had been attacked just last week by a Gar pack might have indicated she was a refugee. She could have been fleeing the Ministry after being deemed genetically incompetent. Carver had been exiled for similar reasons. His only "flaw" was having a Y chromosome.

Jian stood. "Thank you, Bo. We'll take a look at it in a more secure location."

"One other thing," Bo said with a glance at Carver. "I don't know how much you've looked into the pack, but I also got whispers that they have a recent descendent of the Origin among them."

Jian took pause at that. The Origins were the first beings of every race, more powerful than the sum of perhaps the entire population if the legends were to be believed. A close descendant of an Origin would have had immense power—the stuff of myth. That Bo was even suggesting it made Jian nervous. She didn't draw those kinds of conclusions readily.

"More a job for the Professor then," Carver remarked as he stood. "She probably knows more about the lineages of Origins than is written anywhere."

Jian didn't doubt that. He strongly suspected that the Professor was older than she claimed—perhaps the oldest pretern still living. Maybe she was even an Origin or Ancient herself. She'd denied it the last time he'd asked her, but he wouldn't have put it past her to lie about that. There were malevolent things in the world that would jump at the chance to harness the power of an Ancient.

"Back to the Court then?" Jian suggested.

Carver nodded.

Bo wrapped her coat tighter around herself. "Give my regards to the Professor," she mumbled, "and don't get yourselves killed."

Jian offered a terse nod and turned to go. Carver kept pace beside him. His face was hard and unreadable, almost like stone.

"Troubled, detective?" Jian prompted after a moment of silence.

Carver's eyes stared straight ahead. "Where did your contact get this information?"

"She's got an extensive network of spies, both here in the Republic and Tong Bei. They monitor threats to the ICS, so she's probably been watching these Gars for a while."

"And you trust her?"

Jian hesitated before nodding. "She saved my life during the Blood War. She's always been wary of me because of my family, but I trust her."

Carver was quiet for a long moment. "She was a vampire, wasn't she? Weren't demons fighting vampires in the war?"

"In theory," Jian mumbled as his stomach twisted.

Carver glanced at him sidelong. "In theory?"

"Not all of us supported the war. My people had no right to the vampiric land they claimed to own, and I'm glad that we lost ultimately."

"But didn't you fight in the Red Army—the demon army?"

Jian forced his face not to show any hint of discomfort as he trained his eyes straight ahead. "That I did."

◊◊◊

When they got to the Court, the Professor was outside on the steps with Palus. Her spouse had their hair down. It spilled in black streams over their shoulders down to their thighs. Winding, white designs decorated their skin from the tips of their fingers to the base of their eyes. The marks stood in stark contrast to their tawny complexion. A green tunic hugged their slim figure, cinched at the waist with a gold sash. Floral designs in pastel pinks and blues were embroidered along their sleeves and the center fold.

Their high, round cheekbones paired with their long hair often made people mistake them for a woman. The sharp angle of their jaw and nose made others mistake them for a man. Fae didn't have the same concept of gender that most races did, and Palus had long given up trying to make sense of being a man or woman to societies who had such concepts.

The Professor flipped through pages on a clipboard. Palus peered over her shoulder, but they looked up as soon as Jian and Carver approached from the parking lot.

"Something new to report?" the Professor asked without taking her eyes from the papers.

Jian came to a stop near enough to see that she was reading field reports—the rigid, boxy formatting immediately recognizable. Carver hovered close to him, eyes narrowed on the reports.

"My contact did some digging on our wolf pack," Jian explained. "They have ties to the Ministry, which isn't wholly unexpected given our mysterious siren whose location still isn't known. There was also some evidence that one of the pack is a recent descendant of an Origin. We thought you'd know more about that than us."

At the mention of an Origin, the Professor's head came up. Palus stood straighter.

"All of Inugliat's children, grandchildren, and great-grandchildren should be dead," Palus said, speaking the lycan Origin's name too casually for the weight it carried.

"How can you be sure?" Carver asked.

The Professor exchanged a glance with her spouse before speaking. "I was…very close…with Inugliat. I knew her children and their children. I was there when all of them died. The oldest living relative of Inugliat's is her youngest great-grandchild's great-granddaughter, and she's certainly not a Gar. Everyone within five generations is long dead."

Jian didn't doubt she was telling the truth, and he was even willing to overlook the implications about her age if she was old enough to personally know an Origin. What he did have some misgivings about was what this meant for the pack. Where had the rumor come from that they had the recent descendant of an Origin with them?

"Any news on that siren who survived a decay blade?" Jian asked and nodded toward the Court's front doors. "Maybe we should talk in—"

The sound of tires screeching drew everyone's eyes back. An auto came speeding down the street, crashed through the fence surrounding the parking lot, and barreled into the nearest parked vehicle with a loud shattering of glass and the groan of bent metal. The parked auto's alarm blared in tinny rises and falls.

The Professor was next to the crashed auto in an instant. She pulled the driver's side door off its hinges like it was nothing. A woman tumbled out and fell to her hands and knees on the ground. Blood coated her form. Deep lacerations ran across her back and chest. Blue dreads hung around her head. Scales the same color cut with gold emerged from her damp, umber skin. The gray jacket over her had a large hole in one side that had a red stain around it.

Carver jolted into motion, running to the woman. He crouched down and pulled her into his arms. She went limp against him. His hand shook as he swept blood from her cheek.

Jian and Palus ran toward them.

"Do you know her?" the Professor asked as she bent to grip Carver's shoulder.

He swallowed. "This is Saoirse, my sister."

The look in his eyes was cold and unreadable. Jian hadn't thought the already aloof siren capable of being even more expressionless, but it was as if all emotion had disappeared from him while he stared down at his sister. This close, the similarities between them were obvious. They shared the same strong cheekbones and almost pouty lips. If her hair hadn't been in dreads, Jian imagined their curls also would have been the same.

Jian glanced down at the wound just below her ribs where black metal jutted out—a decay blade. His stomach dropped. This was the unidentified siren who hadn't registered in any ICS database.

Carver reached for the decay blade, but Saoirse grabbed his wrist, stopping him.

"Don't," she rasped, voice thin like she could barely speak. "It'll…kill me. Can't…heal."

People were starting to emerge from the front doors of the Court. Palus barked an order to call for emergency medical services, and some people ran back inside.

"We'll get you help," Carver said softly as he smoothed a hand over Saoirse's hair. "It'll — "

"Eye," she interrupted and raised a hand to grip his shirt. "Eye… Killing me."

Her gaze lifted to the Professor before adding, "Like her."

The Professor arched a brow. "Like me?"

"Hers." Saoirse's eyes started to close. "Need…her."

Carver hunched until his forehead pressed to hers. For a few seconds, it seemed their breaths moved together, and then he said, "Behind her left eye is something. It hurts."

The Professor frowned. "Can you determine what it is?"

"I can draw it if you have paper."

She pulled a notepad and pen from inside her jacket. His hands shook when he took them. He drew several lines overlapping each other. It was like a star with six arms, but one of them was longer than the others, seeming to bifurcate the whole thing. He handed the notepad back to the Professor when he finished.

She took one look at it, ripped the paper out, and shredded it into tiny pieces. The color drained from her face.

"Are you sure?" she breathed, voice rough and unsteady. "Are you sure that's the symbol you sensed?"

When Carver nodded, she looked to Palus and said, "Call Damian and let him know to have the hospital on alert. Mobilize the Peacekeepers around it for when we arrive."

Palus ran inside the Court without question.

"I thought your sister worked for the ICS," the Professor said, something sharp in her gaze. "Why isn't she in the database?"

Carver curled his hand around his sister's. "Saoirse is an Inquisitor," he answered, tone flat.

Jian's brows shot up. Inquisitors were shadow agents who investigated government officials. Their information never stayed recorded, so brokers and infiltrators couldn't trace them back to the ICS if their real identities were ever suspected. Most preternatural governments already resented the ICS for holding them accountable for domestic issues. If they knew an Inquisitor was in their midst, that could be grounds to declare war.

"You're not supposed to know about the Inquisitors," the Professor muttered. "They know better than to reveal their job, even to other family members."

Carver let out a long breath. "Yeah, well, it helps that I used to be one myself. Saoirse and I were a team for a while."

Silence followed the statement. There were few groups in the ICS that received more vigorous training than Inquisitors, as they needed to be spies, assassins, diplomats, tacticians—whatever their job required of them. Even the Peacekeepers, an elite force, had less asked of them. And leaving meant changing their identity and living as someone else since the ICS couldn't have any trace of a former agent still in the world.

Carver fiddled absently with his ring. "They didn't know I'd survived my husband's death. Saoirse made sure of that."

Jian wasn't sure if the complete lack of feeling in Carver's voice or the dead look in his eyes was more unnerving.

"We're definitely going to have more of a conversation about your history later," the Professor said as she dragged a hand down her face. "If I'd known she was an Inquisitor, I would have been investigating this differently."

"Unfortunate," Carver intoned.

She looked him over. "The ambulance should arrive soon."

His voice held no inflection when he said, "If Saoirse dies, I will have lost my entire family in the first tenth of my life."

Jian shuddered, discomfort growing with Carver's lifeless demeanor.

The Professor gently lifted Carver's chin with a finger, so he looked up at her. "When you go home tonight," she said evenly, "are you going to kill yourself?"

Carver took a disturbingly long time to answer. "No, not before I know whether or not she'll live."

"And if she dies?"

He was silent.

"Well, I appreciate your honesty at least." She lowered her hand from his chin and took a deep breath. "All right. I don't want to do this, but I think I have to. Brace yourself."

She laid a hand over Saoirse's left eye. Carver went rigid, and a rumble almost low enough to escape Jian's hearing range reverberated through the air. Saoirse tensed. Her face scrunched at whatever sound her brother was making. Jian didn't have much familiarity with siren protective instincts, but they were a highly empathetic species. Any threat to Saoirse probably set off something in her brother.

"Back down, Carver," the Professor said firmly. "It's for her good, and I don't need your permission."

The rumble stopped, but Carver didn't move, a protective curl to his shoulders as he hovered above his sister. His eyes weren't dead anymore. There was something dark and violent behind them. Heat flared in Jian's chest, and he balled his hands into fists against the instinct to bare his fangs. Of all the times his nature could have come out, this was the worst.

The Professor shoved her fingers into Saoirse's left eye. Carver clapped a hand over his own eye when his sister screamed, as if he were also feeling it removed. The Professor's fingers blackened. Dark veins crept up her forearm.

Saoirse's screams abruptly died, and she slumped to the ground with Carver. The Professor lifted her hand. There was no eyeball in her grasp, but there wasn't one in Saoirse's socket either. Blood trickled down her face and joined the rainwater over the pavement.

Distant sirens signaled the approach of the ambulance. The Professor stood and looked up at Jian. Her eyes were darker than normal. All sound seemed to leave the world as she lowered her gaze to Carver. Her lips moved, but she had no voice. Jian didn't know what conversation was being had as Carver responded without making sound.

Something unsettled rose in Jian as he turned around, almost on instinct. Something in him knew that he wasn't meant to bear witness to this. His very blood seemed restless. The feeling got worse and worse over a minute until a scream rang out. It sounded like Carver.

Jian had no idea what the Professor was doing, but he knew innately that he shouldn't try to look under any circumstances. His stomach turned violently. There were many types of screams he'd heard over the years—from battle and torture and grief—but he'd never heard one like this before.

It somehow left the air colder even after it stopped.

The Professor appeared in front of Jian. Her entire arm was black, as was her left eye. Blood dripped from her hand.

"I need a favor, Jian," she said tightly. "I need you to take Carver to your home."

He blinked. "Why is my house safer than the hospital?"

"Because it's away from me."

She disappeared again.

When Jian turned around, he saw Carver lying on the ground beside his sister. The Professor appeared over him and pulled him up by an arm. She virtually shoved him into Jian. Carver was a solid weight, but he seemed to be holding himself up well enough.

"Professor?" The smallness of his voice was uncharacteristic, and that alone would have been unnerving if he wasn't also shaking violently.

"Easy," the Professor said with the same gentleness she had when talking Jian down from panic attacks. "I know you're in pain, but you need to go."

Carver leaned heavily against Jian, body cold and shivering, and still Jian's cardinal fire burned like this sickly siren was a threat.

"What did you do to him?" Jian asked, even as he suspected he didn't want to know the answer.

The Professor shook her head quickly. "Jian, please. We don't have time. Carver needs help."

She patted her coat pockets and then pulled a vial of black liquid out.

"This is Damian's plasma," she explained as she handed the vial to Jian. "It should keep Carver alive until his body stabilizes. You should give it to him while he's still conscious."

She turned and crouched down to lay a hand on Saoirse's forehead without another word.

Well, Jian knew when to be a good soldier and follow orders.

He half-carried Carver through the parking lot to his plain, silver auto. The ambulance arrived just seconds later. Paramedics started shuffling Saoirse and the Professor inside. Jian got Carver in the passenger's seat of the auto and himself in the driver's side.

He opened the vial of plasma.

"Drink this," he ordered.

Carver lifted his hand a little, but it fell limp mid-air.

"Can't." His voice was weak.

Jian released a long-suffering sigh and held the vial to Carver's lips. Barely any liquid had poured out before Carver spat the plasma out.

"Damn it!" Jian hissed. "Why?"

"Burns," Carver rasped.

Jian emptied the vial into his own mouth. The plasma did burn, but it was nothing to a demon who breathed flames. Carver turned his head away, so Jian straddled his hips. That impossibly low warning drone, dizzying this close, filled the cabin. And for a moment, Jian did hesitate while his fight-or-flight threatened to kick in. His entire body practically vibrated with the need to control and subdue.

Jian took Carver's jaw and pressed their lips together. Carver tried to close his mouth when plasma spilled into it, but Jian held his jaw open until all the liquid had been transferred. The choked sounds Carver made only fed the bloodlust's flames. Heat overwhelmed Jian's chest where his cardinal fire burned with the desire to sink his fangs into the softness pressed to them.

But he pulled away and clamped a hand over Carver's mouth.

"Swallow it if you want the burning to stop," he said stiffly and tried not to drink in the raw fear of the blue eyes staring up at him.

The demon in him wanted to force this siren into submission. The rational half of him remembered that Carver needed a friend right now, even if that meant a rough friend.

Carver hesitated a moment before swallowing. Jian removed his hand and slid back over to the driver's seat. Barely restrained aggression burned in him. His chest glowed, and a glance in his rearview mirror showed a glowing ring of gold around his irises.

"I'm sorry," Carver mumbled between coughs. "I can't…think."

The weakness in his voice made Jian's mouth water, and he took a deep breath. Now wasn't the time for this.

Carver's eyes closed slowly. "So…sorry."

Jian glanced at him askance. Carver was so vulnerable right now.

"Don't be sorry," Jian said. "Just rest."

CHAPTER SIX

His sister's pain echoed through his left eye, crushing like the ocean's pressure. The Professor had blackened fingers in Saoirse's eye. Seconds later, the pain abruptly ended. Saoirse went limp. Blood streamed from her eye socket, and water on the ground roiled up to lap it, staunching the bleeding.

Carver hunched over his sister and pulled her into his lap. She still had a pulse. It beat strongly against his hand when he laid it over her chest.

Thomas appeared beside her. "She's not fine," he said softly. "It feels like...something powerful—something beyond what she can hold in her body."

"I didn't want this," the Professor murmured.

A deep instinct to run, to avoid whatever the Professor intended, burned down Carver's legs. He'd never been so sure that he shouldn't be near her than right then.

She crouched down to his eye level. Her hand, black as charcoal, trembled at her side.

"I'm sorry," she breathed, voice light as the air. "Your sister needs more help than this to live."

He could hear his heartbeat in his ears, blood roaring through him with every primal voice telling him to run now.

Thomas appeared behind the Professor, eyes wide and terrified.

"Don't do this," he urged. "You can feel how bad it is."

"What does she need?" Carver heard himself ask the Professor.

"More than I can give her on my own," she said and grabbed his hand. "I need something from you."

The words made his stomach turn, and the refusal was at his lips automatically.

But his sister was dying.

"Take it," he said, surprised by the strength of his voice, despite the tightness in his throat. "Whatever you need, take it."

The Professor wouldn't look at him. "You have to know exactly what this entails before you agree to it."

He didn't think the terms and conditions mattered. There was nothing he wouldn't agree to if it meant Saoirse got to live, but the look in the Professor's eyes stopped him from saying as much.

"What I ask for is the life you've yet to live," she continued quietly, but firmly. "You will be bound to me. If I die, you will perish with me. If I give you an order, you will have no choice but to obey it. My pain will be your pain, and my burdens yours to bear with me. I will own you in body and mind—forever."

He swallowed past the tightness in his throat. What she asked for was his soul. It was worse than slavery.

"Meallán," Thomas rasped, voice small and thin. "Please. Don't do this."

Carver made his mouth move past the stiffness in his jaw.

"Do it," he said.

The Professor stared at him a moment, as if searching for any hint of doubt.

"You won't be the same person after," she cautioned. "You'll become something else entirely, not a siren nor a human nor any known race."

"Like you?"

She was quiet for a beat. "Exactly like me."

His fear didn't feel like his own as it pulsed through him. It belonged to whatever primal part of him recognized this being before him as the true threat that she was. But the fear wasn't his, not really. The part of him that knew how to live and feel had died a century ago.

If he had a soul still, it didn't seem worth saving.

Thomas squeezed his eyes shut and turned away.

"It doesn't matter," Carver mumbled. "Just do it."

The Professor pulled him closer, so he was directly facing her. He immediately lowered his gaze, but she lifted his chin up with a finger.

"Look into my eyes," she instructed.

He met her stare directly. The rest of the world darkened until he could only see two rings of amber. Something pressed against his lips. A metallic tang touched his tongue. It was like ice, creeping into him slowly and unyieldingly. His legs gave out under him until he was falling—into amber like the fires that roiled deep in the earth.

He never felt the ground.

Carver's eyes fluttered open. He stared up at an unfamiliar, red ceiling. Early morning light filtered through a window beside him. A headache throbbed behind his eyes. The vague memory of fire and smoke lingered at his mouth.

He sat up. The cream-colored walls around him were nearly bare, save for a black-and-white picture of a young woman. The hardwood floors were barely visible beneath piles of electronic equipment that looked like machine parts. Something like an altar rested against a wall. It was nothing more than a table with a red cloth on it. A sketch of a man's smiling face sat in a frame on the altar. A stick of incense burned in front of the picture. By the sharp, earthy scent, it was aloeswood.

Carver sat in a bed he didn't recognize. He climbed out of it, narrowly missing the blood-filled bucket on the floor. The world spun for a moment, and when it righted itself, memories of the previous day hit him in a rush. He sprinted out of the room, focused singularly on Saoirse. But he didn't get far.

As soon as he rounded into the hall, something stood in his path. Jian easily stepped aside before they collided. Carver stumbled and slammed his shoulder into a wall.

"Thank you for sparing me the need to check if you're alive," Jian muttered and sipped from the mug in his hand, "but please don't run around my house."

Carver straightened quickly, ignoring every aching protest in his body at the movement. "I want to see my sister."

"I know."

Jian turned into what looked to be a living room with a leather couch, coffee table, and bookcase. A window across the room had a long crack running through it. The woman pictured in the bedroom was shown in a more recent photograph that sat on a table below the window.

Carver glanced at the front door before following Jian. He didn't know where in the city he was or where his auto was. His stomach rumbled the moment he smelled food. But he had to be sure his sister was okay.

"Can you take me to Saoirse?" he asked.

Jian sipped his coffee again. His body language was too relaxed for the anger behind his eyes. No, not anger—restrained aggression.

"No," he said, tone betraying none of his feelings. "The Professor says it's too dangerous right now. You should speak with her."

Don't worry now. Saoirse will be fine with the Professor.

There was only a fraction of a second where he questioned where the thought came from before the panic drained from him. The desire to see his sister lost its urgency. She'd be fine after the Professor took care of her, wouldn't she?

Jian headed into the kitchen, tucked beside a dining area that extended from the living room. The kitchen was just big enough for one person to comfortably cook in it, and the dining area had only a small table with two chairs near a window. A pneumatic tube port was built into the wall by the fridge. It was rare for someone to have one in their house, but then Jian probably needed it for work.

Carver's stomach growled again. Jian took the lid off a pressure cooker and grabbed a ladle from the counter. He stirred the cooker's contents. The scent of star anise, fish sauce, and tomato drifted through the air.

"Damian called me about an hour ago," Jian said flatly. "Your sister is still asleep, but the Professor is certain she will make a full recovery."

He pulled two bowls from a cabinet and filled them with noodles sitting in a colander by the sink.

"How long have I been out?" Carver asked.

Jian didn't answer while he ladled stew into the bowls.

"Almost nineteen hours at this point," he muttered. "Sit."

He added scallions and chopped mint to the bowls, and then set them on the table with chopsticks and spoons.

Carver sat at the small table and breathed in the stew's aroma.

"I feel like I've had this in Lac Kha," he commented. "Is it Tong, too? Or…sorry, I don't mean to be presumptuous. Your name is Tong, isn't it?"

Jian's brows nearly touched his hairline. "You're full of surprises, detective."

His lips twitched, and some of the hostility in his gaze dimmed.

"Half Tong and half Lac," he explained, "but I was raised in Nha Song with my mother. My given name, Tuan, is Lac, but all my Tong family use my middle name, Rong. And then everyone else just uses my family name."

"So Jian isn't your given name." Carver paused to consider that a moment. "I suppose I should have known that with your age. 'Jian' didn't really start becoming a given name until the Sua Hei Li rose to power, and you were definitely born before then."

"History buff?"

"Travel. I regularly sailed around East Sima until the 1820s."

Jian went back into the kitchen to get a bottle of chili sauce and two lime wedges sitting by the sink. Carver murmured a word of thanks when Jian handed him a wedge.

"You must have gotten up early to make this," Carver commented, noting that the light outside the window indicated sunrise wasn't so long ago.

Jian shrugged. "It's not like I slept anyway with you hocking up blood every hour."

Carver's face heated. "I'm so sorry. I didn't want to—"

"No apologizing. I willingly signed up to look after you yesterday. You have nothing to apologize for."

Jian's tone was firm, but not unkind.

Carver chewed his lip a moment. "Then thank you."

Jian gave a small smile. "I would ask you what exactly happened yesterday, but something tells me you know as much as I."

That was a fair observation. In fact, Carver could only vaguely recall yesterday. He remembered the Professor giving him some kind of warning, and then he'd bled a lot. His stomach turned at a dim memory of organs tearing inside his body.

"Probably," he mumbled. "All I know is that the Professor took something from me to save my sister."

"Mm."

Jian didn't say anything else, just stared pensively at his stew.

They were silent while they added various amounts of chili sauce and lime to their bowls. It smelled a little different than what he'd had before, with more star anise than usual, adding extra spice to it. Carver had to force himself to eat slowly.

Thomas appeared abruptly in the living room, peering out the cracked window. He looked different than usual. The white button-down and jeans he'd donned for a century had been replaced by the dark pinstripe suit he'd worn to church every Sunday, and his short curls were almost entirely gray now, as if he'd aged beyond his death.

Carver couldn't help but stare. A hundred years had passed without change to Thomas' appearance, but now it had.

"Detective?" Jian prompted and followed Carver's eyes to the window. "Everything all right?"

Carver pulled his eyes away from his late husband. "No, sorry," he mumbled. "My head isn't quite right still."

Jian looked down at his food, as if he thought nothing of the odd interaction, but Carver knew better than to believe Jian didn't suspect something was wrong. This demon understood more than he let on. He knew how to read people like they were books he could skim through.

"He's not the enemy," Thomas said abruptly. "Is being known such a threat that you need to hide every facet of yourself from anyone willing to look deeper?"

"Eat," Jian said simply. "You'll feel better."

Carver obediently ate a spoonful of impossibly tender beef before mumbling, "You are quite generous."

"On the contrary, I am very selfish."

That wasn't something most people admitted to. Before Carver could respond, Jian continued.

"So the Ministry wants your sister dead, given that they sent Gars after her. Why? I don't understand why they would care about the two of you so much. If their only issue is genetics, this seems like a waste of resources."

"It's not quite that simple," Carver admitted. "My mother was a minister herself. By having me, she tainted her bloodline, which is everything to the ministers. Law dictates that the mother of a male be executed with all her children before the bloodline can continue. They did execute her when they killed my father, but I escaped with Saoirse."

Jian ate a spoonful of noodles before speaking. "I would think they'd be more concerned with you passing on your genes than Saoirse since she's female."

Carver shook his head. "Most male sirens are infertile, myself included. Siren genes aren't really compatible with a Y chromosome. But that's honestly not the main reason that male sirens are hunted. Most of us are khavira."

"Khavira?"

"I suppose you wouldn't know us sirens' dirty secret." Carver took a breath before continuing. "When sirens bond, it intertwines nervous systems, melds two individuals together as one. Some sirens, khavira, have a genetic defect that makes them deadly when they try to bond.

104

There's no gentle meeting of minds. Khavira rend their partner's neurons apart. Most sirens don't even know they are one until it's too late. Male sirens are almost four times more likely to have this genetic defect. The Ministry doesn't want us walking around as a testament to siren genetic fragility."

Jian grimaced. "But you're obviously not khavira if you've successfully bonded. I guess I've never known the Ministry to be particularly reasonable where blood is concerned, though. The whole idea of blood purity is why we have Garsuk at all."

The venom in Jian's voice at the last statement surprised Carver, if only because it revealed a firm opinion on something. Was it the usual hatred for the Gars? Personal stake beyond the case?

"I know that look, detective," Jian said abruptly. "Trying to figure me out?"

Carver lowered his eyes. "Force of habit. Sorry."

Jian shrugged. "I do the same thing. Ask what you want."

"I don't want to be rude."

"Your manners are impeccable, detective." Jian's smile was almost predatory as he spoke. "And if you're curious about something, I would much prefer you ask the question."

Carver swallowed, overcome with the sense that there was something more to the offer than politeness. Never had anyone baffled him so much. What were this demon's intentions?

Thomas peered into the pressure cooker in the kitchen.

"He's just trying to get to know you in the only way that he knows how," he commented. "Strong demons come from strong bloodlines.

You think he comes from a healthy family structure? I'm sure he was raised to dissect people's personalities and exploit their weaknesses, not to form genuine connections."

"You seem to have a strong opinion on blood purity," Carver remarked, keeping his voice level, so as not to reveal the anxiety creeping up his throat. "Have you been affected personally, beyond the Gars?"

Jian's brows lifted. "I'm surprised you don't know my pedigree. It was the talk of the High Court when I first started working there."

"Your pedigree?"

Jian chewed another spoonful of noodles. "There are a handful of demon families that have never paired with other races or even other mixed demons—the Pure Clans. I'm the second youngest member of one such clan."

Carver was familiar with the Pure Clans, if only because he and his sister had worked with someone from them years ago. But he didn't know much more than that they had tried to eradicate the vampires in the north of Tong Bei. He had little cause these days to get involved in world politics like he had when he was still an Inquisitor. There was a Clan Jian, which he vaguely recalled hadn't fared well in the war.

"A pureblood?" he mumbled, which seemed to be the wrong thing to say, as Jian's nose scrunched in distaste.

"I've never cared for the distinction." Jian glanced at the cracked window. "What's the point anyway? Stronger abilities? My power doesn't mean much against bombs and bullets, never mind that most purebloods slowly go insane from bloodlust."

The sadness and fear that knotted in Carver's gut didn't feel entirely his own, and if it was a mirror response of what Jian felt, the emotion had to be strong.

"Rejection of his upbringing, perhaps his entire family," Thomas commented while looking around the kitchen. "Ask him about his family."

"If you're the second youngest," Carver said, "who's the youngest?"

"My daughter." Jian nodded to the photo of a young woman by the window. "As soon as I was of age, my parents married me off to a woman of their choice, and I gave them a pureblood daughter before we divorced. It's fairly common in my family. You marry to preserve the bloodline, and once that's done, no one cares if you stick with your partner."

Carver frowned. "That doesn't sound like a great foundation for any relationship."

Jian's smile was sardonic. The curl of his lips didn't sit right on his face.

"No," he murmured, "I suppose it isn't."

Before Carver could ask what that reaction meant, Jian continued. "I would've sacrificed much more for my family. My parents did their best with the culture they were given, and my aunts and uncles were always there to give me tips on how to be a good husband—some of it bad advice, albeit well-meaning. I didn't really think about my own happiness, especially when everyone else had forgotten their own for the same reasons. Family was everything to them."

"And him," Thomas said with a glance back at the demon in question.

"You're close then with your family?" Carver prompted.

Jian was quiet for a moment. "I was. We're precious few after the war."

Sadness was clear in his voice, but there was something disingenuous about it. His feelings about his family's death were clearly complex.

"I'm not sure you want condolences," Carver observed, "so I won't offer any."

"Much appreciated." Jian sat straighter. "I did toss aside most of my filial piety when I came to work for the Professor. Hard to continue the stuffy, noble act in the midst of Palitz during the twenties."

Thomas had a small smile. "Changing the subject," he remarked, "but giving you plenty of information on something else to obscure his unwillingness to talk. Family is a rough topic then."

And Jian wasn't someone they were here to interrogate. Carver saw no reason to prod at old wounds.

"I just missed being in the Palitz province during the twenties," he said. "My husband and I had a place up in Havitzford that I sold after he died in 1811."

Jian rested his chin in a hand. "I can't imagine being gay at that time."

A cold sorrow, aged and familiar, swept through Carver. "It was a little easier than you might think. I passed as a woman for many,
108

many years until Thomas died."

"Wait, your solution to the problem was just to pass as a woman? Didn't that get exhausting?"

Carver shrugged. "Sirens don't really have a firm concept of gender—all-female normally, so why would we? Males aren't even really regarded as a separate gender, just a genetic fluke. It's all arbitrary rules anyway. Wasn't that hard just to keep my head down and act demure."

Jian opened his mouth to say something when the phone in his kitchen rang. He stood from the table with a sigh and went to answer it.

"Jian," he said tersely.

There was a pause, and then he pressed a button on the phone's cradle. The Professor's voice came through loudly.

"Is Carver awake?" she asked.

"I am," Carver answered as he came closer. "Is Saoirse—?"

"She'll be fine. That's not what I'm calling about. There are…things…we need to discuss." She sighed heavily. "We should speak privately. Can I meet you at your apartment?"

Carver could only imagine how that discussion would go. Yesterday's events were fuzzy, but he could remember that they were significant—that something life-altering had happened.

"You changed," Thomas said, voice so low that it was hard to hear. "She changed you—and me by extension. I feel…"

Carver couldn't stop himself from looking past Jian to his husband.

"I feel like I'm…more than us," Thomas finished after a beat.

Carver wasn't sure what that meant, but he couldn't ask about it just yet while Jian was watching.

"I'll be there soon," Carver promised, and something shot through him. It made his legs tense with the impulse to get up and leave now.

"Thank you, dear," the Professor said, "but take your time and eat. You need your strength. I'll wait."

The phone clicked out of connection.

"I expect a good explanation from her." His voice was low, almost a growl. "You nearly died. She can't just play with people's lives."

"I like this man," Thomas remarked with a wry smile.

Carver strangely couldn't hold any malice for the Professor. She'd saved his sister. He wasn't sure how, but he knew that much.

Instead of saying that, he asked, "Would you mind giving me a ride to my apartment?"

"Not at all." Jian pointed at Carver's bowl with his chopsticks. "But eat first."

Carver nodded obediently and returned to the table. Jian did the same after putting the phone back in its cradle. They were silent for a while, just eating. The food was unfairly good, and Carver hoped that was excuse enough not to talk. As irrational as it was, his manners dictated he act as a good guest and make conversation.

"You didn't have to do so much to look after me," Carver said after a minute. "Thank you."

Jian didn't respond, just stared. Carver didn't usually have problems with eye contact since siren culture demanded it far more than most others, but Jian wasn't just looking. There was always
110

something behind his eyes, something calculating and rapacious. That was probably what made him a good hunter.

After a moment, a warm smile alighted on his lips.

"You're quite welcome," he said.

Carver blinked, transfixed by the expression, and then his cheeks heated inexplicably.

Jian's smile widened.

◊◊◊

Everything was stiff, and Saoirse's head throbbed like it'd been beaten into concrete multiple times. Something was strapped to her face. It pressed over her left eye. The pain she'd come to expect from it was gone, however, and it seemed...absent. Her eye was missing entirely, wasn't it? It hadn't regrown like it did before.

A dim memory of icy fingers enclosing around her eye flashed through her mind. Her brother had been right there at the Court's steps, as if by fate or luck or something else impossible. He'd been with a woman who looked like the one who'd gifted the eye. But it wasn't the same person. The woman had seemed even older despite looking nearly identical. It was in her gaze—a gaze that had witnessed the beginning of all things and waited eternally to oversee the end. The Professor. She had to be the Professor.

Panic started to rise in Saoirse inexplicably.

Zero degrees equaled zero. Fifteen degrees equaled point- two-seven-nine. Thirty degrees equaled point-five. Forty-five degrees equaled point-seven-zero-seven. Sixty degrees equaled point-eight-six-six. Ninety degrees and cosine zero equaled one…

She forced herself to breathe as she repeated the numbers in her head, and the panic faded. Her remaining eye blinked open to see off-white walls and floors. The softness at her back suggested she was on a bed, and its metal railings indicated a hospital bed. White sheets were over her. A digital monitor displayed her heart rate at just under forty beats per minute—a little high for her race. Faint voices speaking in a language she didn't recognize drifted through the air. They seemed sharp, like they were upset.

A man in a white doctor's coat stood by the door to this small room. His silver hair was characteristic of pureblooded vampires, and his eyes were a similar pale gray. He spoke with a tall person who had white markings through their tawny skin—fae slave brands. A thick, black braid wove over their shoulder.

They stopped talking when she forced herself up on her elbows despite how her ribs ached with the movement. It seemed like her wounds had healed. Whatever had been done to her had worked. There was no decay blade in her side or broken bones or claw marks left on her. She didn't have her left eye either, but that seemed a blessing.

"Who are you?" she asked, her tone perhaps too even simply from years of training to hide her emotions. "No, wait. Vampiric doctor. Slave brands from the Ekhabai Occupation. Fae. The Professor's spouses."

The vampire's brows shot up, which didn't surprise her. Most people didn't recognize the tattoos on the fae as slave markings, as the slave trade ended more than five thousand years ago. Only the elder generations remembered it anymore. She knew about it only because she'd had to study it for work.

"Damian Idylla," the vampire introduced. "I've been your doctor since you crashed into the Court. This is my spouse, Palus."

She stared at him. "I'm in a hospital."

"You are."

"Fuck," she hissed and threw the sheets off her.

He rushed over to lay a hand on her shoulder, stopping her before she moved more. "You just recovered from something that's disrupted your nervous system for a long time. Take it slow."

She shrugged his hand off and stood. "I need to see my brother. What's his name now? I keep forgetting."

Palus' eyes narrowed. "Ernest Declan Carver," they offered tightly.

Her heart twisted. She hadn't heard Declan's name in a long time, and Meallán hadn't gone by Ernest since she was a child.

"Of course," she mumbled.

"Your brother mentioned you've concealed that he's alive," Palus remarked. "Why? Was it just to leave the Inquisitors? There are simpler ways to resign."

"No, it was so the Ministry would stop coming after him. They don't like that he's male. That's why they started hunting us to begin with."

She rolled her neck, sending cracks through it. "Fuck," she muttered. "Everything's stiff. How long have I been out?"

Damian looked her over, as if he was trying to figure out how she was related to her brother. That was a common reaction. Meallán was polite and nice and proper, if a bit cranky. She said "fuck" like it was a creative flourish for her sentences and thought manners were overrated unless it got her something.

"A full day," Damian said. "I don't know if you remember crashing into the High Court."

She froze. "We talking the building or the parking lot?"

"Just the parking lot. You obviously weren't in your right mind, and we know that."

She swallowed and gingerly touched her eye patch. "I remember my brother being there. Is he the one who took my eye?"

Palus stepped closer, eyes boring into her. "No, that was the Professor. You had something in your eye. This was the only way to remove it. Do you know how your eye was altered to begin with?"

"Did the Professor not tell you?"

When they just stared at her expectantly, she said, "A woman rescued me from the Gars when they first caught up to me. She said the eye would keep me alive long enough to make it here, even with how severely I was injured."

Damian exchanged a glance with his spouse. "What was this woman like?"

Saoirse glanced between him and Palus. "I mean this respectfully, but you're both ancient. Those of us who are younger can always tell when we're in the presence of people like yourselves. So when I say that this woman was like you, I mean that she had power and age. She also looked an awful lot like another woman who was there when I crashed—identical almost—but I don't think they were the same person."

Palus' gaze was hard. "What happened?"

Saoirse let out a long breath before speaking. "I was investigating the Gars up north when this pack pursued me. They were being paid by the Ministry to capture me. I can't say definitively what for, but I suspect that it was to lure my brother to get me. They want to kill both of us. I escaped after that woman altered my eye. She claimed I'd also need it to save my brother. The Gars have been chasing me all the way here."

When Palus and Damian just stared at each other, Saoirse headed for the door.

"I'm going to see my brother," she said. "He's probably losing his mind over me."

Palus stepped in front of her. "Wait. Let me drive you."

Damian frowned, but the look they shot him made his mouth shut.

"Go home, *aya*." Their tone was light, but the look in their eyes was firm. "You need rest. I'll take it from here."

Saoirse was vaguely amused at the display. It was clear which one of them was used to giving orders in this relationship.

"Do you know anything else about the Gars that are hunting you?" Palus asked and pushed the door open for her.

She stepped through, entering a short hallway with the same white walls and floor as the room. "I know lots. Eastern packs. Most hired hands. No vendetta against me personally. They're obviously just in this for the money and have no qualms killing half-bloods. It's the Ministry's usual choice."

"And do you think they're here?"

"Oh, I know they are, and they'll be looking for me and my brother."

Palus sighed. "All right. Let's get you to Carver, and I'll have Peacekeepers posted on you both until I figure out what the Inquisitors want to do."

Saoirse grimaced at that. They'd probably want to shepherd her away to a safe house or something until they could erase all evidence of her from ICS data, which could take a while. She probably wouldn't be allowed to work on combatting the Gars with Meallán.

Well, maybe he wasn't as bad a detective as she teased him for.

◊◊◊

Carver didn't see the Professor, but he somehow knew she was nearby. The scent of her, like smoke and redwood trees, filled his nose as he stood at his apartment door. Jian had dropped him off after making sure he was fine to walk around on his own. Carver got the sense that Jian hadn't wanted to leave him alone with the Professor, but this was a private matter—more than Carver fully understood, even as he was certain of it.

When he unlocked his door, the Professor was sitting on his couch. Mouna purred in her lap while she stroked her. Carver wasn't angry that the Professor had broken into his place. As odd as it was, he felt like his apartment belonged to her.

"Forgive me for letting myself in," she said softly, "but your cat hadn't been fed since yesterday. I thought she should eat."

Carver shut his door and locked it.

"Thank you," he mumbled absently and glanced at his bathroom. "Do you mind if I shower and change my clothes?"

She didn't turn her head to look at him, just kept petting Mouna. "Not at all. Please take your time."

He headed into the bedroom and grabbed a change of clothes from his dresser before going into the bathroom. His shower was swift. The water felt indescribably good on his skin. He soaked it in, both figuratively and literally. By the time he stepped out, changed and clean, some of his fatigue had lifted. He almost felt normal. Almost.

Mouna was asleep in the Professor's lap when he sat on the couch. He'd found Mouna as a stray kitten, and she'd been slow to trust. That she'd be comfortable enough with the Professor to fall asleep was abnormal. But then the Professor was abnormal, wasn't she?

Thomas appeared on the couch, perched on the back of it behind the Professor. He peered down at her.

"She only shows her belly to you," he commented with an arch of his brow.

The Professor tensed and slowly looked over her shoulder. Her eyes found Thomas', and she leaned away from him.

"Oh, that's new," he muttered.

She hesitantly reached out a hand to him, but her fingers passed through his arm when she tried to touch him.

"You're not alive," she said as she withdrew her hand. "Carver, is this who I think it is?"

Carver didn't speak immediately, too stunned by this turn of events, but he forced his mouth to move after a moment.

"Professor, this is my husband," he introduced. "Thomas Carver."

She glanced between him and Thomas before speaking. "Oh, dear. I had no idea he was still…with you. I suspected that you had hallucinations from time to time, but this is…" She looked Thomas over. "You are a distinct personality."

He shrugged. "I am a complex echo of stimulated neurons who shape the image of a man long dead."

Her brows rose. "Perhaps it is a fluke of repeating electrical impulses in Carver's brain, but he's given you residence enough in his mind to have your own personhood. I can sense that much."

His eyes narrowed. "And how, Professor, can you sense that much?"

"A fair question and one I came to answer." She turned her gaze toward Carver. "But I first want to know what you remember of yesterday."

Carver took a moment to think back, wading through a haze of memories. "I remember you telling me that my sister was dying, and that you could save her if I gave you something. After that…it comes in flashes. I remember waking up in pain and Jian taking me to his house."

She nodded and pushed her bangs back from her eyes. "So you don't remember what I took from you."

Her eyes met his, and for the first time, he didn't feel compelled to look away. The amber boring into him seemed almost welcoming.

"I don't remember." He glanced up at his husband who only offered a shrug.

118

"I know only what you know," Thomas reminded him.

The Professor worried her lip. "I took your life," she said after a beat.

Carver glanced down at himself. "Pretty sure I'm still alive."

"You are, but you are not as you were and never will be again." She let out a breath. "As you've figured out, I am not one of the known races."

He waited for her to continue, inexplicably certain that it wasn't time for him to speak.

She scratched Mouna's head. "I am very old, Carver—older than I claim to be. I was here before the races, and I'll be here long after they're all gone. And now you might join me for the remainder of my life."

Dread tangled in Carver's gut. "What are you saying?"

"You are now a part of me—an extension of my being, in a matter of speaking."

What I ask for is the life you've yet to live. You will be bound to me. If I die, you will perish with me. If I give you an order, you will have no choice but to obey it. My pain will be your pain, and my burdens yours to bear with me. I will own you in body and mind—forever.

The words rushed through Carver's mind. In exchange for his sister's life, he'd sold himself into slavery.

"What are you?" Thomas breathed. "How is what you say possible?"

"I've gone by many names throughout history, none of them my own," she said as she stared down at the cat, perhaps to avoid his eyes. "I don't know what I am honestly. Humans and preterns alike used to think of my kind as gods, and maybe we were. The races collectively knew us as the Ancients. I don't know who's right. I don't think it matters. Most of us... Well, I don't know if we can die, but most of us lost our physical form a long, long time ago."

Carver shuddered. "There are more like you?"

"There's one other who still has form." Her voice was soft, weighted with a sadness that Carver had never heard from her before. "I'm certain she's the one who put the mark on your sister's eye."

Thomas grimaced, the harsh lines of his face deepening.

"And what are you and this...other?" he pressed.

The Professor was quiet for a long moment, and a tightness built in Carver's chest until it ached. It didn't seem like normal sadness. This was older and heavier—grief.

"My kind wasn't always separate," she said, voice barely above a whisper. "When we took our first breath, it was together. We shared one body and one mind. To live, though, is more than just to have a beating heart. It's also to feel—to *experience*—and when we encountered humanity, we knew love and pain and joy and sorrow. Pieces of ourselves splintered off into our children, and then further into bloodlines, which eventually became the races."

She ran a hand down her face before continuing. "The others had lived their natural life, splintered so much throughout their bloodlines that there was no longer a 'them.' It was a death, in a way—perhaps the most permanent one our kind can be allowed. I watched their progeny bloom into societies and felt the absence of

120

what had once been us. But it wasn't 'us' anymore. I was…me."

"Are you saying you are the mother of all the races?" Carver asked incredulously.

"The other Ancients referred to me as such," she said hesitantly, "but it wasn't what I know as myself who fostered the races. I'm not sure how to describe what I was back then. We were many and one all at once. It's only in the last ten thousand years or so that I've developed a concept of 'I' as distinct from the forms that we took through time. The pieces of us that broke from the whole had separate consciousness. Once they left me, they were…people—with their own beliefs and desires and personalities. I never really made the choice to be someone like the others. It was more like how an artist chisels marble away until it takes a shape of its own. I am what was left over, in a sense."

Carver wasn't sure he understood entirely, but he could accept that whoever sat beside him was her own entity. Some part of him could sense how she was whole, with a singular consciousness.

"So this other of your kind used to be part of you?" Thomas prompted as he folded his arms over his chest.

The Professor nodded. "'Sister' is probably the most applicable term. She was the first to leave and develop a sense of self. She didn't have children until very recently, so she never disappeared into a bloodline like everyone else. We've always been cordial. I don't know why she's done this, but I suspect it was to force my hand."

"You needed me to counteract what she'd done to Saoirse," Carver remarked. "Why would she need to force your hand?"

She glanced at Thomas. "Each of us Ancients has a specialty. Hers is a sense for what's yet to come. She does things that support a better future, even if it's not obvious to everyone else and even when it initially seems detrimental. I could sense this is what she wanted. Even apart, we're always aware of each other, like one might be aware of their own hand. We can feel every race as part of us, too— spread out all over the globe, but connected to us regardless."

Carver let the words run through his mind, trying to piece together all this information into something coherent. If she still felt the races as part of herself, then pieces of her—or whatever she'd been—had to still be in them. Sirens, vampires, fae, demons, and lycans were all her in some small part. Could she reclaim them as herself again?

"When I gave you my life," he said, "you reclaimed the part of you that fractured into the siren race, didn't you? Why didn't that change you?"

Thomas stood from the couch. "Too small," he reasoned. "It would be a tiny fraction after this many generations. Even an Origin would be, at most, a twelfth of her."

The Professor nodded. "The part of me that exists in one person is small enough that it only gives me more power if I take it back," she confirmed. "What I am is far beyond the scope of my mortal form. If I am an ocean, you are but a drop in it. That said, the part of me that you held pervaded all of you—everything that you are. In returning it to myself, you had to come with."

Carver pressed his fingers into his knee, half expecting that he wouldn't feel it as his, but the pressure was as it had always felt.

Thomas rounded the couch to lay a hand on Carver's shoulder. The touch still didn't feel quite there, just a memory of the warmth and weight of it. Carver was thankful for it all the same.

"And your sister intended for you to reclaim him?" Thomas asked haltingly, as if unsure of his words. "Why?"

The Professor shrugged. "I wish I could say. Our language in writing was once known as the Sigils of Ancients. The one she put on your sister infused her with our essence. It kept Saoirse alive against whatever injuries the Gars gave her, but if left long enough, it would have destroyed her. No one can bear the power of an Ancient indefinitely, unless they're reclaimed like you were. I assume that the Origin descendent that Jian's contact mentioned was actually my sister meddling in things. I'll be leaving shortly to go searching for her and hopefully get some answers. In the meantime, you'll need to stay here and deal with the Gars. It's clear that they mean to kill you and your sister on behalf of the Ministry. Don't let them, would you?"

Carver sighed and pinched the bridge of his nose. "They killed Thomas the first time they attacked us."

She glanced up at his husband. "I hate to say it like this, but you don't have a weaker human to look after this time. I will warn you that your body is going to go through changes that will be incredibly difficult on you. You need to survive until you are strong enough to wield my power. If you try to rush these changes, you could end up destroying your physical form, and there is only so much I can do to repair you in that instance."

His mouth opened to respond, but she held up a hand stopping him.

"Saoirse is here," she said.

He looked back at his front door just before he heard a knock. When he turned to the Professor again, she was gone, and Mouna lay on the couch—sound asleep, as if she hadn't been resting on a person a moment ago.

Thomas let out a long breath. "I'm sure she'll be back," he said. "She wouldn't abandon you now."

"How can you be so sure?" Carver grumbled as he stood.

"I know what you do."

Thomas disappeared.

Another round of knocks was louder, almost violent.

Carver went to open the door. What he expected was his sister. What he did not expect was a firm shove in the chest.

He stumbled back.

"What the hell are you—?"

He stopped when strong arms wrapped around him, squeezing hard enough to bruise.

"She told me you would die if I didn't get to you in time," Saoirse rasped into his chest. "Fuck you, making me worry like this."

Something like a sob left her. Carver's ribs tightened at the sound. No matter how old she got, he was still her older brother who'd carried her across the ocean, who'd raised her, who'd fought beside her.

He pressed his cheek to her temple and waited while she composed herself. After a minute, she pulled away and wiped at her face.

"I'm sorry," he said gently. "I didn't know you needed me, *ahra*."

"Don't call me *ahra*." There was a slight pout to her lips.

"*Ahra, ahra, ahra,*" he said in a singsong voice.

Her lips twitched. "You better not call me that in front of anyone else."

She pressed a hand to her eye patch and then rubbed her forehead. Something else was wrong. He could almost sense how disquieted she was.

"What's going on, Saoirse?" he asked.

"When I was running from the Gars, I saw…" She took a breath. "Maeva's back."

Just the name made ice run through him.

"The Ministry really wants to kill you, don't they?" he mumbled. "I can't believe they called her in again."

"She's definitely not cheap." She shook her head. "Nothing to be done about it now. I'm just glad you're all right."

"A sight better than you, literally crashing into the High Court."

A small smile touched her lips as she shoved his shoulder. "Whatever. I'm still cool. You've got the worst name I've ever heard now."

He frowned. "What's wrong with it?"

She arched a brow. "Ernest Declan Carver? Really? It doesn't suit you at all."

"Well, my real name was even more recognizable."

"What—you mean Meallán isn't a common name?"

He chuckled and pulled her into another hug. She was real and solid and warm in his arms.

"What—?" she started.

"I'm glad you're okay," he said into the top of her head. "When I saw you climb out of that auto, I thought my heart would stop."

She was rigid for a beat, and then relaxed and wrapped her arms around his waist. They stayed like that for a long moment until she pulled away.

"Okay, that's enough sappiness," she muttered as she wiped at his eyes. "All this emotion is tiring me."

He smiled and ruffled her hair. She swatted his hands away with a grimace, making him laugh, but his amusement was short-lived.

Dizziness struck him suddenly. Saoirse caught him around the middle before he fell.

"What was that?" she asked and held his sides tightly to keep him upright.

He held a hand to his head. "I'm...ill."

It wasn't a lie exactly, but he didn't think now was the time to talk about the bargain he'd made with the Professor. She had enough to worry about.

She led him to the couch and sat him down. Mouna immediately jumped from her cushion and pushed her head against Saoirse's leg.

"You still remember me, do you?" Saoirse said as she scratched Mouna's head.

"Mouna forgets no one." Carver leaned back into the couch and let out a tired breath. "Would it be bad of me to take a nap at seven in the morning?"

Saoirse pushed his hair from his eyes. "Are you having an episode? Vertigo? Fatigue?"

"A bit of everything." He let his eyes close, feeling heavier. "I'm just going to sleep for a bit."

She smoothed his hair back. "I'll be here."

CHAPTER SEVEN

The ocean stretched beyond the horizon. He sunk his feet into the sand as he stepped toward the water's edge. Reds and golds filled the cloudy sky as the sun started to lower toward the horizon line. Light shimmered on the water's surface until it settled into placidity like glass. The sky reflected perfectly on it.

A woman stood at the edge of the water. Her hair fell in tight coils down to her ankles, moving and swelling around her as if she were submerged in water. It was black as a shadow, and her skin was even darker, absorbing light the way black holes did. Only the slight shimmer of scales on her arms and legs gave a hint to her slender form. They glinted almost like stars against her night-dark figure. She kept her back to him, facing the setting sun.

"I gave you life, so you could live it."

The voice came from her, but also from every direction. It whispered with the wind, even as it held the depth of the ocean in it.

Her form started to vanish as the sun lowered under the horizon. He barely made it to her side before the last rays of light disappeared. Tears streamed from her black eyes, falling in heavy streams that spilled into the water below.

Darkness filled his vision, and pressure abruptly weighed on him, forcing the air from his lungs. When he moved his arms, they dragged through water. A point of distorted light shone above him, and he swam for it.

The sun blinded him when he breached the surface. He gasped in a breath of warm air. A figure stood impossibly midair, blocking out the sun. Their features were shadowed from the backlight, but the broadness of their shoulders seemed masculine.

They reached up to cradle his face in gentle hands. He didn't resist as he was pulled toward the figure. His lips met theirs, and the taste of smoke touched his tongue. A force like a wave pushed at him. The world seemed to flip as he landed on his back with the sun beaming down at him. It was slightly obscured behind the figure's shoulder.

Rough fingers pressed into his thighs and pushed them apart. His hands came up to grasp at the strong curves of back muscles over him. They lacked the uneven ridges from whip scars that his husband had, but he didn't stop this figure from pressing their hips together. Want burned hot through him at the first thrust into him. He could barely remember how it felt to enjoy sex, but his body acted as though it had never forgotten.

Shocks of pleasure shot up his spine with every thrust. His breaths came harshly. He dug his nails into an unfamiliar back. A moan left him when the pace increased, and he barely recognized his own voice.

His eyes snapped open to see light streaming through his tiny bedroom window. The sepia walls weren't a comfort on his aching eyes. His room was sparsely furnished with only a dresser and a nightstand. Everything was pristinely clean, save for a pile of clothes on the floor that Saoirse had probably stripped from him when she'd carried him to bed.

He glanced at the clock on his nightstand and groaned when he saw it was six in the morning—almost a full twenty-four hours since he fell asleep. His limbs stretched over his bed in a futile attempt to cool down. Sweat soaked through his boxers and coated his skin. For all the time he spent unconscious, he didn't feel rested at all. His muscles ached like he'd swum the ocean again. Something seemed to burn inside him, setting his blood ablaze.

And then there was the inconvenient stiffness between his legs.

He reluctantly looked down at his erection pressing almost painfully against the fabric of his boxers.

Why now? A century of impotence had been undone, probably because of whatever changes he was undergoing, and he could have done without it. Feeding off sexual energy didn't require his own pleasure, just that he could cause others' pleasure. Sex was hard enough without having to worry about extra sensation that might make his nausea worse.

He almost expected Thomas to appear and comment on his predicament, but his husband was notably absent from the room. Maybe that had to do with nerves. Maybe it was the Professor's changes to his body.

He waited a solid ten minutes, trying to think deeply on the difficult and chaotic future ahead of him, but he did not get any softer. With a long-suffering sigh, he pulled his boxers down and wrapped a hand around himself.

The electric pulse that shot up his spine at the first stroke took him by surprise. He froze for a moment, not sure if he enjoyed the feeling or not, and experimentally stroked himself again. The sensation this time was less intense. He forced himself to breathe through his nose as tingling spread through him. It was almost pleasurable, and he was thankful that it at least didn't make him queasy.

After a few more minutes, the sensation started to feel neutral, and the erection still wasn't going away. He suspected he was going to do this for a while unless he got himself into it. His mind strayed to the dark figure from his dream.

How many years had it been since he'd felt good from penetration? It'd been easy enough for the past century just to lay there and let his partners take their pleasure from his body, but it'd been a neutral, verging on unpleasant, feeling for him. The dream had been different. He'd *wanted*. Desire had run hot through him, and he'd clung to the person filling him and craved more.

His breath caught as he sank two fingers into himself. He was more wet than he'd been in years, and as he stroked himself with his other hand, slick heat dripped down his knuckles. Real, undiminished pleasure shot through him when he curled his fingers up. His thighs trembled, and he swallowed a moan.

It'd been far too long since he'd felt anything like this. He was momentarily surprised that his anatomy could still function this way, but any rational thought vanished under another wave of pleasure.

He could almost imagine the stretch of a man sliding into him. His teeth trapped his lip as he lifted his hips involuntarily and curled his fingers in him again. The fantasy was surprisingly easy to sink into as he imagined lips at his and the weight of another over him. His thighs fell open more, and a whimper escaped his throat at the overwhelming amount of sensation pulsing through him.

The image of burning gold eyes flashed through his mind, and he froze. A vague memory arose of Jian climbing into his lap and pressing their lips together. It burned. Jian had been trying to force-feed Damian's plasma, and it'd hurt. But after Jian had pulled away, the taste of sweet smoke had lingered.

Carver was momentarily too alarmed at how his blood heated at the thought to analyze why Jian was at the center of it. Normally, when he even passingly thought of someone who wasn't his husband like this, he was hit with revulsion. Thinking of Jian only inspired more desire. He could almost feel the pressure on his thighs where Jian had straddled him and the brief scrape of stubble at his chin.

There'd been nothing sexual in how Jian had force-fed him. The enigmatic demon had operated with a mechanical efficiency, bordering on too rough, and still, Carver could not stop his mind from recalling the weight of Jian's hand over his mouth. A shiver ran through him at the image of carefully controlled ferocity in gold eyes.

The illusion of sharp fangs dragging down his neck and nails at his hips left phantom trails over his skin. Pressure coiled at the base of his spine. His breath hitched. He tried and failed not to imagine Jian sliding into him. The memory of sweet smoke mixed with the sea salt of his own scent as it bloomed through the room.

The pressure released all at once. He nearly bit through his lip trying to contain his cry. Pleasure stronger than he had felt in a century burst through him, forcing his back to arch off the bed and his inner walls to squeeze around his fingers. He spilled over his hand as he stroked himself through the waves of his climax.

A full minute passed before his body settled. His breaths came in shallow gasps as the remnants of an orgasm long overdue tingled through his limbs. He carefully pulled his fingers from himself and reached into his nightstand drawer for the box of tissues he'd only ever kept for guests until now. He cleaned himself before flopping onto his stomach.

This wasn't how he'd expected or wanted to spend his first waking hour today. There were many other things he had to be concerned about besides his strange bodily issues. More than that, he didn't want to analyze why he'd picked Jian of all people to make the object of his fantasy. It'd been a tame fantasy, all things considered, but he hadn't touched himself, let alone to the thought of someone, since his mate. He was not at all prepared to consider the implications of what he'd just done.

He groaned in frustration into his pillow. Maybe this was just the effects of the changes to his body from the Professor's influence, or maybe Damian's plasma had brought some long-damaged nerves back to life. Either way, his fascination with Jian was still circumstantial at best—an easy, attractive target for him to focus on in his state of confusion and uncertainty. He didn't really want to fuck

Jian. Right?

"Little late for a panic attack now, isn't it?"

Thomas' teasing tone was unwelcome.

The mattress didn't dip, but Carver could sense that his husband had sat beside him on the bed.

"I can have a panic attack whenever I please," Carver grumbled. "Where were you?"

Thomas shrugged, and while Carver couldn't see it with his face planted in his pillow, he could feel it all the same. Even with an illusion, the bond between them felt as real as the day it'd been made.

"I wanted to give you some privacy," Thomas offered after a beat.

Carver turned to peer up at his husband. Thomas wore the blue knit sweater that Saoirse had made him as a teenager. It was just a little too big.

"We haven't shared privacy with each other in over a hundred years," Carver pointed out with a sigh. "Don't lie to me now."

Thomas' brows rose. "Lie? I could never get away with such a thing with you, but if you mean to imply I had ulterior motives, I absolutely did."

Carver groaned and squeezed his eyes shut.

"It's time you desired someone else, darling," Thomas insisted, voice barely above a whisper. "There's no shame in moving on."

"Sirens don't move on. We love unto death."

"You did."

Carver's chest tightened at the words. A heavy silence settled in the room until he found the strength to speak again.

"I'm not ashamed," he admitted. "I'm afraid."

Thomas' sigh almost felt tangible, like a breeze through a window. "I know," he murmured. "I can't tell you to live, but I wish you would."

Carver grimaced. "I'm still breathing, aren't I?"

"There's more to life than a beating heart and working lungs."

When Carver opened his eyes, Thomas had disappeared. His presence never left, but it seemed subdued, as if he were trying to hide.

Vibrations on wood brought Carver's head around. He grabbed his messenger from the nightstand, and his heart stuttered when he saw the words on the screen.

I hope you're resting, Jian sent, *but I just wanted to let you know that I got some info on the Ministry's involvement with your sister. Can I come over to speak with both of you soon?*

Carver read the simple message over and over again, trying to make his brain form a reply. Eventually, his thumbs moved.

You can come over any time today, he typed. *Is it bad?*

Jian replied almost immediately. *It's not good. I already met with Palus, and they suggested keeping security around Saoirse for the time being. I wanted to talk with you both first before we decide anything.*

Carver's stomach knotted. *I appreciate it. I'll try to prepare Saoirse. When did you want to come over?*

Give me an hour?

That was probably enough time to make Saoirse coffee and prepare her for a difficult conversation. It wasn't enough time for

Carver to brace himself to see Jian, but he'd just have to live with that.

I'll see you in an hour, he typed.

Jian replied a second later. *I'll bring breakfast.*

◊◊◊

Rain was coming down in a light sprinkle when Jian parked in front of Carver's apartment complex. He hadn't gotten the number, but he remembered the unit Carver had gone into when he'd dropped him off yesterday. Saoirse answered when Jian knocked on the faded, russet door.

Even with her black eyepatch, she had the same inhuman beauty as her brother. Her bright blue dreads were tied back into a low ponytail. A black t-shirt too big for her, probably stolen from Carver, hung on her muscled frame, and her shorts were small enough that they barely peeked out from beneath the shirt. Jian made a point not to stare at the smooth, umber skin of her legs.

"You're Jian?" she prompted, narrowing her eye at him.

He nodded and offered a polite smile. "And you must be Saoirse." He extended a hand to her. "It's good to meet you."

She glanced at his hand before shaking it firmly.

"I brought breakfast," he said as he lifted the canvas bag in his other hand.

Her gaze surprisingly softened. "Come in. My brother is finishing a bath. He's still recovering from…whatever happened to him."

Jian stepped in when she moved aside. He looked around the little apartment, unsurprised to find it minimalist—bordering empty. It only had a leather couch and a bookcase on one side and a kitchen with a tiny dining table on the other. The two doors at the back probably led to a bedroom and a bathroom. Carver's hardwood floors were scuffed, but extremely clean. There was nothing on the walls, not even a family picture. It was the home of someone who didn't consider it home.

A black cat trotted from behind the couch. It hissed as soon as it saw Jian, hair raising down its back. That was the usual response pets had to him, so he just stood still and tried not to spook the poor thing more.

"*Lati, lati,* Mouna," Saoirse said gently as she shut the front door. "Don't mind her, Jian. Even if you weren't a demon, she's always been a testy bitch."

He shrugged. "I appreciate her honesty. Most people hide that reaction when they first meet me."

The cat sprinted away, and Saoirse went into the kitchen to pour herself a cup of coffee from the half-full pot on the counter.

"Your daughter is Jian Li Anh, yes?" she said lightly. "And you're Jian Rong Tuan."

Jian had worked with Inquisitors before. Most of them were hardened with years of seeing the worst of government officials and witnessing war crimes that they couldn't stop without the ICS's intervention. Even in a baggy t-shirt and shorts, Saoirse held herself with the rigidity of someone who had survived horror after horror and now perpetually waited for the next one.

Jian set his bag on a kitchen countertop.

"Are you familiar with my daughter?" he asked.

Saoirse sipped her coffee black and turned to face him. "We met briefly during the Blood War. I'd been deployed to investigate your family for conspiring to commit genocide against the vampire population in Weiqi. Imagine my surprise when I discovered most of Clan Jian had been thrown into a flood channel. Even purebloods can't survive being submerged in water."

Jian's gums ached as his fangs threatened to elongate, but he calmly unpacked glass tubs of broth from his bag.

"It was awful," he mumbled. "My daughter and I escaped the assassins with only a few cousins."

"A few cousins who also opposed the war?" Saoirse said with an arched brow.

Jian pulled out a container of chopped cilantro, scallions, and thinly sliced onion. "Am I under investigation, inquisitor?"

She sipped her coffee. "Just sating a longstanding curiosity. I know enough to recognize that you're no threat to anyone on our side at present."

"Why not, if you seem to know so much about my history?"

She swirled her coffee in her mug absently. "There's a saying where I was born to never look into the brightest stars because they have cores forged in iron. I didn't know what it meant until I joined Meallán as an Inquisitor. The kindest people, the brightest stars, have known the greatest suffering, and they know how to inflict it."

When Jian narrowed his eyes at her, she added, "You and my brother aren't so different, you know."

He lifted the tubs of broth from the counter. It was none of his business what Carver had done to make his sister compare them. If she truly did know Jian's crimes, she wouldn't have made such a statement so lightly.

"I wouldn't presume to know your brother better than you," he said, "but he doesn't seem anything like me."

She arched a brow. "He doesn't seem violent, you mean?"

Jian's jaw clenched before he offered a short nod.

"He was always underestimated," she murmured. "Did you know that they give our call signs to us based on the roles we play for the Inquisitors? They called him 'Ihret.'"

"Ihret?"

"In siren folklore, ihret ka-duul are creatures from the depths of the ocean that drag people down into the dark, drowned and crushed by pressure. Their name roughly translates to 'death's grasping hands.'" She swirled the tip of her nail in her coffee. "That was my brother. Death's hands."

Jian couldn't read her body language to glean what she was thinking. Everything about her had practiced ease—giving away nothing. Whether that was intentional on her part or not was unclear. Her lack of expression could easily have been habit after so many years as an Inquisitor.

Jian couldn't recall another time he'd gotten such conflicting information about a person. The Professor seemed to think her apprentice was a kindly soul, albeit tortured, and Jian could certainly understand that impression from his interactions with Carver. There were also shades of the person Saoirse seemed to know—someone terrifying in their own right who faced life without flinching. Who had Carver been before that his own sister would speak of him like this?

"I'll take care not to cross him," Jian mumbled as he opened his tubs of broth. "May I use a large pot?"

Saoirse pulled one from the top shelf of a cabinet and set it on the stove. When he emptied the broth into it, she said, "You like star anise, don't you?"

He lit the burner and set it on high. "Not a fan?"

"On the contrary." She took a long sip of coffee. "You do know that my brother will have to make you food for this, don't you? I was too young when our mother died to remember all the siren customs, but he holds them dear. I think it feels like keeping Yama with him."

Jian nodded. "Well, I'm sure he'll have more opportunity to cook for me, if he wants. We still need to figure out what to do about the Ministry and the Gars."

He slid his fingers through the fire under the pot, so flames covered his hand. He ran it through his hair. The water in it sizzled as it steamed out, leaving it dry.

"Do you have a smaller pot?" he asked.

Saoirse pulled one from the same cabinet, and he filled it with water.

As he lit another burner for the pot, she abruptly said, "Are you trying to fuck my brother?"

Jian blinked, surprised by the bluntness of the question. Evidently, she lacked her brother's tact and manners, but that wasn't a bad thing. People hid behind propriety. He much preferred the ones who said what they meant and meant what they said.

"What if I were?" he responded, meeting her stare directly.

She shrugged. "Well, you wouldn't be the first war criminal that my brother has made cow eyes at. Just don't fall for him. He will absolutely break your heart."

That wasn't the response he'd expected. Usually, siblings demonstrated a level of protectiveness, especially if a prospect was an identified war criminal, but perhaps this was one area she didn't think Carver needed protection.

"I have no intention of falling in love," he admitted, "nor do I intend on sleeping with your brother. He doesn't seem to enjoy the act, from what I've been told."

"Hmm, you should still be careful." She waved her hand at the coffee pot, and a stream of coffee flowed into her cup, filling it to the top again. "You're his type."

He cocked a brow. "His type?"

"He's always liked the tragic ones."

Before Jian could ask her to elaborate, the sound of a door opening brought his head around. Carver stepped out of the bathroom in a thin tank top that clung to a lean, muscled chest and plaid lounge pants. Scars littered his shoulders and the hint of skin where the tank top didn't meet the top of his pants. The silvery lines were obviously from claws, most appearing in parallel sets of three.

"I thought I heard your voice," he remarked as he headed for Jian. "Do I smell bo hai soup?"

Jian resisted the urge to step away as some part of him sensed that novel, immense power in Carver. It was easier to be around now. The energy seemed gentler, or maybe just less erratic. Jian could even meet Carver's eyes without the innate aversion that he experienced with the Professor's gaze.

"It is a breakfast food," Jian said as amiably as he could. "You look better. Did you manage to get some rest?"

Carver shuffled to the coffee pot with a nod and poured himself a large mug.

"He slept for almost a full twenty-four hours," Saoirse said as she absently ran her fingers through her brother's curls. "You still haven't explained why you were ill."

His mug stopped midway to his lips, and he let out a long sigh. "In order to heal you, the Professor needed my energy. It was hard on my body. It will continue being hard on my body, according to her."

He spoke with ease, giving no indication of lying, and as far as Jian knew, he wasn't. It still didn't seem like the whole truth.

"Whoever that woman was who altered my eye," Saoirse said with a scowl, "she had ulterior motives, but she definitely wasn't with the Gars. She looked a lot like the Professor."

Carver nodded, as if this was old information. "Do you have any idea where the Gars are now?"

She sighed. "Depends on the scale of their forces. I wasn't able to gauge how many wolves were part of this operation. If it's more than one pack, I would expect that they'd be encamped outside the city. A pack or smaller would probably find lodging in town. That's not a guarantee. A lot of Gars choose to stay shifted for long periods because they think it's more natural or something. They couldn't do that in a city. The tactical thing to do would be to split the group to have some in Vespera and some in the surrounding forest. That way there's always some available to surveil the outskirts and some doing work in the city."

"I actually wanted to talk to you about that," Jian said. "How familiar are you with the Gars?"

"You're talking to the primary expert among the Inquisitors in the Republic," Carver said. "The only person who might know more than Saoirse is based in Lac Kha. We could reach out to him, but I'm pretty sure he's busy."

"So what's your professional opinion?"

Saoirse rubbed her forehead. "I think they're going to have the vast majority of their people outside the city. The only people who have any business being here are agents who are good at recon and maybe undercover, if they have anyone cut out for it. Is there a part of the city that's more rundown?"

Carver tapped his fingers on his mug. "There's Redcliff—part of the old town. A lot of the buildings out there are almost as old as us and condemned."

Saoirse nodded curtly. "That's where I'd focus for now then. Easy to have agents holed up there without attracting attention."

"I don't know how much investigation I'm going to be up for. The Professor warned me that I'd take a while to recover."

The memory of Carver vomiting copious amounts of blood for

most of a day passed through Jian's mind. Just how long would this recovery take? Days? Weeks? Months?

"I'll let Palus know," Jian said. "There is one other matter we should discuss. The ICS is very unhappy that the Gars are pursuing you, Saoirse. As an Inquisitor, people having your information is not good for them, even if you probably have a thousand aliases."

Saoirse cast a withering look at him. "Is this your nice way of saying that they're going to shuffle me to a safe house until someone can scrub all evidence of my existence?"

"That was the main option that was passed to me." Jian glanced up at Carver. "The other is shipping you back to Balfour in a heavily armored convoy."

Carver looked down at his sister when she hissed, "Fuck."

"Saoirse, just stay here," he said tiredly. "Better than getting shipped out."

She shook her head. "They'll still be after you, and I'll be housebound while you're in harm's way."

"The Professor wouldn't let anything happen to me," Carver insisted.

Saoirse scowled. "How can you have so much faith in her?"

"She saved your life." His tone was uncommonly firm, almost chastising. "Mind what you say."

The muscles of her jaw flexed as she glared up at him, but eventually, she lowered her gaze.

"Just don't do anything stupid," she grumbled.

He bent to press his forehead to her temple, and she visibly

144

relaxed. All the fight seemed to drain from her as she leaned into him. Her intact eye closed as they took a breath together.

"I promised I wouldn't leave you alone in this life," he whispered. "I keep my promises."

She didn't respond for a long moment, and when she did, her voice was soft. "You better be fine."

He pulled away and waited until she looked up at him to speak. "I will."

Carver turned his eyes to Jian, and with it was the instinctive urge to look away—less intense than yesterday, but still present. Jian forced himself not to break eye contact, the demon in him unable to back down from the perceived challenged. The scent of sea salt grew as soon as Carver stepped closer to peer into the pots on the stove. A rush of heat shot through Jian.

"Can I get you anything while it warms?" Carver asked, voice low and gentle. "Coffee?"

Jian swallowed the smoke creeping up his throat.

"Coffee would be lovely—and chopsticks, if you have them," he said with a polite smile.

Carver stepped away to pour a cup of coffee and grab wooden chopsticks from a drawer, giving Jian a moment of reprieve from their proximity. As soon as he returned, though, Jian's heart picked up. He took the coffee and chopsticks with a mumbled word of thanks. Carver didn't step away again.

"Two meals," Carver remarked. "By your own admission of selfishness, I have to assume you have ulterior motives."

Jian's lips twitched. He set the chopsticks on the rim of the water pot. "Maybe I just like good food and good company."

Carver cocked a brow. "Is that so?"

Jian caught Saoirse shaking her head with a smile out of the corner of his eye.

"I'm going to take a shower," she muttered as she headed out of the kitchen. "Don't be a brick, Meallán."

She disappeared into the bathroom.

"Why am I a brick?" Carver asked with a frown.

Jian only offered a shrug in reply.

Carver sipped his coffee with a sigh. "Doesn't matter anyway. I'm sure you have questions about yesterday."

"I have a feeling it's above me at this point," Jian said, "so I won't ask my questions."

Silence stretched between them for a long minute. Carver was the one to break it.

"I wield the Professor's power now." His voice was strained. "She said that I shouldn't try to rush my recovery, and that I'll be weak for a long time. But if I hold off long enough to get my strength back, I'll be able to handle the Gars on my own."

Jian wasn't sure how to respond. The extent of the Professor's power remained a mystery that she kept close to her, and that she could share it with someone else, fundamentally altering them, implicated she could do it to others. More alarmingly, Carver didn't seem to relate to it as a gift. He'd called it a cost. The strain that it'd put on his body supported that the process wasn't purely beneficial, which then begged the question as to how much this had changed him and would continue to change him.

"What did she do to you?" Jian asked haltingly, almost afraid of the answer.

"I can't explain all of it, not without her." Carver stared at his coffee as he chewed his lip. "But I'm not the same."

Jian's eyes narrowed. "I sensed as much, but how are you different?"

Carver shook his head. "Again, I can't explain it all without her, but I'm more... like her."

More like her? What did that mean? More like whatever she was? More like her in soul?

"If you're more like her," Jian said after a beat, "then are you less like you?"

Carver shrugged. "Bodily, I feel very different, but I still feel like myself mentally."

"You do seem to be acting the same." Jian glanced at the bathroom door. "Have you told Saoirse?"

"Not yet. I will today." Carver let out a heavy sigh. "Thank you for everything, by the way. I feel better knowing that she'll have protection when I can't look after her."

Jian offered a small smile. "Just doing my job."

"I'd say coming over with food to personally discuss our options is beyond your job description. I appreciate it." Carver worried his lip a moment before lowering his head. "I can't help but wonder why you would go this far for me, especially after the first day we met. I was…not myself."

Jian took a moment to consider his response. "I broke a friend's arm accidentally once—couldn't separate what was happening from my memories of the war. You bend your head too readily, detective. You didn't even hurt me."

"I could have, though."

"And I imagine if you had, you'd be kneeling in front of me, begging for forgiveness."

That sea salt aroma bloomed in a wave that Jian felt from his chest to his fingertips. Carver's gaze darkened when his eyes lifted, as if he were imagining begging on his knees. The image was a pretty one, and Jian immediately forced it from his mind before he could get any other dangerous ideas.

"Besides," he continued, "you'd have to do a great deal more than set my instincts off to offend. I am a pureblood, after all."

Carver blinked. "What does being a pureblood have to do with anything?"

There were so few Pure Clans now that Jian wasn't surprised their quirks weren't common knowledge.

"Demons have a strong urge to hunt, as you know," he explained. "My clan is the worst extreme that we know of. We have to hunt frequently to maintain our sanity—or rather, to slow the insanity of bloodlust. In general, purebloods struggle more than any other demons to contain their urges. Unlike my father, I found…other outlets…than violence, but I'm still not immune."

Carver cocked a brow. "Other outlets?"

148

"Was it not obvious from the interrogation?" Jian smiled when Carver averted his eyes. "Bounty hunting, tracking suspects…social games—all forms of the hunt, in a way."

Carver chewed his lip before replying. "I was wondering how you could always maintain cordiality while…testing people."

Jian forced himself not to smirk. "Do I test you, detective?"

"That question alone traps me. If I confirm that you do, that lets you continue on this topic, providing more opportunity to test me. If I deny it, I'm dishonest." Carver narrowed his eyes. "What are your intentions with me, Jian? Is this simply your way of interacting with people, or do you have other motivations?"

Jian knew his eyes had to be shining with gold. He rarely found anyone bold enough to lay out his conversational tactics like this. Most were too afraid to challenge a pureblood demon directly. But then, what did Carver have to fear? He wielded the Professor's power now, by his own admission.

"As I told you, detective, I'm a very selfish man," Jian said evenly. "I confess that originally I was curious as to the extent of your effect on me and mine on you. Was it purely biological? Would time prove to lessen the severity? And then, as I got to know you more, I was intrigued by who you were. You are filled with complexities and contradictions."

Carver didn't respond immediately, perhaps not expecting the candor. "What kinds of complexities and contradictions?"

Jian let his eyes roam over the mess of scars on Carver's shoulders. "Well, detective, you are a siren who despises sex. You demonstrate so much kindness and empathy for someone who approaches the world with enough pessimism to drown in. Your attachment to life is tenuous at best, and yet you continue to do everything you can to keep going."

The silence that followed wasn't unexpected. The laughter that broke it was. Carver clasped a hand over his mouth to stifle himself. A few beats passed before he quieted enough to speak.

"Well, all right then," he said between chuckles. "I suppose you've got me down to the letter. Did you get all that from observation?"

Jian shrugged. "More or less."

"I suppose I should have expected as much." Carver's lips pulled up slightly. "You hide behind transparency better than anyone I've ever met."

Jian's chest heated. "Do I now?"

"I admit that you've baffled me time and time again. You're open, but you're only ever truly candid when you know it will fluster me. You tell me you're selfish. I believe you, but I don't believe it's your primary motivation."

Jian cocked a brow. "And why's that?"

"Because you're not in my bed."

Jian was momentarily floored by the assertion. It wasn't arrogant or even confident. Carver had spoken matter-of-factly, as if he knew that Jian desired him—at least at a physical level. Perhaps a siren could always comfortably know that they were attractive, but Jian doubted Carver had such a simple justification for his statement.

"What makes you think it's selfless of me that I don't take

advantage of you?" Jian asked tightly, trying to keep his fangs from elongating. "I'm not that much of a monster as to ignore consent."

Carver tilted his head slightly, as if Jian's question confused him. "Would you have followed through if I'd given consent?"

When silence met the question, he added, "By your own admission, you think I don't like sex, and I doubt you're selfish enough to test that, despite how much you test everything else."

Jian took a breath before his chest could start to glow. The heat behind his ribs grew almost uncomfortable.

"You like testing back," he observed. "You're doing it now. Trying to make me show my true colors, detective?"

Carver shook his head. "You took me to your home, cared for me, fed me. And now you're here, caring for me again. There's nothing you could want from me, besides sating curiosity, and that seems a poor reason to go to these lengths. If your true colors are as dark as you seem to insist they are, you're welcome to prove me wrong."

It was the kind of challenge that could be left alone without shame. Jian knew he could keep his secrets, but then, what was the point? So long as Carver had the Professor's power, few things could truly hurt him. If anything, Jian could try having genuine connection with another person.

"Why do all this for me?" Carver asked softly. "Why are you here?"

Jian let out a breath as a defeated smile pulled at his lips. "I suppose that I want you to feel cared for."

Red managed to bloom through Carver's dark skin as he blushed up to his ears.

The water in the small pot started to boil over, drops hissing as they fell over the rim. Carver leaned over to shut the burner off. Jian didn't move, letting them get within inches of each other. He knew he was testing something he shouldn't have. Carver was a widower with a complicated relationship to attraction, and pushing him would have been unforgiveable. But no one had ever held Jian's interest like this—overcome with the desire to hunt, but without the drive to kill.

Carver didn't move away after turning off the burner. This close, Jian smelled hints of lavender under the overwhelming scent of sea salt.

"Are you hungry, detective?" Jian murmured, almost too quiet to hear over the rain outside.

Carver didn't take his eyes off Jian when he whispered, "Very."

Jian forced his breaths to stay even, despite the way his heart flipped. He didn't think they were talking about food. That thought alone was making heat creep into his throat.

"You must be starving," he offered, giving Carver an excuse for his behavior—a way to absolve himself of responsibility.

Carver's gaze roamed over Jian before tentatively making eye contact again.

"More like a craving," he said. "I don't want to eat just anything."

Jian gripped the handle of the oven until the metal groaned. "How unusual."

Carver lowered his eyes almost coyly. "It's a…recent development."

"I see." Jian caught the bright gold of his eyes in the reflection of the window over the sink.

The click of the bathroom door opening made Carver tense, and he straightened, pulling away as he did so.

Jian slowly released his grip on the oven handle and set his mug on the countertop. Carver's scent slowly faded, and Jian took a deep breath before releasing it in a plume of gray smoke.

This siren made him feel voracious—like he was just a look, a touch, a word away from losing control. Was this only siren allure? Or was it Carver? Did it matter, in the end? The outcome was the same, regardless of the cause. And maybe the desire was reciprocated.

Jian glanced at the pot of water on the stove. It had stopped boiling.

CHAPTER EIGHT

Sand stretched in one direction past the horizon. It glittered like silver dust, nearly blinding even in the light of the moon overhead. In the other direction was an endless expanse of dark water. Little waves lapped gently at the sands. The dead washed up on the silver shores of Aheru. That was what the siren scriptures said, at any rate. Carver had believed it when his mother taught him as a child, but after being so viciously exiled from siren society, his faith in the Great Goddess was near non-existent. Still, he'd longed for the silver shores following Thomas' death.

Carver crouched down to scoop a handful of sand. It was soft, almost liquid, as it slipped between his fingers.

"You belong here."

The voice was soft and warm. It seemed almost inviting, like the warmth of a hearth.

Carver glanced up to see the shape of a woman standing at the water's edge. Her form flickered in and out of focus, almost like how reflections warped on flowing water. Hair dark as the night fell in thick waves down her back. Her face was turned away from him, but something in him knew he shouldn't try to look too closely at her.

"You've stepped on these shores once before," she said softly, "but you didn't stay."

Carver cautiously came closer. "Who are you?"

She crouched down to dip her fingers into the water. Her skin was black, but bright white freckles like stars stood out against it.

"I've gone by many names," she said, "as you have, Meallán."

He held his breath when she turned her head to look up at him. Her eyes were as silver as the sands, almost disappearing into the luminous white of her sclerae. High cheekbones sloped at a sharp angle down to lips made of shadow. Those bright white freckles on her black skin dotted the slope of her nose and the tops of her cheeks.

Carver couldn't hold her eyes for long before he was compelled to look away. There was something ancient in her gaze, as there was with the Professor.

"You are an Ancient," he murmured. "Which one?"

She sighed and looked over the ocean. "I don't know what name the waking world has given me, if I have any at all now. My mother would call me Salwnsu."

Carver's mind involuntarily supplied a translation of the name: Little Night.

"Why have you returned here, Meallán?" Salwnsu asked before he could speak.

He glanced around. If these truly were the shores of Aheru, then he was dead. Saoirse would never forgive him if he stayed.

"I don't know," he answered honestly. "I can't stay."

Salwnsu had a small smile. "I know. Your sister called for you as you let the waters take you back to her."

He stared over the dark sea. "I couldn't leave her alone in life."

"Yes, you could." She stood to her full height, towering over Carver by several feet. "You bonded with a human. She was prepared to lose you before your life had really begun. Why did you truly return?"

He blinked. Her words didn't seem wrong, but he had always maintained that he'd survived Thomas' death for his sister. What other reason could there be?

"I... I don't know," he mumbled.

She peered down at him. "Think, little one. What happened when you were last here?"

He glanced between the water and the sands. Something buried deep within him seemed to claw at the base of his skull.

"I came to the shores," he whispered, unable to make his voice any louder, "and Thomas was waiting for me. He was crying. He..."

Salwnsu lowered a hand to wipe at his cheek. Her thumb came away wet.

"He told me something," he continued, louder now. "He said I had... I had to..."

The blurry image of Thomas' face against the night sky. Tufts of silver sand flying up in a breeze. Thomas' lips moving. No sound.

Sharp pain shot through Carver's skull, as if a blade had lodged through his eye. He clutched his head with a groan.

"It's all right," Salwnsu cooed. "You have walked the worlds of life and death—a journey not easily taken. It will return to you with time."

He rubbed his forehead as the pain faded. "I don't have time. The Gars are coming for us again."

She bent to be eye level with him. "Then we must give you the strength to fight."

His brows furrowed. "I don't know how to use the Professor's power."

"You are an extension of the Mother of Ancients and a child of mine. You cannot wield our strength yet, but until such time, I will teach you to survive." She smiled, making her eyes light. "I will find you when you dream, but our time has run out."

She pressed cool lips to his forehead and whispered, "Wake up."

His eyes snapped open to see his room. He lay in bed with Saoirse. She was still asleep with her back to him. The clock on his nightstand flashed 6:43. The beginnings of sunlight filtered through his window.

He got up, careful not to disturb Saoirse, and padded into the main room. Thomas was waiting for him in the kitchen. His brows were knitted together, as if deep in thought.

"What a strange dream," he commented. "It seemed…real."

Carver sighed and trudged toward the coffee maker. "It's probably just a weird symptom of being reclaimed."

Thomas arched a dubious brow. "Really, Meallán? You're not even going to entertain the possibility that it was real?"

Carver grabbed the can of coffee grounds from the cabinet above the coffee pot. He frowned when he opened it. They were running low.

"Meallán," Thomas said, drawing out the name disapprovingly.

"What?" Carver muttered as he scooped grounds into the coffee maker's filtration basket.

Thomas' brows lowered. "Are we back to ignoring me when you're mad?"

"I'm not mad. I just don't know if I believe it." Carver grabbed the coffee pot and went to the sink to fill it with water. "If I didn't return from the silver shores for Saoirse, then what did I return for? It doesn't make sense."

"Doesn't it? You definitely thought about her before you bonded with me." Thomas folded his arms over his chest. "It makes more sense that you were prepared to leave her behind than not."

Carver took a breath and poured the water into the coffee maker. "So what was the reason? According to my alleged memories, you had told me to do something."

"I don't know." Thomas shrugged. "I know what you know."

Carver set the coffee to brew. "I'm actually going insane," he muttered as he ran a hand down his face. "Dreams about Ancients and arguing with my dead husband about a conversation we maybe had when we died."

"Is it any weirder than being reclaimed by the Mother of Ancients?" Thomas waved a dismissive hand. "Never mind. I'll drop it for now, but at least consider the possibility that this dream wasn't just a fabrication of your mind. Can you do that?"

Carver nodded instead of trying to speak. He wanted nothing more than to set himself on fire and return to the silver shores, but that wasn't going to happen. He had promised to—

He blinked as his thoughts came to an abrupt halt. He had something to do? What did he have to do?

Thomas said something beside him, but there was no sound. His lips were blurred, as if out of focus. Carver stared, trying to figure out the shapes they were making.

"Meallán?" Thomas' voice was sharp. "Meallán, are you all right?"

Carver blinked multiple times as he snapped from the trance and looked up at his husband. Thomas was in focus again.

"What was that?" he asked.

Carver shook his head, as if it could dispel the vision. "I don't know. Something strange is happening to me."

"The Professor did say you were going to become something else." Thomas glanced out the window over the sink just as rain started to fall. "I guess we have to wait and see."

◊◊◊

Jian sat in the Court's archive rooms, occupying himself with tracking Garsuk movements on the ICS's records. Maps and reports laid on a table before him. Half were pulled from the archives and the other half he'd collected from his personal records. The alcove he occupied had a small window overlooking the city. Rain fell in thick sheets, obscuring the view through the glass. It was further blurred by the rising sun rays coming over the ocean.

The only people who worked here were the archivists who spent most of their time on their terminals, hiding in the maze of bookshelves containing files upon files of historical and legal documentation. The scent of old paper and ink filled the spacious room. Only a couple terminals dotted the edges of the archives. They were tall, boxy structures covered with bronze buttons and dials. Most had a long feed of paper running in and out of their sides to catalog current computations.

Jian hunched over his documents, looking through them as he had a thousand times. The Gar pack that attacked Saoirse was largely a family group, but only five of them were mercenaries who regularly went out to take jobs. None of those five had any experience with assassinations. They were more the type to run out and solve their problems loudly and messily. Tracking them in the city should've been easier, but there wasn't a sound or any indication from his contacts of unusual people around.

There was also the fae that Saoirse had mentioned in a report she gave him: Maeva. Jian had encountered many fae through his life. One of his closest friends was one, but she'd run off somewhere to do only gods knew what. The head of security for his clan was also fae, and he was back in Lac Kha to protect Jian's daughter. Reaching out to them might have been helpful, but there wasn't much they could do on the other side of the world.

Fae were some of the oldest preterns in existence and held knowledge of the old ways. Jian had never wanted to be on the receiving end of their ire. They could lay curses and produce illusions, trap people in the memories of their pasts or otherwise alter their senses. They made fearsome colleagues, and they would have made horrifying enemies.

Saoirse had suggested focusing somewhere in Redcliff. It was largely condemned, which meant there weren't modern security systems in the area to watch if there were Gars. Any monitoring would have to be done in-person. An abandoned cannery there was large enough to house multiple people if needed. A small team could watch it and the surrounding area for activity.

Jian ran a hand down his face tiredly. Pulling all-nighters had been normal when he'd been a Peacekeeper, and it'd been too easy to fall back into the habit. He probably should sleep soon. His mind was approaching its limits.

The phone on the desk rang. He'd told the receptionists where he was, so they could direct calls to him. But he wasn't sure who'd be contacting him now.

"Jian," he answered.

"What are you doing at the Court this early?" Palus' voice was stiff, as if they were annoyed with him.

He leaned back in his chair. "The Professor hired me to track the Gars. I'm doing my job."

"I know for certain you've barely slept all week." Palus sighed. "Look, I'm not interested in dictating everything you do. I have to trust that you know your body, but the Professor is out for the foreseeable future, meaning everything falls to me. Don't be something else I have to manage."

Jian pinched the bridge of his nose as the beginnings of a headache started behind his eyes. "Point taken. I was just finishing here anyway. We should deploy some agents to watch the old town in

Redcliff. Carver's sister suggested it, and there's an abandoned cannery there that could hold several Gars. How many Peacekeepers can you spare me?"

"How many do you want?"

"Seven."

"Done. I'll send them out now."

Jian rubbed his eyes and started gathering the documents on the desk. "Thank you. Is this all you called me about?"

Palus didn't reply immediately. "No, I have something else for you. It's been sent via tube to your house. The Professor compiled a complete history of Carver and his sister for you. She said that it might help you figure out what the Ministry intends with them, if it's not just to kill them outright."

"Oh." Jian sat straighter. "Does Carver know she gave me this?"

"I don't know." Palus' voice was heavy with tiredness. "The Professor requested you watch Carver—an unofficial bodyguard essentially. I don't know how much you know about their situation, but Carver is going to be weak for a while. The Peacekeepers will be shuffling his sister off to a safe house later today. That leaves just him unprotected. And the Professor and I are of the mind that he shouldn't be kept under strict security in order to draw the Gars' attention. There's a chance we can deal with them before he finishes his recovery, and then he won't need to worry about trying to wield the Professor's power. But he needs to survive. He needs someone looking out for him."

It had been a long, long time since Jian had been given a

babysitting job like this, but it wasn't like it was the only thing he needed to do. He would still need to conduct his investigation. Carver would just need to be close by while that went on.

"I'm not like I was, Palus," Jian warned. "I'm…more fragile."

Palus' voice was gentle when they spoke. "You're not fragile, dear one. You're recovering, too. It's hard work to heal from mental wounds, as it is physical ones. I understand your reticence, but Carver shouldn't be completely infirm. He just needs someone else looking after him."

Jian let out a slow breath. "All right. I can do that."

"I thought so. Get some sleep, for my sanity please."

They hung up.

Jian rubbed his eyes. Fatigue weighed on him. The rains had ensured that he couldn't spend one moment sitting still. If he wasn't working, then he had too much time to think about the war and all he'd lost to the water that streamed from the sky.

He stared at the phone resting in the wall and hesitated another moment before dialing. It rang only once.

"Hello?" Carver answered.

Jian took a breath before speaking. "Good morning, detective. Are you well?"

There was a pause before Carver responded. "Sleeping on and off against my will, and my sister hasn't let me leave the house because of it. But I'm feeling better. What's wrong?"

"Nothing wrong, per se." Jian glanced down at his stack of documents. "We should discuss the Gars. I've found a few things, and

I could use another perspective."

"Of course," Carver agreed readily. "Do you want to meet at the Court?"

Jian grimaced at the idea of staying at the Court any longer. He just wanted to get Carver's input and then immediately go to bed. Besides, the documents Palus sent were at his house.

"Would you mind coming to my home?" he asked. "Palus just sent more materials there, and I'd rather not have to grab them and then return to the Court, if it's all the same to you."

There was a long silence before Carver responded. "Yes, I can meet you there."

Jian gave his address before hanging up. He set the phone back in its cradle and pulled his messenger from his pocket. There were a handful of reports from Peacekeepers about wolf sightings near the edge of the city, which wasn't unexpected. The amount of Gars was more than had been anticipated, but then, the Ministry had a lot of money to burn. They really wanted Carver and Saoirse dead and were willing to pay for the wolves, it seemed.

He typed brief orders for his agents along the coast to give geographical surveys of their areas, so they could map out probable routes for Gars to take. He'd just gotten through his final message when a distant rumble drifted through the ceiling. His spine stiffened immediately, and the hairs on his arms and the back of his neck rose.

Light flashed through the windows seconds before a louder rumble rolled through the air. His legs felt unsteady underneath him while he half-ran out of the archives and into a long, white corridor.

164

The footfalls of his frantic steps echoed loudly off the walls. They reflected back sound twice as loud, and the fluorescents along the ceiling cast heavy shadows. He almost tripped when he caught one move along the wall. His heart skipped at the fleeting sight of long, dark hair. But when he focused on the shadow, it wasn't there. No other sound except his own footsteps echoed back at him.

He stopped at the end of the corridor where it intersected with another and made a fist in his hair. Thunder reverberated in the walls, muffled by their thickness but no less perturbing. He dragged a trembling hand down his face and forced himself to take a breath.

Driving in this state was asking for an auto accident. He could call a cab, but then the idea of being in a confined space for any length of time made his stomach knot. His house was five miles away, within walking distance. It'd hurt from rain exposure alone, and he wasn't confident he wouldn't just sit on his kitchen floor when he got there and bleed through the cracks in his skin until he could seal them up. Then again, Carver was on his way over. Relying on his assistance wasn't ideal, but it'd have to do.

Thunder vibrated through his bones when he finally started moving again. He hoped Carver could forgive this.

◊◊◊

The house looked much like many others in the city. It was an old colonial-style with white columns framing the front door and boxy eaves. The russet wood paneling on the exterior almost appeared pleated. A cobblestone path led from the driveway and curved around a small magnolia tree to the front door. There wasn't much of a yard. Instead of grass, the front yard was lush with clover and flowers.

Carver parked on the street out front. Thunder rumbled overhead when he climbed out of his automobile. Rain came down in thick sheets.

Thomas leaned on the auto, watching the water fall.

"I think I first kissed you out in a downpour like this," he mumbled. "You'd crawled out on the roof to soak in the water. I was sure you'd slip off and break something."

A small smile touched Carver's lips as the warmth of the memory seemed to bloom through him. Soft lips. The taste of rainwater. Heartbeats louder than the thunder.

"I barely spoke enough Imperial then to understand your panicked shouting," he remarked. "How funny to be worried about a siren in the rain."

Thomas chuckled. "You'd only been with us for a few months. I had no idea."

"It was sweet of you, all the same."

"You deserved sweet."

Carver let the water run over him as he headed for the front door. The scent of blood hit him as soon as he got close. The door was ajar, and a red handprint dripped on the frame.

Cold dread ran down Carver's spine as he palmed the pistol at his hip. He carefully pushed the door open. The living room was readily visible and empty. Blood streaked along the wall nearest the door. Carver pulled his pistol out and crept inside, half-expecting for a Gar to come lunging for him.

The sound of labored breaths preceded the sight of Jian on his kitchen floor. He was soaked and lying in a puddle of water. Cracks ran through his skin, seeping blood steadily. Red smeared along the stove beside him. One of the burners was lit, but there was nothing atop it. Had he lit it himself, but didn't have the strength to get to the fire?

Carver immediately holstered his gun and rushed closer.

"Gods, you're soaked," he breathed. "What were you doing?"

Jian just bowed his head and huffed a breath of smoke. He was shaking from head to toe.

Carver immediately pulled off Jian's soaked jacket and the damp shirt beneath. He pointedly didn't stare at the expanse of bare, muscled chest revealed. Bloody cracks ran through Jian's hands and arms from water exposure. A tattoo of a long snake wound up his side, over his shoulders and arms, and the head rested just under his sternum. It had a pair of fangs bared. One black eye was visible, seeming to peer up at Carver.

He hesitated when he got to Jian's pants. They were also drenched and needed to come off, but that seemed like a line he should hesitate to cross, especially when he could already feel heat creeping up his chest.

"Can you take off your pants while I get you a towel?" he asked.

Jian's hands shook violently when he reached down to the front of his pants. His fingers were clumsy, trying to grasp at the buttons and fumbling repeatedly. The cracks in his skin tore more with the movement.

Carver took a breath. "Let me," he said. "Please."

Jian pulled his hands away and pressed them to his sternum. Carver carefully unbuttoned the jeans and pulled the zipper down, keeping his movements clinical. Sliding the jeans down damp legs proved the most difficult portion, but Carver eventually shimmied them off. More cracks split through the skin underneath in harsh, red lines.

Jian lay in only black boxers, still shivering viciously. He needed to get dry.

Carver lit all the burners on the stove and pulled Jian up. The fire virtually leapt toward the demon as Carver draped him over the stove. Flames licked across Jian's skin, slowly sealing the cracks in it.

Satisfied, Carver rushed for the bathroom. There was a cabinet in a corner that had yellow towels. He grabbed one and ran back to the kitchen.

"Sorry," Jian rasped when Carver came closer. "I was careless."

Carver was about to ask why when a bout of thunder rattled the window over the sink. Jian tensed immediately and squeezed his eyes shut. A shudder ran through him. Was he afraid of thunder?

Carver wrapped the towel around Jian's hips in an attempt to dry the part of him that wasn't currently soaking in fire.

"Why thunder?" Carver asked softly as he patted the towel to a bloody calf.

Jian let out a shaky breath. "The war." His voice was uncharacteristically thin. "Sorry."

168

"Don't be."

Jian didn't respond, and Carver stood when the cracks started to flesh over.

"What can I do to help?" Carver asked.

Jian took a deep breath, and his pupils dilated almost instantly. "Why do you always smell so good?"

Carver averted his eyes as the scent of sea salt saturated the air even more. This really wasn't the time for his allure to get the best of him, but it was impossible to control this close to Jian. Some part of him recognized the power in the demon before him, even in this state.

"It's an oil I produce over my skin," he explained stiffly. "Reacts to air and instigates a serotonin and dopamine response when inhaled."

"Makes people want to be around you," Jian concluded with a humorless chuckle.

Carver swallowed as more of his scent filled the air. "Do you want to be around me?"

Jian straightened and switched off the burners. When he turned to face Carver squarely, the gold in his eyes had completely eclipsed the brown. Smoke seeped from his lips as he let out a slow breath.

"It seems I do," he admitted and took a step, getting close enough that Carver felt the heat radiating off him.

Carver instinctually stepped back. His hips met countertop, preventing him from moving further as Jian got closer. Their chests almost touched. Wisps of smoke escaped Jian's nose and mouth on each quickened breath.

Light flashed through the window, followed immediately by

thunder. Jian barely flinched as he drew a deep breath.

"Is it all biology?" he rasped. "Why does just your proximity help?"

Carver's breath caught when Jian leaned forward. Mere inches separated them. Jian brought his face to Carver's neck, breath hot on the skin there. The heat of him was almost searing this close.

"If being near me helps," Carver heard himself say, "then feel free to use me."

Jian froze. "Are you really okay with that?"

"You were just bleeding on the floor." Carver hesitantly lifted a hand to Jian's shoulder. "You've taken care of me. This is the least I could do."

"Care..." Jian mumbled the word like it was foreign in his mouth.

Carver took his elbow. "C'mon. Let's get you warm. My body temperature is too cool for you."

Jian didn't protest and let himself be lead to the couch. Carver pulled all the blankets he could find from under the coffee table and laid it over Jian who numbly wrapped himself in the layers of fabric. Steam started to rise off the exposed skin of his head and through his hair.

He flinched when thunder rumbled overhead, so Carver sat at his side and wordlessly pulled him closer. Jian tensed briefly before pressing his face into Carver's shoulder. Using siren skin oil to calm a panic attack was unorthodox, but it seemed to be working.

Thomas appeared behind the couch, peering down at them with almost sad eyes. "Doesn't feel so long ago that I held you through your terrors. It's good you found him."

Carver wasn't sure about that, but he understood PTSD well. If Jian found relief with him through the storm, then that was enough.

"Be good to him," Thomas said as he faded, "and yourself."

Gradually, minute by minute, the tension eased from Jian's body. His breathing evened. Even with the thunder booming every so often, he didn't tense again. Carver let himself feel the pressure against him, knowing that his allure would continue to do its work like this. The oil on his skin used similar chemical components as antidepressants and sedatives, and he didn't doubt that it was helping to regulate the overly anxious state that Jian was in.

"I'm sorry for this," Jian whispered. "I am...not myself."

Almost by instinct, Carver pressed his cheek to Jian's temple. "Do you want to talk about it?"

A shiver ran through Jian, and he curled slightly. "No, but I should. If we'll be working together more, I feel obligated to let you know who you're with."

Carver was doubtful his opinion of Jian would change, and his curiosity burned to know more. "You told me once that you thought your family and the other demon clans were wrong," he said slowly, picking his words with care. "Did you fight for them anyway, even knowing what they were doing was horrible?"

Jian let out a humorless chuckle. "I let them think I was fighting for them. I let them think that for a long time, up until my team and I got caught."

He was quiet for a moment before continuing. "They tied my

people to posts outside. It was monsoon season. The rain stripped their flesh from them. I was made to listen to their screams over the thunder all night."

Carver's heart twisted. "That's why you don't like thunder."

"One of my cousins, Vanh, was on my team. She kept telling me not to look at her, didn't want me to remember her like that—mutilated and in pain."

Carver's chest grew tight. He'd suspected that whatever sins Jian was reluctant to talk about had to do with the war, and maybe they had more to do with survivor's guilt than anything. Jian seemed like the type, taking responsibility for things that weren't his to own.

"I'm so sorry," Carver murmured. "You don't have to talk about it, if it's too painful."

Jian absently ran his fingers over the tattoos on his arms. "The Professor may still think well of me, but we're alike in a lot of ways. I don't think she could judge me without reflecting on her own crimes first."

Carver's brows knitted together. "Whatever you think is bad enough to scare me away, I promise you it won't."

"You can't promise that."

"I can." Carver glanced at his wedding band. "If the Professor can't judge you, then neither can I."

Jian was quiet for a long moment. "My family summoned me to help them commit genocide against the vampires who refused to surrender their ancestral lands in Tong Bei. I couldn't do it, and I couldn't let them do it."

Carver's heart dropped as he realized where this was going.

"'If you must choose a side, commit,'" Jian added softly. "Old demon saying."

Carver didn't speak or move, not sure if any kind of comfort would be welcome just now. Nothing seemed appropriate.

Jian took a deep breath before speaking again. "I killed most of my family—grandparents, aunts and uncles, cousins—before one of them put a dagger through my ribs. My daughter took him down before he could finish the job. The cousins who'd sided with me took care of the rest, and then we gathered them in the back of a truck and dumped them into the nearest flood channel for the water to dissolve them. Many of them raised me and educated me. That was how I repaid them."

He peered up at Carver.

"Still want me around?" he asked flatly.

"Yes," Carver said without hesitation. "If anything, I'm sorry you had to make that choice."

Jian sighed. "You really aren't fazed, are you?"

"I don't see why I should be." Carver shrugged. "I would have done the same."

"Is that so?" Jian shifted until he was virtually lying atop Carver. "I probably should have known when your sister warned me about you."

Carver arched a brow and made a mental note to call Saoirse. She never could leave well enough alone.

"What did she tell you?" he asked.

"That you were compared to the ihret," Jian said. "Deadly creatures in siren folklore, right?"

The shame that tightened around Carver's throat at hearing his old sign was unexpected. "She talks too much, but she didn't lie. Ihret was my sign. It was a bit dramatic, I think, but maybe fitting. I was sent out exclusively for assassinations toward the end of my career with the Inquisitors. I don't remember most of them honestly, but I know not all of my targets could have been deserving of their fate. There were…too many…to believe that."

Jian craned his head back to hold Carver's eyes. "What an odd change of career you made. The Peacekeepers are largely defenders."

"Fewer moral quandaries that way."

Carver smoothed a hand over Jian's hair thoughtlessly. He was going to withdraw his hand and apologize when Jian closed his eyes.

"I think," Jian mumbled, "that I may pass out now."

Just a minute later, his breathing evened with sleep. He really had been tired.

Carver pulled the blankets higher and settled into the couch.

CHAPTER NINE

The silver shores seemed brighter than the last time he'd come here. A strong breeze swept through, kicking shimmering dust into the air. Salwnsu stood at the water's edge. Her black hair billowed around her like a cloak. She took a fighting stance, planting her feet shoulder-width apart, and raised her open hands up. He intuitively took his own stance, almost mimicking her form. There was no way that he stood a chance against a being several thousand years his senior, but he supposed that was why she wanted to train him.

She moved with blinding speed. He sensed more than saw her before she lunged forward. Her arm swung toward him. He stepped aside, barely dodging the strike. His hand darted for her throat on instinct, his own training taking over. She blocked it with her forearm. Faster than he could react, her hand shot toward his ribs. They gave with a crack, and he staggered back.

She waved her hand toward him, and his ribs snapped back into place with a painful crunch.

"Again," she ordered.

He lunged first this time. As expected, she brought an arm up to block her strike, and he took the moment to bring his other hand into her side. All his weight went into the blow. She grunted. Any human and most preterns would have ruptured an organ or two from the strength of a siren. Salwnsu just took a step back. Her hand darted out to grab his throat while her knee swung into his.

He fell back on the sand, neck crushed under her weight. How was he supposed to fight her? She was significantly stronger than him.

She eased her hold on his throat and straightened. "The Professor's enemies are as strong as her," she said, as if reading his thoughts. "You need to draw on her power to compete."

He scowled as he got to his feet. "I don't know how that works."

"And you won't until you try."

She lunged for him. He barely sidestepped her in time to avoid the fist that came for his jaw.

They traded blows over and over again. Each time she inflicted a severe injury, she healed it instantly. Broken arms and legs and jaws—wounds that Carver barely flinched at anymore after so many years of enduring worse with the Inquisitors. He only grew frustrated with his inability to inflict any injury in return. How was he supposed to fight an enemy that didn't even flinch at strikes that were typically lethal?

The tips of his fingers started to blacken when he raised them to block a swing. His bones cracked under the force of the strike, but as soon as he stepped back, they snapped together. Salwnsu jabbed at his throat. He knocked her hand to the side, and her fingers diverted to his shoulder. They buried into the flesh and forced the joint out. It wrenched back into place with a pop when she withdrew her hand.

His hands darkened, as if dipped in ink. Despite the dry air, black scales emerged along the backs of his arms. The wind picked up around him, sending metallic granules of sand whipping up. Droplets of water from the ocean lifted into the air.

Salwnsu swung her knee up. He moved to swipe at it. Water drops coalesced around him, forming a stream that followed the motion of his arm. It thinned to a blade as his hand connected with Salwnsu's knee. The blade of water ran through her flesh and nearly through her bone.

She jumped back. A massive gash exposed the femur beneath. Black blood oozed from the wound. Her flesh started to knit together almost immediately.

"Not bad," she said. "Learning control of water will also help you. It's better suited to slow an Ancient, though, not to do harm. Think you can use it to throw off my footing?"

He shrugged. "I don't know how I used it in the first place."

She glanced up at the night sky. "Our time is up anyway. I suggest asking your sister for assistance with your new affinity for water."

"Will I see you again?" he asked as the edges of his vision darkened.

She smiled. "I'll be waiting here as always, child."

His eyes opened to an unfamiliar ceiling. He moved his hand to rub his face, but something heavy held it down. It was almost uncomfortably warm atop him. His eyes lowered to see Jian sleeping. Blankets draped over his back. His head rested on Carver's chest. Light still shone through the windows, so it wasn't yet nightfall.

Carver didn't even remember falling asleep, as was becoming common. His recovery was ongoing, and he kept sleeping in unpredictable intervals.

Jian stirred. The weight of him shifted lower as he moved. He pressed a knee between Carver's thighs, and the next shift of weight created unexpected friction. The scent of sea salt bloomed in the air immediately as heat rushed through Carver.

Damn his reactivity. There was nothing sexual about this situation. For the gods' sake, he was supposed to be providing comfort and safety after a stressful situation.

A low rumble, almost like a growl, vibrated up from Jian's chest. Smoke escaped his lips as he lifted his head. The gold in his eyes had almost completely enveloped the brown. He ground his hips into Carver's, earning an involuntary groan. The heat coming off him was near scorching as he stretched to bring their faces within inches of each other. Sweet smoke lingered between them.

Their lips brushed briefly before coming together. Carver arched up into the kiss before he could think better of it. A hand grasped the back of his neck, drawing him closer. The tongue that passed over the seam of his lips made him draw a sharp breath. Electric pulses rushed through him. They weren't painful, as they normally were when he was starving. But then, he wasn't starving. His body seemed like it was waking up. Processes that had been dormant made his blood heat. His scent built around him, saturating the air with sea salt. He wanted more.

Jian abruptly jumped off the couch. He rushed to the kitchen and turned on the sink. A hiss escaped him when he ran his hand under the water. Steam plumed in the air with a sizzle. His skin started to crack within seconds.

Carver launched himself over the back of the couch. He pulled Jian's hand from the water and turned the faucet off.

"I'm so sorry," Jian said quickly. "I didn't— Gods, put the water back on. I need to cool off."

Carver clamped a hand over the faucet, holding it down. "No."

Jian went unnaturally still, as if every muscle were tensed. "What are you doing, detective?"

The blood rushing in Carver's ears seemed to get louder and louder. "I'm not letting you hurt yourself."

"You won't like the alternative."

The stiff words, almost snarled, made heat rush through Carver anew. His own scent grew more around him. The smart decision would have been to run to his auto and drive far away. They didn't have to cross any more lines today.

"You should leave," Jian murmured as he took a step closer.

Carver took a step back. He swallowed against the thrill that tangled around his spine and warmed the apex of his thighs. The pair of gold irises staring up at him were filled with such raw desire that his knees weakened.

"Do you want me to leave?" he murmured.

Jian took another step forward. "It's not about what I want."

Carver's next step was cut short by the counter behind him, making him press into it. "Don't make me beg for it."

Jian closed the distance between them, pinning Carver's hips with his own. The heat of him was almost uncomfortable, but Carver melted into the contact immediately. His breath left him in a rush when a knee pushed between his legs. Jian craned his neck to ghost his lips over Carver's jaw.

"I wouldn't hurt you," he whispered, as if to give reassurance.

Carver let his legs open more. "It's fine if you do."

He didn't hear so much as feel the growl in Jian's chest. It vibrated from the lips that trailed up to his mouth. The shiver that ran through him was as much anticipation as unfettered want. Jian's breath tasted of sweet smoke. He lingered, not moving any closer—as if he couldn't bring himself to make the final, damning move.

Carver leaned forward, bringing their lips together fully. The taste of sea salt and smoke mixed between them. There was so much heat. Demons were all flames and smoke and light, like the sun itself brought to the ground. It almost burned.

Carver dragged his tongue along the seam of the mouth on his, eliciting another silent growl. He imagined that if fire had a flavor, it'd taste like the spicy sweetness at his lips. Jian slowly licked into his mouth. There was a deliberateness to all of Jian's movements, exploring and testing. He took his time until he could curl his tongue just so, bite just hard enough, push just deep enough to elicit little moans.

Carver's blood sang in a way he'd forgotten it could, impassioned and overwhelmed. Nerves he thought long dead were suddenly alive where fingers bit into him. He *wanted*. There was no nausea or pained

180

waves of hunger, just the basal desire to touch and be touched.

When Jian rolled his hips, Carver gasped, breaking the kiss. The second roll made him groan.

"If you keep making that sound," Jian whispered, "I'm never letting you leave my house."

At the next roll of his hips, Carver groaned again, louder and higher. He was rewarded with a fist in his hair and teeth at his neck. A shiver ran through his whole body at the memory of sharp fangs with smoke seeping between them. The teeth on his skin were blunt, but he wouldn't have minded if they weren't.

A yelp escaped him when Jian abruptly lifted him by his thighs. They got to the bedroom easily. The show of strength was impressive, and Carver half-expected to be tossed around. But Jian was gentle in laying him on the bed. He pulled at Carver's shirt until he could get it off, and then his lips were tracing a path from clavicle to sternum. They strayed to the side, heading for a hardening nipple.

Carver bit into his lip when that overheated tongue found its mark. His fingers sank into Jian's hair, just to have something to hold onto. The heat pooling between his legs was growing uncomfortable. He strained against the front of his pants. Every pass of Jian's tongue made the ache between his hips worse and stole a little more of his sanity. And when a hand ground into the growing bulge in his pants, coherent thought vanished. All he could do was moan and clutch the sheets.

It seemed too long and too soon when Jian trailed his lips down. He nipped at the cords of muscle framing Carver's abdominals and licked a path down. The end goal was obvious enough, and nervousness snuck up Carver's throat.

When fingertips teased at the top of his pants, he blurted, "Wait."

Jian froze. His eyes lifted.

"I'm not... I'm different from most men," Carver explained haltingly. "Sirens don't really have the genetics for male anatomy."

"Meaning?" Jian prompted.

"I have male and female anatomy."

"And how do the parts you have feel about tongues on them...or in them?"

A breath Carver hadn't realized he'd been holding left him at the obvious eagerness in the question.

"Very favorably," he murmured.

Jian's eyes seemed to brighten. "Then may I continue?"

"Please."

Carver kept still while his pants were pulled off with the undershorts beneath. It'd been a long time since anyone but a consort had seen him, and they all had sensitivity training for intersex and transgender clients. There was always a chance that a partner wouldn't be able to see past the oddness.

He wasn't sure what he expected when he was finally naked, but Jian came back up to kiss him. Fingertips grazed over Carver's hardening cock, making his hips buck. The sound that left Jian was almost like a deep purr. He nipped a line down Carver's throat. The scrape of teeth on skin elicited a shiver.

A hand slid lower, heading for the heat between Carver's thighs.

Deft, gentle fingers slipped through the folds there. A gasp left him at the first press at his entrance. His thighs shook at the tongue that ran up the side of his neck to his ear.

"So wet for me," Jian breathed.

The ache in Carver grew stronger, creating an emptiness that demanded to be filled. He couldn't stop his moan at the finger that slid into him and curled deliciously. It wasn't nearly enough, and he canted his hips up. But before he could start begging, Jian pulled away and slid down the bed. He seated himself between Carver's knees. His eyes dragged over every inch of skin in front of him, like he was trying to decide where to take the first bite. When his gaze met Carver's, he held the eye contact, even as he ducked his head to plant kisses along a thigh.

Carver couldn't remember the last time someone had paid him so much attention. Usually, he was the one trying to elicit as much pleasure as fast as possible from his partner, just to get it over with. This wasn't to feed, though. This was indulgent. There was no starvation or vaguely nauseous desperation to produce pleasure for rapid consumption. In fact, he had no desire to get this over with quickly. He would have been happy to draw it out as long as they could handle.

Jian made slow work of inching up Carver's thigh. He stopped at the joint where leg met hip and dragged his teeth maddeningly over the skin there.

"Please." The one word left Carver brokenly, and he felt Jian's answering shiver between his legs.

Unnaturally warm breath passed over the base of his cock, and then lips grazed the sensitive skin. He gripped the sheets to stop himself from trying to buck his hips up. Jian dragged the tip of his tongue over Carver's length and then circled the head. The electric shocks that seized Carver's spine made him arch back helplessly.

Fingers pressed inside him just as heated lips enveloped the head of his cock. His vision dimmed. He could almost feel himself coming undone under every touch. His thighs tightened around Jian's shoulders. Every beat of his heart rang in his ears and pushed against the back of his ribs.

Jian didn't rush, mouth and tongue slow and attentive, while he stretched Carver open more and more. Sometimes he'd dip his head down to pass his tongue between the soft folds below, as if he just wanted to taste the slickness there. His mouth was almost painfully hot when he took Carver's length in it fully.

It was too much. Each pass of tongue and lips made breathing difficult. Carver nearly bit through his lip as he felt himself unraveling. He had forgotten this. It'd been so long, and he'd forgotten how anything could feel this good. His heart beat against his sternum like it was trying to break through. Each breath burned. The way it was supposed to be.

Jian brought him to the edge embarrassingly fast, but he backed off at the last second, only to wait for Carver to settle and then bring him right back to the edge again. The process repeated over and over and over. Carver didn't know how long he was kept in this torture. Time blurred. His entire body seemed like a taut wire, waiting to snap at the lightest pressure. And when frustration and overwhelm stung at his eyes, Jian leaned back and pulled his own shorts from his hips.

Carver forgot how to breathe for a moment. More serpentine tattoos ran down the side of Jian's leg and wrapped high on his thigh before disappearing behind his waist. The indents of his hips formed a sharp V, leading directly to dark curls. Carver probably shouldn't have been surprised to find a full erection when Jian was clearly enjoying himself, but it made any kind of doubt in him vanish. And when Jian settled over him, their bodies came together easily.

Their lips found each other again. Carver tasted himself, salt and rainwater, in the kiss. He whined when Jian rocked their hips together. His fingers curled into the sheets as he felt as though the small movement would undo him.

"Please," he rasped into Jian's mouth, not even sure what he was pleading for. "Please."

Jian made that purring sound again. "Please what?"

Carver moaned at the next roll of their hips. "Please."

A chuckle vibrated through Jian's chest, and he pulled his hips back slightly. Carver lost all ability to breathe when he felt hard heat press at his entrance. But Jian didn't move more, just stared down with expectant eyes.

Carver's voice trembled when he rasped, "Yes."

The initial push was shallow, barely breaching the first ring of muscle, but when Jian pulled back, his next thrust went a little deeper. He wasn't small, and Carver felt every inch that sank deeper into him and filled him so completely. Part of him was still waiting for the nausea to set in and ruin this. But it didn't.

Their hips met as Jian buried himself fully. He stilled for a moment, as if savoring the feeling, and then started an achingly slow pace. Carver's eyes stung with the threat of frustrated, overstimulated tears. Pleasure so intense it verged on painful flooded him, and it only got worse when Jian reached between them to stroke him.

The pressure of release grew at the base of Carver's spine, even with how slow they were going, and when he started gasping, the hand around him released. He groaned in frustration, but couldn't muster the strength to protest much more.

It was too much and not enough. Every thrust into him kept him on the edge, but never quite enough to tip him over. His hand sank down, reaching for his own cock. Jian caught his wrist and pinned it to the bed. Seemingly just for good measure, he grabbed the other wrist and held it down. Carver only struggled for a moment until Jian abruptly thrust harder and faster, hitting that bundle of nerves inside that stole what little breath he had left.

The hands at Carver's wrists slid up, and their fingers threaded together. His face pressed into Jian's neck as he felt the seams of himself come undone. And then with a whispered curse, Jian truly pounded into him.

Carver muffled his voice in the fevered skin at his mouth. The pressure at the base of his spine made him arch back as it released all at once. Near violent waves of euphoria arrested him. Jian rode him through every crest until his thrusts grew uneven, and the familiar heat of another's pleasure burned where their bodies were joined. Jian started to pull away, but Carver quickly hooked his legs around him to keep them together.

A tidal wave of feeling hit him. Pulses of pleasure rippled up his spine. They gained strength as they got faster and more frequent, repeating like echoes overlapping each other until they blended into one, powerful wave. He couldn't do much more than writhe under the force of it.

All strength left him as soon as the pulses faded. He virtually melted into the sheets, breaths heaving from aching lungs. Jian panted into his shoulder. He was heavy, but not uncomfortably so. Warmth centralized at his chest, showing no sign of dimming. Their hands were still clasped together.

After a beat, Jian started to rise, and Carver automatically squeezed his hand tighter. An unexpected knot of anxiety clamped in his gut as he waited for the leftover sensation in his body to become too much and repulse him. He hadn't been nearly desperate enough to take someone's energy like this, and his body would surely reject it.

But the revulsion never came.

"It's all right," Jian said softly. "We'll take it slow."

He eased out, and the absence left a hollowness behind. But then he laid down and gathered Carver against his chest. The heat behind Jian's sternum was almost searing, but Carver still pressed his face into it and took a deep breath. He couldn't get his thoughts to form anything coherent and couldn't make himself worry about it.

They lay wrapped together for several minutes. Carver just kept breathing, his anxiety easing beat by beat. His faculties steadily returned until he could make his mouth move.

"Are you all right?" he whispered into the silence.

Jian rubbed the base of Carver's skull absently. "Better than all right," he said. "I don't think I've ever experienced anything like that."

Carver craned his neck back. The gold in Jian's eyes had dimmed, giving way to brown again. There was something warm and fond in his gaze.

"Are you all right?" he asked.

Carver swallowed. "I think so. I… I haven't felt this since… Well, maybe not since I was unmated."

Jian's brows furrowed. "Is that a bad thing?"

"No, it's just been a very, very long time since I was able to enjoy sex, let alone lose myself like that." Carver absently traced the outline of the snake on Jian's chest with a finger. "And I've rarely had someone focus so much effort on my pleasure."

"Don't the consorts try to please their clients?" Jian asked disbelievingly.

Carver shook his head. "Not for me. I'm not… It was hard enough for me to feed. Being touched always repulsed me. Besides, I feed off another's pleasure, not my own."

Jian frowned. "But this was good for you?"

"Very." Carver chewed his lip for a moment. "You are methodical and relentless. I suppose I should've expected that from you. I just didn't know I'd enjoy it so much."

"Neither did I. You are exceptional."

188

Carver swallowed as an ache started low in his belly. Did he still want more?

Jian ghosted a hand down to Carver's hip. "I'm sorry, though," he murmured, "that I came in you without permission. You got your legs around me and—"

"That was intentional."

"Oh." A corner of Jian's lips pulled up. "Is that something you like?"

Carver resisted a shiver at the glow in the eyes boring into him, clear with the intention to give an encore.

"It was instinct mostly," he explained. "Orgasms are the most intense wave of energy, and it feels even better when the contact is also internal."

Jian's lips spread more. "I'll keep that in mind."

Carver stared up at the glittering gold in the demon's eyes, his heart speeding up just at the sight. The hum of fresh energy pulsed through him comfortably. He could take in more, he knew. No queasiness. No disgust. This had only felt good, the way it was meant to—the way it once had.

Carver craned his neck up until their lips met. He hooked his leg over Jian's as he pushed him onto his back, keeping the kiss together as they moved. His thighs bracketed Jian's hips, and he ground down. The siren pheromones were still strong in the air, so he wasn't surprised to find Jian getting hard again. They moaned into each other's mouths.

"I should be too sensitive for this," Jian said when he pulled away.

"Is this more of your siren magic?"

Heat burned through Carver as he ground into Jian shamelessly.

"The oil in our skin shortens refractory periods," he explained breathlessly. "No good if our prey can only feed us once. It'll go away when I'm no longer hungry."

"Is that so?"

Jian held the hips above his still. The head of him pushed at Carver's entrance, eliciting a groan.

"And your own pleasure doesn't feed you," Jian said with a wicked smile, "just mine."

Carver's brows lifted.

"So you can keep going until you're fully fed," Jian continued as he pushed a little deeper. "You could come again and again and again."

Carver put his weight back, taking Jian fully in one motion. It only made the ache in him worse.

More. He wanted more.

"I never should have told you that," he breathed as Jian pulled back only to thrust into him again.

His thighs shook, and he collapsed into the overheated chest beneath him when the fullness in him got to be too much. Jian just took that as incentive to wrap his arms around Carver and thrust faster.

It'd been so long since sex had felt anywhere near this good. This was the desperate, fevered kind of pleasure that Carver couldn't control even if he wanted to. As it was, he could only succumb to it while he was flipped onto his side, leg lifted onto a shoulder while Jian pushed into him at an angle that made him see stars.

He suspected that this demon was going to try to catch him up on a century's worth of starvation.

CHAPTER TEN

Blue curls highlighted with bright blond filled Jian's vision. He didn't remember falling asleep, but then he had never fucked someone until his back threatened to give out and fatigue forced him into unconsciousness. Not that he was complaining.

Carver was curled into him. His head lay in the crook where Jian's chest met his shoulder. The sheets had been tossed to the foot of the bed, but Jian doubted Carver had needed them when the difference in their core temperatures was almost thirty degrees. Demons were walking furnaces for everyone else.

Sunlight crept over the floor from the window across the room. The clock on the nightstand flashed 7:13, almost two hours later than Jian usually woke up. He didn't wonder why as the ache in his muscles reminded him of what he'd done the night before.

The sex had been better than any hunt he'd ever done. Watching Carver come apart over and over again, finding new ways to make him gasp and moan, earning scratches and bruises—they all satisfied that predatory urge Jian spent bounties and investigations trying to quell. He had almost been disappointed when he came for the fourth time and couldn't find the strength for a fifth.

Carver sluggishly pressed closer until their limbs were thoroughly entangled. A little sigh left him, evidently content to keep his face in Jian's chest despite it having the highest concentration of heat. The gesture was so unbearably cute that Jian almost missed the significance of it.

Carver seemed to hold almost everyone at a distance, never lowering his walls made of professionalism. This was an immense display of trust and intimacy.

He will absolutely break your heart.

Jian hadn't thought much of the warning at the time, but as he carded his fingers through blue curls, the words came back to him roughly. Saoirse had probably thought her brother incapable of enjoying sex and perhaps suspected he could never reciprocate romantic love again. Maybe she was still right about his capacity for love. Sex was just biology. To love someone was another thing entirely.

Jian ghosted his lips over Carver's forehead. How one man could have so thoroughly consumed his attention like this in such a short time was baffling. Jian was adept at figuring people out—their motivations and habits and aspirations—and rarely was he impressed with what he discovered after he'd uncovered everything. More often than not, he saw the same petty concerns and fears that everyone had, himself included. But Carver didn't seem to know how to be selfish.

"You're too good for me," Jian whispered into the quiet.

Only Carver's soft, even breaths served as a response. A small hum left him when Jian wrapped an arm over his waist, and he curled even closer.

Fifty years ago, Jian might have been intimidated by someone like this—a genuinely good person—but these days, he knew that there always had to be people like himself who were willing to get dirty to preserve the bits of light in the world. At least, that was what he told himself to sleep at night. He knew it was as flimsy a justification as any, but how else was he supposed to hold Carver with hands that had committed atrocities?

He pressed his face to Carver's hair and breathed the traces of sea salt and lavender in it. Minutes ticked by like that, just breathing in the comfortable quiet of the morning. Eventually, Carver stirred and craned his head back to look up. A beat passed before bleariness turned into comprehension, and he glanced down at how close they were.

"Ah, sorry," he mumbled and started to roll away.

Jian held fast to Carver's waist, stopping him. "Hold on. What's to be sorry for?"

A faint red bloomed through Carver's cheeks. "I didn't mean to crawl over you while we slept."

"You don't like cuddling?"

The red grew.

"That's not... I mean..." Carver took a breath before continuing. "I do...like it."

Jian smiled, amused at how cute this man could be. "Then I don't see a problem."

Carver relaxed when Jian pulled him closer. They lay in silence for a long moment, and Jian allowed himself to enjoy the feel of another person held close to him.

"We really did that," Carver mumbled abruptly.

Jian rubbed his thumb into the scarred hip under his hand. "Did what? Sex? I can confirm that."

Carver let out a half-hearted chuckle. "You don't seem to have as many anxieties as I do."

"What are you anxious about?" Jian asked, honestly concerned now. "Did I do something bad?"

Carver took a moment to answer. "I don't know how to say this without sounding arrogant, but if I had felt uncomfortable or unsafe at any point, there is nothing you could have done to stop me from rectifying that."

Jian wasn't sure if that confidence was born of having the Professor's power or simply the martial training of an Inquisitor. Either way, it did come as a comfort.

"Point taken," he conceded. "So what are you anxious about?"

Carver lifted his eyes. "I guess I'm anxious about…what this is. I haven't done anything like this in a very long time, and while it was good, I don't know if it'd be a good idea to repeat it."

"You want to leave things here?" Jian didn't bother to withhold the surprise and disappointment from his voice.

"I guess I'm just not sure what continuing this means for us. These aren't exactly safe times, and I…" Carver glanced away. "I'm changing. I don't know if my body will allow me to do this indefinitely. I could revert to what I was before."

While sex was good, Jian found that it wasn't much of a consideration for him to be around this enigmatic siren.

"Maybe I just like your company," he confessed, "without expectations as to what we do with our time."

Carver's cheeks darkened immediately at the words, even if they hadn't been intended to be romantic.

Jian trailed his fingertips up Carver's sternum. "I can't begin to understand your condition," he murmured, "but if you took my energy, that seems to be progress."

Carver's eyes closed for a moment. "One night doesn't mean I'm cured."

"No, but I'm not looking to be a cure, just companionship. If you don't want it, that's completely fine. I won't push for anything you're not up for."

Carver was quiet for a long moment before speaking again. "I feel like my body is going to betray me again, but I'd still like to try."

The way Jian's heart fluttered would bite him later—he was sure of it.

"If you can tolerate me," Carver added. "I'm very rusty with anything…intimate."

Jian offered a small smile. "Could've fooled me."

Carver flushed down to his chest. "You know what I meant."

"I think you're doing just fine," Jian offered earnestly, "but even if you weren't, it's difficult to get me upset. I'm more concerned that you're going to get tired of me and my antics, which would be understandable. I know I can be challenging."

"I actually appreciate being challenged. Most people treat me like glass."

"Well, you didn't seem delicate to me last night."

Carver chuckled. "Did you reach that conclusion before or after you pinned me against the headboard?"

"Well before." Fresh heat rose in Jian's chest. "I had an inkling when you told me I could hurt you."

Carver shifted almost nervously. "You didn't hurt me."

Jian wasn't sure how to interpret the words. They sounded disappointed, which immediately made his fangs ache. Few people wanted the kind of damage that demons were delighted to inflict.

"I don't make it general practice," he said, "to cause harm without discussion of methods beforehand."

When Carver didn't respond, he added, "Do you want me to hurt you, detective?"

Carver lowered his gaze. "It has…crossed my mind."

Jian swallowed the rumble that tried to leave his chest. "Mm, you should tell me over breakfast, so I don't get any ideas while we're in bed."

"What if I want to give you ideas?"

Smoke left Jian on his next exhale. He climbed atop Carver.

"I'd say we have time for that," he murmured, "but you need to eat first."

Carver rolled his hips up into Jian's, eliciting an involuntary groan. "I'm not hungry."

Jian enclosed his thighs around Carver's hips to stop them from moving more. "You're a brat."

"Am I?" Carver whispered primly.

The words made Jian's cardinal fire burn hotter, and he bent until his face hovered just above the lips he'd kissed almost to bruising just hours ago.

"Brat," he whispered before slotting their lips together.

Carver let out a little moan and opened his mouth readily. Jian was nice enough to indulge the kiss for a moment, but then he pulled away and climbed out of bed.

"Breakfast first," he insisted again.

Carver narrowed his eyes. "Fine, but I get to make it."

Jian chuckled. "Deal."

Carver stood and stretched his arms over his head. In the light, evidence of scratches covered his hips, thighs, and shoulders where Jian had been a little too rough. They'd disappear as soon as Carver made contact with water. Jian tried to quash the disappointment that rose at the thought.

"How does a pureblood scar?" Carver asked abruptly. His eyes were trained on a raised line along Jian's hip.

"A knife wound that had water poured into it," Jian answered with a shrug. "Almost killed me."

Carver circled him, eyes scanning over the myriad of other scars. "This was during the war?"

"Yes." Jian held his breath when Carver stopped at his back. "Those are all from bullet wounds that got rain in them."

"I knew the Blood War was horrible," Carver said softly. "But this… There are so many."

Jian laid a hand over Carver's when it got to his shoulder. "They've long healed. I'm not in pain."

"I know." Carver passed fingertips down the raised spots and lines littering Jian's back. "I've just never seen anything like this on someone who was still breathing."

"Admittedly wasn't breathing much at the time." Jian stepped away and out of reach. "We should get dressed. I'll make coffee."

He planted a kiss on Carver's jaw as he passed to soften the abruptness of his dismissal. This morning was good, and he didn't want to sour it with talk of the war. He spent enough time ruminating on it already.

Carver didn't offer a protest, just gathered his clothes from the floor and pulled them on. Jian dressed in undershorts and sweats that he gathered from his dresser. They padded out to the living room. Jian's messenger, abandoned on the floor by the kitchen, was buzzing. He grabbed it before grimacing at the blood stain that'd dried on the tile.

"Let me help," Carver said as he grabbed a sponge from the sink. "Quicker with four hands."

Jian took paper towels from a rack on the counter, and they spent a couple minutes just scrubbing his blood out of the floor. Embarrassment warmed up his neck. He tried to remind himself that Carver had already witnessed him bleeding out on the floor, which was much worse than cleaning it. Still, some irrational part of him bristled at having the evidence of his weakness scrubbed by someone else.

"The Professor wrote a condensed history on you," Jian said as they tossed the towels and sponge into the waste bin by the fridge. "She sent it to me, thinking it might help the investigation."

Carver tensed.

"I haven't read it," Jian added after a beat.

Slowly, some of the tension bled out of Carver. He opened the fridge and started pulling out ingredients.

"Why not?" he asked stiffly.

Jian took the canister that'd been sitting in the pneumatic tube port of his wall since yesterday. "Didn't have time, but even if I had, it seemed wrong without your permission."

Carver set various vegetables and a carton of eggs on the counter. "Read it aloud. I want to know what she said."

He looked through the cabinets until he found a pan, cutting board, and a knife. His expression was as stony and unreadable as the first day they'd met.

Jian sat at his dining table and opened the canister. There were just two papers inside. The Professor's perfect, winding script covered them. She hadn't written proper paragraphs, just bullet points with information she likely thought was relevant.

"'Born in 1748 to Minister Fayruz Nahoumazti and the pirate captain, Niall O'Fogladha,'" Jian read. "'Carver's mother renounced her title to hide having bore a son and moved to live at sea with her husband. They had Saoirse almost twelve years after. Carver was fifteen when the Ministry discovered him and executed his parents.

He then carried his sister across the ocean to the new world while the Ministry pursued them.'"

Jian paused, reading that last line repeatedly. There were several thousand miles of ocean between continents. To carry a child that distance while pursued by assassins at fifteen was astonishing. Most people that age would have simply died.

Carver was chopping an onion, but he stopped abruptly. "Everything all right?"

"I just didn't know you'd traversed an entire ocean with your sister," Jian murmured. "She would've been just three or four. You had to have been taking care of her while you fled."

"It wasn't as bad as it sounds." Carver resumed chopping. "Our mother had taught me to hunt by then and how to cover our tracks."

Jian shook his head. That was no less impressive, but he didn't think explaining that would have been welcome.

"'They were taken in by Declan, a human blacksmith in the Palitz province of the Republic,'" Jian continued. "'Declan's son, Thomas, would eventually become Carver's husband.' Ernest Declan Carver. You took your father-in-law's name."

Carver nodded. "They would call me Ernest because my real name was too difficult for Republic tongues. I didn't speak or read any Imperial then. Thomas taught me with the few books we had."

Jian could imagine coming to a foreign nation with no grasp of the language, as he'd done the same, but to do so as a refugee with a small child to look after added a degree of complication.

"'The ICS in Havitzford granted Carver and his sister asylum in

1763,'" he read. "'He found work with them as a defender, and then he was scouted to join the Inquisitors at nineteen. He worked with them until he was twenty-eight when he married and bonded with Thomas.'"

Carver slid onions in the pan he set on the stove and then started chopping mushrooms. "I was a worse partner when I was an Inquisitor. It became obvious to me that I couldn't be one and Thomas' husband, so I chose Thomas."

Jian could understand that. He hadn't been pleasant to be around during the war.

"'The Ministry hired Garsuk in 1811 to kill Thomas.'"

It was a simple line, a fact spoken as such, but the weight of it sat oddly in Jian's chest. It was 1912 now, over a century later. And Carver was still dealing with the impacts of his mate's death.

"They succeeded," he murmured. "I came home to Thomas bleeding out in our kitchen while Saoirse held off the horde, but she wasn't going to make it either. The Ministry had hired a fae to help, distracting me and making escape difficult. I couldn't save both Thomas and Saoirse."

"And you chose her." Jian's voice was barely above a whisper. "You chose her over yourself, too."

"Easy choice. Thomas was sixty, and we didn't have many more years left. Saoirse had the rest of her life ahead of her."

Jian stared at the words for a moment. "If you knew it would come to this, would you have chosen the same?"

Carver's hands paused, but only for a beat. "Without reservation."

The answer was expected. He would have done anything for Saoirse, if the last few days were any indication.

Jian continued reading. "'Carver survived the death of Thomas. Saoirse continued a career as an Inquisitor while he joined the Investigative Division of the ICS. He took medical leave in 1834 following his third…'"

Carver glanced at him. "You can say it."

Jian had to take a breath first. "'He took medical leave in 1834 following his third suicide attempt.'"

"They called in Saoirse for that one." Carver slid the sliced mushrooms into the pan. "She made me promise not to do it again. I kept my word."

"Just like that?"

Carver grabbed some cloves of garlic from a basket on the counter. "Do you remember what a khavira is?"

The question seemed irrelevant, but Jian didn't think this was an attempt at deflection. "A siren with a genetic defect that makes them deadly to the people they try to bond with."

Carver nodded. "Saoirse is one. She found out shortly before I tried to kill myself the third time. Most khavira kill their partners when they find out what they are. She was fortunate enough that she didn't, but knowing that you can't be with the person you love—that just being near them might kill them—is too much for most khavira. After the third attempt on my life, she said that she was living for me. If I died, then she had no reason to stay either. It was either we lived together or died together."

Jian's brows rose. He'd known Carver's attachment to life was nearly non-existent, but it was somehow even less than he'd anticipated. If anything happened to Saoirse, her brother had no reason to stay in this world.

"Continue," Carver said as he crushed garlic under his knife blade.

There was nothing Jian wanted to do less at present, but he returned his eyes to the papers and read aloud.

"'In 1840, the Ministry hired Gars to kill Saoirse. They tried again in 1863, and then again in 1872. The ICS declared her dead after and provided her the alias Rain Andreacchi. Carver wasn't targeted, having been assumed dead by the Ministry after the death of his mate. It is unclear if they still think him dead or not.'"

Jian grimaced at the last line. The Gars did seem focused on Saoirse, not Carver. There was also a possibility that they were so obsessed with her because she was a khavira. They could have found out back in 1834, and they had just been going after her ever since, despite having been granted asylum and the backing of the ICS.

"You think the Ministry knows she's a khavira?" Jian asked.

Carver cut into the garlic, chopping it into fine pieces. "I wouldn't have told you if I thought they didn't. She hates people knowing."

"Understandable." Jian leaned back in his chair and set the papers on the table. "So the Gars have a long history of pursuing you both at the Ministry's behest. I think if they didn't know you're alive, they do now. They might try to get Saoirse by going through you. I'm glad we chose to shuffle her to a safe house."

Carver pushed the garlic into the pan and lowered the heat of the burner to a simmer. "If we only knew where they were, we could just be done with this."

Jian rested his chin in a hand. "I've been looking, but maybe you can see something that I can't."

"Leave for the Court after we eat?"

"Sounds like a plan, detective."

Carver tilted his head curiously. "Why do you always call me 'detective'?"

Jian shrugged. "Well, forgive me, but I believe we've established that your name isn't Ernest Declan Carver. In fact, I think the name your sister called you by was Meallán."

Carver tensed, but only for a moment. "I go by Carver because it's the one name I can still use that's mine. I took my husband's name when we married."

Jian turned slightly to meet Carver's eyes. "So what is your full name?"

"Meallán O'Fogladha Nahoumazti Carver."

"That is quite the name. Would you prefer I call you Carver, then?"

The question didn't seem to be one Carver expected, as he took a long moment to respond.

"You can call me Meallán," he said finally. "Do you have a preference for yourself?"

Jian hadn't thought too much on that in a while. Very few people knew him as anything other than his clan name, but he didn't have a right to it anymore, nor his Tong name.

"Technically," he said haltingly, "I gave up everything but my given name when I killed my family."

"Tuan?" Carver supplied.

Jian averted his eyes immediately and rubbed the back of his neck. It was such a small thing, a name, but his heart skipped at hearing it.

"Ah, so you remembered it," he mumbled.

"Should I continue to use Jian?" Carver asked with a smile, seemingly amused at the display of embarrassment.

"No, Tuan is fine."

"As you say...Tuan."

A soft pink touched Jian's cheeks in an uncharacteristic show of emotion. "Perhaps sparingly."

"I can do sparingly." Carver lifted the pan from the stove and shook it briefly. "Do you have plans today beyond our work at the Court?"

It sounded too close to an invitation, and Jian was already looking forward to spending more time with this siren who quieted the storm in his mind and made the bloodlust tolerable. He'd take whatever he was given.

"Only if they involve you," he said earnestly.

Carver's eyes lowered, but his smile didn't slip. "We can make that happen."

CHAPTER ELEVEN

Jian had barely gotten dressed for the day when he got a message from Palus. There were wolves spotted around the abandoned cannery in Redcliff, as he had predicted. Palus sent the coordinates and told him to check it out. Carver had to come with as both bait and the one who needed to be protected.

Old, colonial houses blurred by in the early morning light. In this part of Vespera, many of the buildings were derelict. Chipped and peeling paint accompanied shattered glass and splintered roofs on the houses. Yards overgrown with weeds or rotted to bare dirt lined the streets. Factories and warehouses dotted the skyline. Some of the warehouses still got use, but the factories were largely condemned.

A sprinkle of rain fell. Drops accumulated on the windshield as Carver drove. There was no way to know what to expect out in Redcliff, so they would have to wait around and surveil the place until the wolves showed up. The ICS had agents all over the city to keep constant surveillance, and they'd seen surprisingly little so far. Maeva was still nowhere to be found. That made Jian more anxious than anything else. The fae were nothing to trifle with.

"Are those our agents?" Carver asked when he turned onto a

narrow street.

Jian sat up straighter. A group of people stood out front of a mostly intact house. Among them was a tall woman. Blond curls fell in tight coils over one of her shoulders. Braids close to her scalp ran across the side of her head. Her ochre skin had cool highlights where the dim light touched it. She wore plain jeans and a black coat — clothes that wouldn't stand out. Spies did their best when they could move freely in plain sight.

Irsa was an exceptional agent. As with most sirens, she could charm anyone into loosening their tongues, and her attention to detail was admirable. She would've made a good spymaster. But she was too smart to accept such a position.

The other two agents with her were also familiar. One was an exceedingly tall person — taller than even Carver. He had pale patches in his tawny skin where vitiligo had reduced pigmentation. His black hair was tied back behind his head. The angles of his face were hard and then soft, almost like a trick of the light. Sanya was a shifter, an exceedingly rare race that had next to no population at present. He could change his appearance at will, but rarely did unless he was undercover.

The third agent was a lean man. His brown eyes had a ring of gold around the pupils. A dark goatee encased his lips and chin. He wore a hood and gloves, protecting him from the rain. Demons were rare in Vespera, but Zhihao had followed Jian out here after their other cousin had died in the war.

Irsa approached the auto when Carver pulled up and parked at the curb.

"Director," she greeted as Jian and Carver climbed out. "It's been quiet, but we have long-range scouts around the perimeter, armed and ready whenever you need them."

Jian inclined his head. "Thank you, Irsa. Let's hope we won't need them at all."

Zhihao offered a warm smile. He looked so much like their great-grandfather sometimes, with the same severe angles to his face and square jaw, but his eyes were much softer.

"Good to see you back, *tahe*," he said with a nod at Jian.

"I wish I could say it's good to be back," Jian admitted, "but I'm glad to see you anyway."

Zhihao held out a hand toward Carver. "Lieutenant Jian Zhihao."

Carver shook the offer. "Jian?" he echoed. "Any relation?"

"Zhihao is my cousin," Jian supplied. "One of two who survived the war."

"Generous to even be called a cousin," Zhihao said with a wry smile. "I'm his father's great uncle's second son's son, which is a long-winded way of saying that we have the same family name, but I got none of the political responsibility like he did."

Jian grimaced. "Lucky you."

Sanya offered a terse nod. "It's been a while, director."

His Yuvom accent was slight, but weighed his tongue down and forced his vowels to the back of his mouth.

"It has," Jian said gently. "How are your kids?"

"Adjusting." Sanya's tone was stiff. "You hear anything from Eji about my…ex-wife?"

The uncertain way he said 'ex-wife' seemed to indicate he wasn't sure if the term was applicable.

Jian shook his head ruefully. "You'd be the first to know."

Sanya didn't respond, just stared with hard eyes.

"Ah… Detective, this is Sanya," Jian introduced haltingly. "He's… Well, his ex-wife is the sister of my clan's head of security, Eji."

Zhihao rubbed the back of his neck. "Eji's sister actually introduced him to our clan."

Carver glanced between them. "I'm sensing some tension," he said after a beat. "Messy divorce?"

"It's not official yet," Sanya muttered bluntly. "Fumi left me a note three months ago that said there's someone else, and she's not going to try to visit the kids."

When Carver's brows climbed his forehead, Sanya added, "We don't need to dig this up right now. It's not relevant."

Jian ignored the mix of resentment and guilt stirring in his chest. He hadn't kept up with friends while he dealt with his shattered mind, and it seemed like things had fallen apart in his absence. He'd thought of Fumi as a friend. She hadn't said a word to him before she disappeared and abandoned her family. Maybe if he'd been better, if he'd been around, he could have helped her through whatever had her leave. Well, it was too late now.

Irsa took a deep breath with her nose scrunched. She narrowed her eyes at him. He wasn't sure what she smelled, but he suspected it had something to do with the persistent scent of sea salt on him. Other sirens could probably tell he had recently been with another siren.

"Please don't ask," he said before she could speak.

"*Iidha eurif alsabab batal aleajab*," she muttered with a wave of her hand.

When Jian's brows furrowed in confusion, Carver said, "It roughly means that she knows, and she's worse for it."

"Know what?" Zhihao asked as he glanced between everyone. "What am I missing?"

"Siren stuff," Jian answered tersely.

Carver said something in Ireadia. The clipped consonants paired with round vowels gave the language an almost musical quality, like staccato notes along an otherwise fluid song. Irsa replied in Ireadia. The conversation was short, with only a few words exchanged back and forth, and then Irsa spoke in Imperial again.

"We've got bigger problems," she said. "Let's get to the cannery, director, so we can brief you properly."

Jian was all too eager to start work. His relationship with Carver wasn't anyone else's business, and it felt too new, too delicate, to face scrutiny right now.

He trailed behind Sanya and Irsa when they headed down the sidewalk. Carver fell in step beside him, and Zhihao took up the back.

"What were you talking about?" Jian asked with a glance at Carver. "Anything I should worry about?"

Carver shook his head. "I just asked for her discretion. Irsa knows you well enough to be curious about your personal life, it seems."

Jian couldn't fault them the curiosity. He'd gotten a reputation after coming to the new world as a chronic bachelor and persistently commitment-averse curmudgeon. His longest relationship after his divorce lasted less than a year, and he often went decades at a time without a committed partner. Working at the ICS wasn't conducive to keeping a relationship. He'd travel for months at a time, and sometimes without proper communication equipment.

"Why are you here, *tahe*?" Zhihao asked abruptly. "I thought you wanted nothing to do with this life anymore."

Jian sighed. "Palus asked me, and I can never say no to them. My resignation is already drafted and set to send as soon as all this is over."

"I can't say we won't miss you, but it's good to know you'll take care of yourself." Zhihao looked up at Carver. "I heard you're my cousin's partner now, detective. He acts tough, but he's a sap with no self-preservation. You have the hardest job in the ICS right now."

Jian scowled without any real chagrin. "Who are you calling a sap?"

"You listen to disco."

"Chang is an icon."

Zhihao sputtered into a chuckle. "Sure, thirty years ago."

Carver's smile sat on his face oddly, like he was trying to stop the expression and failing miserably.

"Got something to say, detective?" Jian said with narrowed eyes.

Carver shook his head. "Of course not, sir."

Jian ignored the pang of need that shot through him at the honorific. When he let his eyes wander up Carver's body, the scent of

212

sea salt bloomed in the air, almost indistinguishable from the rain currently falling. But Jian could detect the slightest difference.

Irsa glanced back at them. They didn't meet her eyes.

"We're close," Sanya grumbled, and then added under his breath: "Thank the gods."

They rounded a corner. The street here sloped up. At the top of it was a large, concrete building. The cannery sat at the edge of a cliff. Time had brought the edge closer and closer until the location was deemed hazardous. Rust clung to the metal pipes running along one side. The logo of the canning company was just white streaks now. A dilapidated chain link fence encircled the property.

"We'll be stationed through the surrounding area," Isra said, "but Palus was adamant that Detective Carver should always be accompanied and monitored."

Jian sighed and shoved his hands in his coat pockets. "I'll go inside with the detective. Better to get an idea of the place first, and maybe we'll see how the Gars are set up."

Sanya unclipped two radios from his belt and handed them to him and Carver. "Should be set to the correct frequency," he said. "Range is a mile. It's connected to our entire team, but I'll be taking point if you need anything."

Jian nodded and hooked the radio to the leather strap of his gun holster. The lapel of his coat concealed it when he pulled it in place. Carver did the same.

"Good luck out there, *tahe*," Zhihao said with a nod at his cousin.

He headed back the way they'd come with Irsa and Sanya.

"What does he keep calling you?" Carver asked as he started toward the cannery with Jian.

"*Tahe*. It literally means older brother," Jian explained, "but it's more like a teasing title the way he means it. It can also mean something like 'gang boss.' I'm technically his clan head, even if he's not part of the main family."

"The main family?"

"The 'outside' family, as we say in Tonghua, aren't considered to have pure enough blood to pass on our name." Jian didn't bother to conceal the venom in his tone. "If Zhihao were to have a kid, he couldn't give them the Jian name. The only reason he has it is because we share a great-grandfather."

Carver chewed his lip—a habit he had while thinking. "But you could pass on your name."

"I could. I did. I wouldn't again." Jian gave a humorless chuckle. "They tried to marry off my daughter when she was twenty, just like they did to me. I refused. The thought that she'd end up in a marriage like mine... Well, I thought she deserved better."

Carver's eyes were soft, not quite pitying but close. "You deserved better."

Jian lowered his gaze as heat rose in his face. "It's in the distant past."

There was a beat of silence, and then he felt a hand wrap around his. It was such a small, simple gesture. But Jian's heart sped away.

They didn't let go until they got to the fence enclosing the cannery. A large hole had been cut in the chain link. They ducked through.

214

Leaves squelched underfoot. Water pooled over the ground. A pair of heavy, metal doors were locked at the front of the building. The window beside them was nearly opaque from how clouded it was.

Sparks jumped from Jian's fingertips as he approached the doors. The padlock holding them closed was old and brittle. Sparks flew off it when he brought his fingers to the shank. The metal whistled and groaned a moment before it shattered, sending a spray of red shrapnel to the ground. Smoke drifted off Jian's fingers. He pulled the lock off and pushed the doors open.

The hinges groaned with how rusted they were, but miraculously, they didn't snap. Jian stepped in with Carver. The interior looked much the same as the exterior. Dust and dirt covered the floor. Water fell through a hole in the roof. Most of the machinery in here appeared to have been gutted, leaving only cavernous space and a smattering of broken machine parts. The catwalk overhead was little more than a rusted length of grate that hung off one wall at an angle. The windows at the back looked over a vast expanse of ocean.

"See anything of note?" Jian asked as he stepped deeper inside.

Carver looked around the interior. "Nothing yet. It—"

He stopped as his eyes set on a window in the back wall. A woman stood at the cliff's edge. She wore a white cloak that clung to her shoulders with the water soaking through it. It contrasted harshly with her dark skin. There was nothing remarkable about her outfit. It was just a white blouse and black pants. A braid of dark hair draped over her shoulder.

"Jian," Carver said tightly. "Run."

Jian's brows lowered. "What are you—"

"Now," Carver bit out, never letting his eyes leave the woman.

The radio crackled to life.

"Director!" Sanya's voice had an edge of panic. "I don't know what you did in there, but we have wolves coming up from the sewers! They're heading your way!"

The sewers? Was that how they were getting around the city?

Growls and snarls sounded distantly. Jian cursed and pulled his gun from his hip.

The woman at the cliff seemed to move directly through the wall, passing through it like it didn't exist. Her speed was almost too fast to track as she collided with Carver. They went flying back across the cannery. One of the walls gave like tissue paper under the force they slammed into it, and they tumbled outside.

Gunshots rang from out front of the cannery. Yelps cut through the noise. Heavy footfalls followed. Jian took a deep breath. The fire in his chest burned hotter until a faint glow emanated through his ribs and throat. He was going to have to fight his way out and hope that Carver could handle the woman.

The doors burst open. Wolves clawed at the metal, gnashing their fangs. He blew out. A stream of fire burst from his lips. The two wolves at the front flew back with a whimper as the force of the flames struck them. They landed on the concrete out front. Three more wolves rushed inside.

Jian raised his gun and fired two shots. They tore through one wolf's chest and head. It collapsed to the floor just as another charged forward. There wasn't enough time to get another shot off. Jian lifted his arm against the open maw that came for him. Fangs clamped down on his elbow. Pain nearly blinded him. His bones crunched under the force of the bite.

He reached up with his other hand and grabbed the wolf's throat. Fire erupted from his fingers, searing through its neck. It writhed with a yelp, and its bite loosened.

Something struck Jian in the side, sending him to the ground. Pain burst through his ribs. He looked up to see the third wolf standing over him. It snapped at his head. He just barely struck it across the face in time, pushing those fangs away from him. His hand shot up, sliding between ribs, and heat burst from his fingers. The wolf couldn't make a sound. It just jerked wildly and then fell limp as its innards burned.

Jian pushed himself out from under it. Creaking overhead brought his head up. Another wolf had appeared on the catwalk. He'd barely gotten a spark in his lips when it jumped, heading directly for him. Claws sank into his chest as fangs clamped around his already shredded shoulder. The wolf jerked its head to the side, slamming him back into a window. Glass shards sprayed up around them. Something like tar oozed from the wolf's mouth. The black, oily substance spilled thickly over Jian. It smelled of decay and infection. His nerves started to numb as whatever poison the wolf spilled soaked into his wounds.

He got his arms around the wolf's neck and pushed back through the window. Damp rock met his back. Rain fell heavily over them.

The crash of ocean waves roared from below. Just a few feet away was the edge of the cliff. He got his legs under the wolf and kicked them out with all he had. The wolf skidded across the ground and tumbled over the edge of the cliff.

Rainwater was already cracking Jian's skin when he stood.

"Pity."

He'd barely turned to see the source of the voice when the woman from earlier shot toward him at impossible speed. She abruptly morphed into the shape of a wolf. Nails like razors dug into his flesh and dragged him to the ground. His skin burned on contact with the puddles below. But then something pulled the wolf away and slammed it into the ground.

The creature was unlike anything Jian had seen before. It crouched on all fours, but still stood well over eight feet. The scales covering its body were black as the night, and the rain spilling over them almost gave the illusion of ichor emerging from it. Spines like the rays on fish lined its arms and back. The head was distinctly humanoid, but it lacked any visible eyes or mouth—that is, until a slit opened to show rows of sharp fangs dripping with blood.

Jian lay frozen as it stood over him, shielding him from the rain. The surrounding water seemed to fly away from them, as if repelled by an unseen force. A siren could do such a thing.

The woman's form appeared amongst the growing group of wolves in the cannery.

"All right," she said. "Let's try this again."

The creature over Jian crouched lower, almost protectively, as it bared its fangs. A low drone that he'd heard before emanated from its chest.

Was it Carver? But how? Was this what he'd meant when he said the Professor's influence would cause changes?

"Director!" Irsa called into the radio. "Director, what's happening out there?"

Jian rushed out from under the creature and backed away, giving himself space from it and the wolves. He'd just started looking for ways to escape when a screech preceded a loud slam and the crack of bone giving way. Jian glanced back to see the woman with her fingers embedded in the creature's chest while she held it down. It lifted a clawed hand and dragged it across her chest. She hissed as bright red bloomed through the tears in her white blouse. The beast lunged up and clamped its teeth around her arm. She laughed as she grabbed its jaw and crushed it. A high screech left it, but its bones snapped back into place almost immediately.

"Director, can you hear us!" Irsa called through the radio.

Several wolves were starting to pile on top of the creature. The woman had its head pinned to the ground while she stared at Jian. Her eyes seemed to draw him in as soon as he met them. The rest of the world darkened. He blinked, trying to dispel whatever strange effects were upon him, but it was futile. His eyes opened to familiar, geometric wallpaper.

Gold hexagons contrasted starkly against the black backdrop. Blood spotted the dark floorboards. Thin ribbing ran along the edges of the ceiling. The single window to one side showed the ocean beyond it. Broken glass and jewelry lay atop the dresser at the back of the room. Jian lay on the bed, taking up half the space. A woman sat atop him with a hand at his throat.

Xiuying was beautiful. Her long, black hair fell heavily over one shoulder. Brown eyes ringed in gold peered down at him between long lashes. Blood smeared across her lips and trickled down her chin. Jian's wife had been known for her strength as much as her beauty. Everyone had told him he was lucky to be given such a match.

His head snapped to one side when she struck his face. Her nails tore across his cheek.

"Fuck you!" she hissed. "If you weren't such a fucking coward, we wouldn't be in this position."

Heat rushed through him as the predator in him grew indignant. It wanted to lash out—to cow her the way she tried to cow him. But he only stared blankly at the wall and didn't respond.

Her hand tightened around his throat. "If you don't get me pregnant, we're going to stay married for longer. Is that what you want?"

The idea of bearing a child with this woman made his stomach turn, but he wouldn't say that. His obligation was to his family, not her. She'd probably give up the child for him to raise anyway while she continued her career outside Tong Bei.

"Why won't you fucking speak!" she growled.

His jaw clenched against the urge to tear her throat out with his teeth. He was stronger than her. If he truly wished her harm, he could make her bleed like she did him. But would it stop there? He didn't trust himself not to kill her in his rage. Better to stare at the wall and wait for her tirade to end.

She pulled at the waistband of his pants. "Fine. I'll do everything myself."

His stomach dropped. He caught her wrist, stopping her. She sneered at him while he wrenched out of her hold and threw her off him. A hiss escaped her when she nearly fell off the bed.

"I don't owe you anything," he said stiffly. "I don't owe you my loyalty, and I certainly don't owe you my body."

An odd sense of satisfaction rushed through him. He never told her his true feelings, and he certainly never defied her. But he was done now. He'd leave her finally and never look back.

No, that wasn't what happened.

Pain shot through his head as his vision seemed to split in two. There was his wife glaring at him from the bed. And then she was also straddling him with her nails digging into his neck. The images overlayed each other, as if happening simultaneously.

It wasn't real. None of it was real.

He drew in a deep breath, letting the flames in his chest burn hot. Fire erupted from his mouth on an exhale. The illusion dissipated like ash peeling off charcoal until the cannery returned.

The fae and wolves still clawed at the creature. They jumped back as the fire encroached on them, but the creature stayed where it was. Flames spread in a wide cone, searing through the puddles and rain. Thick plumes of steam and smoke rose into the air.

Jian closed his mouth as his fire dimmed behind his sternum. His breath came harshly from exertion. There was too much water here dampening his power, but he'd at least provided cover for them. The steam and smoke were dense enough to obscure vision past a few feet. Sparks and embers drifted through the air.

A wolf emerged from the haze. It caught his arm between its teeth, pulling him with it as it slid across the ground. They tumbled over the edge of the cliff. Jian grabbed a piece of rebar jutting out from the ground. A growl below was quickly covered by the crash of waves against the cliffs. He glanced down to see the wolf clinging to the rocky face. It was slowly inching its way up. His fingers burned from the rainwater falling over him. The numbness coursing through him was getting worse, loosening his grip.

"Jian!"

Carver's voice cut through the air. Jian was about to call back when pain shot up his leg. He cried out and looked down.

The wolf had sunk its claws in his leg. It tugged.

His grip slipped.

◊◊◊

She'd launched herself at Carver and sent them careening back through the cannery wall. They landed outside among cracked, damp concrete. Her eyes were a bright green like the kelp forests back home. She had high, severe cheekbones like most fae, tapering down to a narrow jaw. A raised, silvery line cut through her eyebrow where Saoirse's knife had dragged through her skin many, many years ago.

"Maeva," Carver hissed.

A corner of her lips twitched.

He planted his feet to the ground when her hand shot toward him. Icy fingers burrowed between his ribs with the same ease of cutting through butter. It burned, but he didn't flinch. He caught her wrist before she could slide her arm through his body. Blood welled around her hand.

"It's been a long time, Meallán." Maeva's voice was smooth, with a slight Vaulair accent that rounded all her vowels and blended her words into each other. "Miss me?"

"I should've killed you a century ago," he all but growled.

She chuckled. "You're welcome to try again."

Something dark and violent roiled in his chest. His fangs ached in his gums. He tasted the metallic bite of blood on his tongue. All he could hear was his heart in his ears. Webbing grew between his fingers, but it wasn't blue and gold. It was black. Scales as dark as the night erupted under his skin. Motes of white from their sheen glimmered like stars.

Maeva pulled her hand from Carver's chest. There was no sign of harm on him. Fae could be so annoying. As an illusionist, she could make herself look like anyone and make him feel whatever she wanted. Sustaining large illusions for long periods of time, however, was beyond the scope of her abilities. The wolves pouring into the cannery were probably real, but she could have been anywhere. He doubted she was as he saw, just meant as a distraction for him. She was likely hidden nearby.

His legs abruptly gave out from under him. He barely felt when his knees and hands hit the ground. His fangs elongated as he gasped in air that was too dry. A warning drone rumbled out of his chest, filling the air like thunder. The concrete beneath his hands cracked when he curled his fingers. Heat pulsed over his skin, and he barely resisted the urge to peel off his flesh in an attempt to cool off.

Maeva crouched down to hold his chin in a hand. Her touch was gentle.

"You're different," she remarked. "Someone's been playing with the old ways."

Her gaze turned to the back of the cannery. Jian was wrestling with a wolf. He managed to kick it over the edge of the cliff, and it tumbled down to the ocean below. Carver couldn't afford to let her take his attention again.

The rest of the world seemed to slow around him as he sprinted forward just as Maeva did. He got ahead of her. Her strike landed against his shoulder with force beyond what should have been possible. Bone crunched and shattered as blood burst out of his back. He hissed at the pain, but stood his ground. His dreams with Salwnsu had never felt more relevant. She broke his body repeatedly and expected him to hold firm, like he was now.

The illusion of Maeva dispersed as the wolves inside the cannery scrambled. Carver's broken bones healed over, having never been injured to begin with. The spines at his back and along his arms stretched. A burning pain writhed in his bones, making them shift under his skin and muscle. Cracking drowned out the pounding in his ears. He dimly recognized that the sound was his own skeleton moving in him.

The rain diverted toward the cannery, droplets sharpening to points, but then Maeva darted for Jian. There was a chance that her form concealed something. Carver couldn't take the risk that it was dangerous and got in her path. Her form gave way to that of a wolf with its fangs bared. He hissed when it bit into his arm, but the pain was negligible. His hand wrapped around its throat. He slammed it into the ground, sending cracks bursting through the earth around it. Its yelp sounded for only a moment before it was cut short.

His arm continued to bleed where it'd been bitten. The wolf had been real.

More surrounded him. Maeva's form reappeared among them. Her eyes were narrowed as her jaw set, calculating and analyzing.

Carver barely recognized his own hands as he planted them in the ground. They had blackened entirely, and his fingers had elongated with an extra joint. The nails grew into sharp claws. He was vaguely aware of Jian under him. The rain falling over them streamed to the sides, away from the vulnerable demon.

Jian was smart and scrabbled out from under Carver and backed away several paces.

"All right," Maeva said and tilted her head curiously. "Let's try this again."

She got Carver's jaw in her hands and crushed it. A cry left him, but when he wrenched out of her hold, his bones snapped in place again. Wolves tumbled out of the cannery to swarm on him. He blindly tore at them, claws rending flesh indiscriminately.

And then fire erupted toward him. The rain seemed to automatically surround him like a shield. Steam and smoke burst through the area, enshrouding everything with the flames. The surrounding world was obscured beyond only a few feet. Seconds later, the stream of fire ceased. Only the smoke remained. Carver couldn't see through it.

His bones seemed to move in him again. He shrunk into a more humanoid form as he looked around frantically.

"Jian!" he called.

There was a growl and a cry—by the edge of the cliff. His blood ran cold. He didn't think before he ran through the smoke and launched himself over the edge. A mass of blue opened to him as soon as he was out of the haze. There was a circle of foam in the surface of the water, marking where something had fallen through.

The water seemed to rise up to meet Carver, and he slipped readily into its depth, not even feeling the cold. His eyes adjusted immediately to being submerged. Jian was sinking just a few feet down. Cracks were open all through his skin, leaving trails of blood in the water as he descended.

Carver was upon him in a moment, pulling him into his arms. The water roiled around them. It propelled them directly to the surface and then across the waves to a flat section of rocks at the base of the cliffs. Carver laid Jian down carefully and started stripping wet clothes off him.

There was so much blood. A myriad of scratches and bite wounds joined gaping cracks from water submersion. Jian wasn't breathing.

As if on its own, water dispersed from around them, pulling away from Jian and the surrounding stone. It slid out of the cracks and cuts and punctures. For a moment, nothing seemed to change. And then Jian gasped in a breath and coughed out water. It was tinged with blood.

This wasn't enough. He needed fire.

The bang of a gunshot rang out. Carver glanced back to see a wolf at the bottom of the cliffs slump into the waves.

"Detective!"

Zhihao's voice came from above.

Carver gathered Jian into his arms. Water coalesced around his legs, as if knowing what he needed. It swelled, pushing them up the cliff. Zhihao was at the top, gun drawn. He nearly dropped it when he saw his cousin.

Carver stepped onto the ground, and the water that'd lifted him sank back to the ocean.

"Please," he rasped. "Help him."

Zhihao quickly shrugged his coat off and laid it on the ground. Carver set Jian on it.

"I need med evac now," Zhihao said into the radio on his shoulder as he pulled his gloves off. "The director fell in the ocean."

"Fuck," Sanya hissed through the radio. "Medics incoming. Hold your position."

Fire erupted on Zhihao's hands. He pressed them to Jian's chest. Flames spread from there, licking at the cracks and injuries. Most would likely scar from the water exposure.

Carver knelt with his hands clenched so tightly in fists that his knuckles paled. If he wasn't still recovering, this wouldn't have happened. Even now, fatigue pressed on him, making his limbs heavy and vision darken. Sheer force of will kept him focused.

"Meallán."

Jian's voice was barely above a whisper.

Carver's head snapped down. Jian was staring up at him. The ghost of a smile touched his lips.

"You're okay," he murmured.

A choked chuckle escaped Carver. Only one of them was on death's door, but Jian was worried for him.

"I'm not a demon who fell in the ocean," Carver pointed out. "I'm just fine."

Jian frowned. "I thought you couldn't go in the ocean. The terms of your asylum with the Ministry—"

"Damn the Ministry. Nothing could be worth more than your life."

"I'm sorry."

Carver lowered his head to Jian's. The body heat of a demon was normally scorching compared to a siren, but it felt lukewarm now.

"I told you to go," Carver murmured.

Jian huffed. "And leave you on your own to take all the glory?"

Carver's skin lightened slowly, changing from inky black to its normal umber. His scales took their usual blue and gold as well.

"Maeva could have killed you," he bit out. "You're not equipped to handle her. *I* wasn't equipped to handle her."

The muscles of his jaw flexed, and his voice was strained when he added, "She killed Thomas."

If they hadn't before, the Ministry certainly knew Carver was alive now, and after today, they'd know he had more power than before. This had been meant as an ambush for him. It might have worked, too, if Jian hadn't been here.

As if on cue, Maeva's figure appeared a few paces away. Zhihao stood and raised his gun at her immediately.

"Relax," she said flatly. "I don't have the stamina to keep fighting. I just want to talk."

Carver glared up at her as he straightened. "About what?"

"You went in the ocean, dear boy." She tilted her head. "Naughty, breaking the terms of your asylum."

Was that why she'd lured him here? To get him to go in the ocean?

"You could, of course, give yourself over to the Ministry voluntarily," she continued, "but if not, they'll have to take it up with the Superiors."

Carver didn't think the Professor would allow the Ministry to take him, but she wasn't here at present. And refusing to turn himself over would just cause problems for the ICS when he'd voluntarily broken the terms of his asylum.

"I'm afraid we have no idea what you're talking about," Jian said abruptly. "Meallán O'Fogladha Nahoumazti died a century ago with his husband. What siren could survive the death of their mate for this long? It's unheard of."

Maeva's jaw visibly clenched. "Really? That's the argument you're going to make? I'm looking right at him."

Jian shrugged. "The way I see it, it's your word against mine, and I promise that my word carries more weight with the ICS than a mercenary on the Ministry's payroll."

She stared at him a moment, and then a chuckle bubbled up from her throat.

"All right," she said as her form started to fade. "Let's see how long that lasts."

She disappeared.

Carver's stomach turned. It was bold to claim that he was dead, but quite technically, Meallán O'Fogladha Nahoumazti had been declared deceased over a century ago. He'd been living with a different identity for a long time. And there were lots of people with the name Carver. Maybe not so many male sirens, but then, was he still a siren?

Paramedics came running up a minute later. They got Jian on a gurney. Carver followed them out to the street where an ambulance waited. The back had a heart and oxygen monitor. A medic wrapped Jian in an electric blanket and set it to the highest setting while they started driving. Carver sat on one of the benches lining the interior.

"You're so reckless," he muttered as he rested his elbows on his knees. "Maeva won't give up. She works best by splitting our attention, so she can get around our defenses. That's how she killed Thomas, and she nearly killed Saoirse multiple times that way."

His shoulder throbbed. When he lifted his arm, Jian flinched, as if expecting a strike.

Carver froze. "I wouldn't... I was only stretching my shoulder."

His voice was soft now, all of his frustration from earlier gone in an instant. "I'm not angry."

Jian took a breath. "I didn't truly think you'd hit me, detective. I'm just...on edge. Maeva showed me a memory of my ex-wife. It was unpleasant."

"Your ex-wife?" Carver's brows knitted together. "I thought fae could only show enticing things. How was it unpleasant?"

"It was an altered memory. My ex-wife was..."

"What did she do?" Carver asked, even as he feared the answer.

Jian swallowed before speaking again. "We were under pressure from my family to produce an heir. The sooner she got pregnant, the sooner we could divorce. Neither of us were happy with our arrangement, but that made making an heir difficult. I just didn't want her. Eventually, she got fed up with trying to appease me."

He was quiet for a while, but Carver didn't speak, intuiting that there was more.

"After a meeting with my parents went badly," Jian continued, "she cornered me in our bedroom, intending to force me to be with her. I'd always dreamed of leaving her and defying my family. And in the memory Maeva showed me, I did just that. I pushed her off me."

A mix of rage and sorrow made Carver's blood icy. For a long moment, there was just the sound of the ambulance engine revving and the paramedics in the cabin up front talking into their radio.

"You didn't push her off, did you?" he said so quietly that his voice almost disappeared under the ambient sound.

"No," Jian mumbled. "Not even once."

Carver had to swallow the unexpectedly intense wrath that shot through him. Before he could reply, Jian said, "It doesn't matter now. Maeva's a problem. How do we want to deal with her? I can help Palus hold off the Ministry for a while, but she'll likely persist on the off chance that the ICS can't offer you protections."

Carver sighed. "There's a chance that she didn't truly think she'd kill me today. How she got to Thomas before was ambushing me outside our house while she caught him and Saoirse inside. My sister is in a safe house now, and we'd know if she were attacked. It could be Maeva's trying to find the house and just needed us out of the way for a while."

Jian glanced through the windows in the back doors of the ambulance, as if expecting to see Maeva through them, but there was only the rain-soaked street.

"I'll have the Peacekeepers increase their guard for Saoirse," he said stiffly. "We should assume Maeva is monitoring all forms of communication. If we need to discuss anything, it should be in person."

Carver looked him over. "You seem accustomed to this. And why does everyone call you 'director'?"

Jian sighed. "I guess there's no harm in telling you since you're effectively the Professor's right hand. Before I left for the war, I worked as the Director of Covert Operations for the High Court."

Carver's brows climbed his forehead. "As in the head of all of Covert Operations for the Republic?"

"Please don't make this into anything. I'm not the director

anymore, nor am I well enough to take the position again."

"The Professor made you sound like just another analyst in her retinue." Carver ran a hand over his face, making water cascade down his neck. "I guess I should have known. Your connections and knowledge seem extensive...director."

Jian grimaced. "Don't."

"Would you prefer 'sir'?"

Carver had used the title earlier, and the look on Jian's face then had been almost...voracious. That same look was on him now, as if Carver were the first meal he'd encountered in days

"Try it again and see what happens," Jian challenged. "At your own risk."

Carver hummed tersely, content to drop the matter for now, but he knew his eyes were light with mischief.

"You had a different form," Jian remarked, seemingly eager to change topics. "I don't think sirens can typically grow significantly in size and alter their skeletal structure."

Carver flexed his hands as he stared at them, almost expecting them to grow an extra joint again. "I wasn't aware I'd changed that much. What did it look like?"

"Nothing I've ever seen before. Vaguely humanoid, but much taller. Black scales and spines. No eyes that I could see. A lot of teeth, all of them sharp."

There was a beat of silence, and then Carver laughed. He couldn't help it. This was just too absurd.

"Care to explain the joke, detective?" Jian asked and arched a brow.

Carver got his chuckles under control before responding. "It's not actually funny. I'm sorry. You've just described an ihret."

"The monster you got your sign from?"

"Fitting, isn't it?"

Jian didn't seem convinced, brows pinched together and lips pressed to a thin line, but he didn't make further comment on it.

"Whenever they're satisfied I'm not dying," he said instead, "we should discuss more in-depth how to keep you safe. You're not looking well yourself right now, and we cannot keep up having you confront Gars while you're still recovering."

Carver resisted the urge to grimace. His fatigue was only getting worse, and he suspected he was probably going to pass out for another few hours as soon as he let himself.

"Do you mind if we meet up again at your house?" he asked. "I don't like the idea of leaving you alone either. Maeva took an interest in you."

Jian nodded shortly. "You're always welcome in my home, detective."

"Thank you."

Jian lowered his gaze. "I should be thanking you. It was my job to protect you, and you ended up saving me."

"Just maybe leave from imminent danger when I tell you to?" Carver suggested with a wry smile. "And no more diving into the ocean."

Jian chuckled. "I make no promises, detective."

CHAPTER TWELVE

The week passed quietly. Too quietly. None of the ICS's agents encountered anything to indicate the Gars movements or encampments. It was as if Maeva had pulled away entirely from Vespera Bay, but that didn't make any sense. Besides, Carver could sense that she was near. He couldn't explain how he was so certain of that, but he was disinclined to question any of his new otherworldly intuition. There were things he didn't—and probably would never—understand about the Professor's power and its effects on him.

Palus had held back the Ministry with Jian's continued insistence that Carver was dead. It wasn't a permanent fix. Carver would likely have to be moved to a different Court and restart with a different name again, but he couldn't just yet while he didn't know where Maeva was or what she planned. She would still be hunting his sister as well. Her silence over the week might have indicated that she was plotting something else, regrouping for a different assault.

In the meantime, Carver and Jian had been trying to investigate places the Gars could be—with no success. None of the motels and hotels big enough to hold a large amount of wolves had a sudden influx of clients. If the Gars were in the city, they had spread out to

236

limit how many were in any given location.

Carver didn't go anywhere without Jian these days, not that he was complaining. He had virtually moved into the reclusive demon's house for how he frequented it. If they weren't at the Court to look at maps and records, they were at home and planning. Jian was paranoid about using phones or messengers for discussion, so that meant Carver had to be near in order to talk. He really only left to grab clothes from his apartment or to visit Damian who wanted to check on his health.

Carver had gone from sleeping sixteen hours a day to twelve. He still didn't feel entirely himself, and his body seemed drained of energy within a day if he went without sex. Whatever changes were happening in his body were being fueled by feeding. Jian didn't seem to mind offering himself as sustenance. If anything, he was usually the initiator, and Carver was all too happy to indulge in the attention and care.

Muffled music drifted through the front door when he returned to Jian's house after visiting Damian at the hospital for the second time this week. The upbeat melody mixed with synth in a distinctly old style.

"Disco?" Carver muttered incredulously.

"*Thi lau lieu yeu co chan khong,*" a woman crooned in Tieng Lac. "*Biet khong doi khi nen.*"

He arched a brow. "Lac disco?"

The music swelled around him when he opened the door. A phonograph sat on the coffee table in the living room, playing the song at top volume. He shut the door behind him and slid his shoes off before stepping further into the house.

Jian was in the kitchen. His hips swayed as he stirred something in the wok on the stove. A slightly off-key rendition of the lyrics passed his lips as he sang along. He glanced back as Carver approached, and a smile spread his lips.

"I was wondering when you'd show," he said. "Lunch is almost ready."

Carver's chest felt like it was too tight for his heart, but it strangely wasn't a bad feeling. He leaned against a countertop. The smell of ginger and garlic was thick in the air. Chicken and various vegetables simmered in the wok. A rice cooker by the sink had a green light to indicate it was done.

"What did Damian say?" Jian asked. "Are you still all right?"

Carver let his eyes follow the sway of Jian's hips. "I'm the healthiest I've been in a very long time."

"Oh? I can't imagine why." Jian's face was turned away, but there was a smile in his voice.

Thomas appeared, perched atop a countertop. "He's flirting," he said with a wry grin. "You remember how to do that, Meallán?"

Carver rolled his eyes and folded his arms over his chest. "I miss anything while I was gone?"

Jian sighed. "Unfortunately not. The Gars have been silent."

Maeva had to be planning something. She didn't give up, and Carver didn't think that had changed just because he could become an ihret-like creature now. Not in a century had she ever backed

238

down from a fight.

"Thinking hard, detective?" Jian said with a glance back.

Carver's thoughts were useless, so he took a chance on some boldness. "More just enjoying the view."

The rumble that left Jian seemed pleased. "Well, I'm happy to provide."

He lowered the heat under the wok and put a lid on it. The phonograph transitioned to something jazzier, and he headed towards it to adjust a dial on the side of the base. The volume lowered. A saxophone droned low and smooth through the air.

Thomas' arms wrapped around Carver's shoulders—the weight of him intangible. "Reminds me of the eighties," he said. "I loved to watch you sing at the clubs."

Carver stepped forward, out of his husband's reach, and leaned a hip on the couch. "How long until lunch is ready?"

"Needs to simmer for a few minutes," Jian said and extended a hand.

Carver hesitated before he took it. Jian pulled him closer and swayed to the beat. Some long-forgotten instinct had Carver following in step. He hadn't danced in years, but the muscle memory was still there.

"I think a song or two should be enough time," Jian said with mirth in his gaze.

Carver didn't know where this lighter mood came from, but he wasn't about to complain. The last few years had seemed like an endless stream of dour days. He couldn't even remember the last time he'd been this at ease with someone who wasn't his sister. Maybe not since Thomas.

They spun around each other, letting the music guide their steps. Carver pressed his cheek to Jian's temple as they moved. The heat coming off the demon seemed to burn hotter. For being a creature beholden to bloodlust, he was surprisingly good-humored and charming. That had probably made him a good spymaster. The man could wield wit and manners like a weapon when he wanted, and he didn't seem to care about appearing silly or strange, just did as he wanted—like playing disco and dancing in his living room. Carver might have even described him as whimsical.

"You're doing a terrible job of appearing demonic," he remarked as they turned in a slow circle. "Who else knows the dreaded former Director of Covert Operations dances?"

Jian chuckled. "No one will believe you. And if you really want me to act demonic, I'd be happy to bare my fangs."

"I think you'd do more than bare your fangs, and then we'd get distracted. I know you hate to waste food."

"I hate to leave you dissatisfied more."

"How would you know? You never have."

The rumble that vibrated through Jian's chest was almost a purr. He preened under praise apparently. Carver mentally filed that particular detail away for later.

"I know you want more from me," Jian said, voice lower than it had been. "You have an exceptionally high pain tolerance."

Carver wasn't sure if there was reticence in the words or not. "I'm content with whatever you're willing to provide. Most people are hesitant to inflict what I want, my late husband included."

Jian was quiet for a moment, and when he did speak, his voice was soft. "I can give you what you want. I just worry that it'll engage a part of me that's much harder to control."

The admission was unsurprising. For all his softness, he was still a demon with all the instincts that came with it.

"I don't want to ask for anything you don't want to give," Carver reassured. "I'm happy with our current arrangement."

Jian leaned back enough to make eye contact. "You misunderstand. I'm not unwilling. I just worry that you won't be in the right headspace to stop me if I go too far. I recognize that you have the power to do that, but I also know that there are a plethora of reasons in the moment why you might not."

Carver recognized when a concern came from experience. "Did you hurt someone, and they didn't tell you until it was too late?"

Jian nodded stiffly. "I was still junior to love. It ended our relationship instantly, and I would not want to do it again."

Carver could imagine the guilt of doing what he thought a partner wanted, only to find out it was not. "Is my word not enough that I would stop you if I didn't like it?"

"It's enough, but I worry anyway."

They turned around each other a few times while Carver gathered his thoughts.

"Why don't we just take it slow?" he suggested. "Start small and work up?"

Jian brought them to a stop as the song faded to an end. "I think I can manage that."

"And we can always go slower if you're ever uncomfortable." Carver lifted a hand to Jian's cheek unthinkingly, but then found the gesture felt natural for him. "How do you feel about being on the receiving end of things?"

Jian had an almost pained expression as he lowered his eyes. "Anxious. I don't trust myself not to react poorly if something happens that I don't like. Every fiber of me detests feeling out of control."

How odd that they could be on such disparate ends of the spectrum. Carver resented how often he had to control every facet of his existence, managing his symptoms with work and feedings. Having just one part of his life where he didn't need to think or be in control of anything seemed a luxury. But Jian probably spent most of his time feeling like his control was an illusion he had to entertain, so he didn't tear someone's throat out.

"I'll keep that in mind," Carver said. "I never want you to feel pressured into anything."

Jian turned his lips into Carver's palm. "I can't imagine you would."

Carver bent to bring their foreheads together. This probably wouldn't end well for either of them. He had no idea what the Professor's power would do to him or if he stood any chance of improving more from the damage of losing his husband, but contentment settled in him like it belonged there all the same.

It almost felt like healing.

◊◊◊

Jian ate lunch while answering messages. His agents were largely in position around the city. They wanted permission to comb through the surrounding forest. He was disinclined to let them. If he and Carver had barely made it away from Maeva and the Gars with their lives, regular scouts certainly didn't stand a chance. They just needed to bide their time until Carver felt better.

The sound of the kitchen sink faucet stopping preceded near silent footsteps on the old hardwood floor. Carver rounded the couch and laid across the empty space. His head rested on the edge of Jian's lap, not enough to make typing difficult, but enough to show passive comfort.

Carver was so tall that his legs would hang over the edge of the couch in this position, so he planted his feet on it, propping his knees up. His shirt hiked up, showing the dip of his hipbones. Jian forced himself not to think about nibbling them. Carver pulled out his own messenger and started typing—likely to his sister.

Jian absently ran his fingers through the blue ringlets in his lap while he typed with his other hand. The little hum that left Carver was unfairly cute. He seemed to press back into the touch, or maybe he was just relaxing. A small smile touched Jian's lips. He reluctantly took his hand back to type through his messages faster.

Minutes passed in quiet, save for the clicking keys, until Carver adjusted himself on the couch. His head moved higher. Jian had a sharp intake of breath when the barest pressure grazed the front of his jeans. Carver stilled immediately. His eyes slowly lifted to Jian's.

"Accident," he said. "Sorry."

Jian returned his attention to his messenger. As soon as he started typing, Carver turned onto his side, putting him eye level with Jian's zipper.

"Getting comfortable," Carver explained when Jian looked down at him quizzically.

Jian didn't think it was just getting comfortable, but he continued typing again, spreading his elbows out to accommodate the head on his thighs. Not a minute later, something light brushed against his jeans again. A slight shock ran through him, and warmth started to build low in his abdomen. He didn't move his eyes from his screen, disinclined to protest any amount of touching.

The pressure against him built until he could feel the shape of Carver's mouth through his pants. A low groan started in his chest. His fingers faltered on the keypad. The scrape of teeth nearly made his hips buck. He started to harden, cock straining against the denim of his jeans.

Carver's teasing dragged on for several minutes before he took mercy and unzipped Jian's pants. His lips ventured up the bulge contained behind the thin cotton of boxers. It was torturous—not quite the skin-to-skin contact Jian craved, but so close. He rushed through another message as his ability to type sentences rapidly escaped him.

He'd just opened the last message he needed to read when Carver pulled down the waistband of his boxers. Dexterous fingers wrapped

244

around his cock. Lips found the bare skin of the shaft, and he cursed through his teeth at the heat that burned through him. His breaths came harshly while he typed out a response that was probably too terse to be polite. He couldn't bring himself to care.

Strong hands pressed one of his hips to the couch. The slickness of a tongue slid up the length of him and swirled around the head. Sparks escaped with his next moan. He barely got a moment to breathe before soft lips enveloped him. The messenger almost slipped from his hands while he hastily sent off his last message, and he tossed the device onto the coffee table.

Carver swallowed him down without warning. Jian's hand sank into the blue curls splayed over his thighs and made a fist, tugging lightly. The muffled whine Carver made was sinful. Vibrations of it reverberated through Jian's cock to the base of his spine. He rocked his hips, moving in and out of Carver's mouth minutely. He probably could have used more force, but didn't want to try without permission.

The question was on his lips when Carver dug nails into Jian's ass, swallowing him to the hilt. Jian took the hint and started moving more, still not thrusting enough to be forceful, but he was tempted when it earned a moan low and long around him. There was a hint of teeth with every press deeper, scrapes adding sharpness to the pleasure. The tongue sliding over him, combined with the tightness sucking him in, was almost too much.

He was embarrassingly close to coming already. The heat of his release simmered low in his gut, and he yanked Carver's head back by the hair before it could build further.

Dazed, blue eyes lifted to Jian's. Carver's lips were slightly swollen, flushed pink and inviting. The arc of his throat was exposed in this position, and Jian fought the urge to sink his teeth into the skin laid vulnerable just for him. He instead wrapped a careful hand around Carver's neck, squeezing just enough to be uncomfortable.

The effect was immediate. Carver was perfectly pliant when Jian lifted him by the throat to bring them face to face. Their lips brushed, but didn't move closer, just sharing air.

Part of Jian had hoped that he might scare Carver away with his crimes. He didn't know what to do with acceptance. And he certainly didn't know what to do with the lips now moving over his cheek tenderly. The gesture made his heart stutter, and he swallowed past the sudden tightness in his throat.

What was this? How could someone make him feel like his skin was on fire, while the same touch was a balm to the burn?

"I wanted to do something for you," Carver whispered, breath cool. "You spoil me too much."

"Impossible," Jian murmured, and he meant it.

He released the delicate neck in his grip and instead slid his hands under Carver's shirt. His nails scraped up the cool, scarred skin he found. It was just enough to hurt, but not enough to draw blood. The answering shiver he got seemed to indicate that Carver liked the pain. He'd yet to show pain he didn't like.

Jian's tiredness from the day had vanished. He was wide awake now, with his heart beating against his sternum. The fingers that

246

swept through his hair elicited a shiver down his spine, and when they tugged lightly, his mind went blank. A small moan escaped him. Gentle lips pressed to his, stealing what little breath was still in him. He tasted the salt of himself in the kiss.

Weight settled over his thighs, and his head was pushed back as Carver straddled him. The tongue that slid over his made his limbs weak. He shivered under the fingertips pressed to the back of his neck. His hands gripped scarred hips, clinging to them like he'd drift away otherwise. Heat crept up his throat with a whimper.

The sound of his own voice, uncharacteristically desperate, sparked him into alertness through the haze of need. He grabbed the thighs bracketing his and lifted them. Carver fell back on the couch, and Jian went with, climbing atop with more roughness than was necessary. Their lips pulled apart at the sudden shift in position.

Jian's breaths came in stuttered pants as smoke slipped from his mouth. He wasn't sure if it was alarm or want that made his heart pound in his ribcage. Carver seemed unaware that anything was off, staring up through hooded eyes.

Was the allure stronger? Jian hadn't felt like this before—like he was losing himself in a person. Even when he had trouble keeping his eyes off Carver, he still felt in control of himself. This was different. This felt like his being had narrowed down to sensation and desire.

Whatever wiles had been acting on him were probably involuntary, if the lack of change in Carver's behavior was any indication. Maybe they'd get stronger the more Jian fed the siren sexual appetite. He'd have to be careful about it in the future, not trusting himself enough to lose his senses like that. People got hurt when demons lacked control.

"Tuan."

Jian's given name pulled him from his darkening thoughts. It sounded like a prayer on Carver's lips, reverential and pleading. Jian couldn't stop the rumble in his chest. Few people had known him by the name his mother's people had given him—a name separate from the Pure Clans and everything they stood for.

Carver was unfairly stunning. Blue curls highlighted with bright blond splayed wildly over the dark couch cushions. His shirt was pushed up to reveal one pec. The muscles of his abdomen flexed with each breath he drew. Reddened lips parted, shining with the remnants of their kiss.

"Hands above your head," Jian said softly.

Carver obeyed without question and crossed his hands at the wrist over his head.

"Don't come," Jian instructed as he unzipped Carver's jeans and ducked his head down.

It was mean. He knew that, delighted in it even, as he pulled out the hardening ridge straining against Carver's undershorts. His tongue dragged up the solid length in his hand, and he wasted no time with teasing, especially as he let his fingers dip lower to find wet heat. Carver's head tossed back when Jian swallowed him down. The taste of sea salt was in the air and at Jian's tongue while he started a slow rhythm. His fingers easily slipped into Carver and curled, earning a shiver.

It wasn't long until he felt a touch in his hair. He pressed his free hand to Carver's hip and let heat burst through his palm. The sound of flesh simmering preceded a hissed curse.

"Hands up," Jian reminded gently as he lifted his head.

Carver raised his hands again. The skin on his hip had cracked open from the heat that burned it. Blood seeped from the cracks. He swallowed as his breaths seemed to grow more ragged. Sirens were susceptible to high heat, and true fire would scar. This much could be healed with water still. The threat of permanent damage, however, remained, and Carver had never shied away from it.

Satisfied, Jian took him into his mouth again. The pace this time was faster, intending to get Carver to the edge. Within minutes, Jian had to press a hand to the hips below him to stop them from squirming too much. Walls of warm muscle squeezed the fingers he had in Carver as he curled them in time with his movements.

"I can't," Carver rasped.

Jian didn't believe that and made no move to slow his efforts at all. His touch was soft while he spread his hand over rapidly flexing abdominals, and when Carver inevitably tried to stop him with a hand, Jian let heat burn through his palm.

"Fuck!" Carver hissed and rapidly brought his hands over his head again. "I'm going to stain your couch."

Jian glanced up to see bleeding cracks in the skin he'd heated, and he took a moment to lick the blood away before it could drip onto the cushions. It tasted of sea air and fresh rain.

"You're going to kill me," Carver murmured between rapid

breaths.

Jian's lips twitched. "Unlikely."

"May I come?"

"No."

The whine that came out of Carver was musical. His hands balled into fists when Jian swallowed his cock down again. Those blue eyes shimmered before they were squeezed shut. He writhed to limited effect. Jian needed only apply some heat at his hand—not enough to burn, but enough to threaten—to keep him from squirming away.

"Please," Carver begged. "Please may I come?"

Jian just hummed tersely in response.

The squirming got worse. Carver's spine was a taut line arching back over the couch. He really was trying his best to do as he was told.

"Please," he repeated, and then softer: "Sir."

The rumble that left Jian was involuntary. He had often held positions of authority, and as nobility, most people had used respectful honorifics for him. From Carver, though, who didn't care for any of those lofty titles, it seemed so much more significant.

Jian lifted his head enough to say, "You may."

He put his mouth on Carver again, and something seemed to shift. Sea salt saturated the air. Every breath Carver drew was stunted. He moved his hands forward, and then froze and gripped the couch behind his head. His hips rolled with barely restrained need. The way he bit his lip threatened to draw blood.

He spilled into Jian's mouth with a cry. There was again that taste of salt and fresh rain mixed with something tart. Jian swallowed through the pulses until they stopped, and Carver lay limp and panting. He still had his hands up while he turned his face into an arm.

"Thank you, sir," he whispered.

Jian could get used to that. He crawled up to pull Carver's hands down and kiss them.

"You earned it," he murmured. "I'm impressed."

"Mm, haven't you made me enough of a puddle?"

Jian let his eyes wander over the expanse of dark skin beneath him, some of it cracked and bleeding.

"Not enough," he said honestly. "Not nearly enough. You're so beautiful."

Carver didn't seem to expect the answer. He averted his eyes with uncharacteristic shyness. Jian leaned down to bring their lips together. The taste of them mixed in the kiss sent a possessive pang through him, and he pushed it down as best he could.

If only they'd met sooner. He would have cherished every additional second given him.

CHAPTER THIRTEEN

They eventually got a lead from an agent who saw a wolf spending a lot of time around the aquarium. Being around massive tanks of water voluntarily wasn't Jian's idea of a good time, but he took Carver with him, as he did everywhere now. Maybe those water manipulation lessons that Saoirse was giving her brother would pay off. Aquarium glass wasn't easy to break, but Jian wouldn't put it past a wolf to try.

The familiar discomfort of being in close proximity to large amounts of water prickled over Jian's skin. He walked through the aquarium's deep sea exhibit with Carver. It was kept dark here. The only light sources provided were LED strips along the walkways and around the windows into the tanks. Fish of various shapes swam through the displays. Most of them had too many teeth or spines, and they were largely white or clear. There wasn't much cause to have color in pitch black.

Young people wandered the halls. Many of them were couples, using the dark to linger in the shadows. A pang of envy shot through Jian as he passed a pair holding hands while they leaned against each other. He'd been married at twenty and forbidden from having any

252

kind of romantic entanglements before then. His relationship with Xiuying could hardly have been considered sweet or loving. There were never any intimate moments stolen in dark corners, and as an adult now, he lacked the drive to steal kisses or whisper sweet nothings to a partner.

"You seem more interested in the people than the fish," Carver remarked as they passed a large tank of eels.

Jian glanced up at him. "I just wonder what it would have been like sometimes. I wasn't allowed a relationship before I was married, and by the time I was divorced, romance seemed more of a hassle than anything."

They came to a circular room. It had a long tank that wrapped the circumference, displaying squid and silvery fish that almost seemed to sparkle in the dim light.

"Your first relationship was with your ex-wife?" Carver said as they headed for a bench at the back of the room.

Jian shrugged. "My family wouldn't have risked letting me throw away our pure bloodline on just anyone."

They sat on the bench, giving them a full view of the room. Jian's agent was due to arrive soon. She had suggested meeting in the aquarium proper to show them her findings on site, which was just as well if they were going to confront the wolf here.

Jian looked over when silence met him. "Something wrong, detective?" he asked, noting the tension in Carver's jaw.

"Your ex hurt you," Carver said tightly.

That wasn't what Jian had expected. He tensed for only a moment before resignation made him relax. There wasn't a point in hiding anything, and he didn't fear being judged.

"She did," he admitted. "I was too afraid of losing control over my prey drive to ever fight back."

Carver leaned back against the tank behind him and released a slow breath. "So you had no experience with relationships at all, didn't know anything about love or sex, and your first time was…"

There was something sharp in his tone, almost like he was biting back anger.

"It was a long time ago, detective," Jian said lightly. "I have since had much better relationships."

Carver took a breath. "That doesn't make what you endured any less cruel."

Jian stared at a young couple swinging their clasped hands between them. "So what did I miss out on? What was it supposed to be like?"

There was a long silence where Carver seemed to gather his thoughts. He worried his lip between his teeth, and gradually, his face softened.

"It's…intense," he said haltingly. "It's all new—new feelings, new sensations, new everything. Every glance feels like the first and last. Every touch lingers long after it ends. Every kiss leaves you floating."

His hand crept across the bench to Jian's. Their fingers hooked around each other.

"You'd take any chance," Carver murmured, "for just one more."

The air seemed thinner as Jian's heart picked up. He was barely aware of how close they'd gotten until Carver's breath grazed his lips. The scent of sea salt, intimately familiar now, was thick in the air, but something else mixed with it. It was like fresh rain after a dry spell, earthen and crisp.

Jian's eyes slid closed as Carver leaned closer. Gentle fingers trailed along his jaw. He had been touched more intimately than this, but it didn't feel like it now. There was something in the way his chin was tilted up and the soft brush of lips on his that made his chest ache. He was caught in a current, pulling him irrevocably toward the man at his side. It'd surely drag him under.

"She's here," Carver whispered.

Jian took a moment to decipher the words. He was breathless when he pulled away and turned his attention toward the entrance to the room.

Irsa stepped in. She was dressed in plain black jeans and a red sweater. Her beauty still drew attention, but her outfit wouldn't. She stopped at the entryway, and her nose scrunched slightly before her eyes snapped toward Carver. He wouldn't meet her gaze.

"Director," she said with a short nod of her head. "You look better. Thought you'd have more scars after falling in the ocean."

Jian glanced between her and Carver curiously, unsure what silent communication had just transpired. But there were more pressing matters at hand. He'd need to ask about it later.

"Well, you've called me a cockroach before," he said. "Even the ocean couldn't kill me. Got something for me that will?"

She glanced at Carver again before turning back the way she'd come. "This way."

Jian fell in step beside her. Carver trailed behind them a few paces back. His posture was oddly stiff, and he kept his head bent. Jian almost wanted to stop and ask what was wrong so suddenly. But here wasn't the time or place.

"Gar has been coming nearly every day," Irsa said as they walked through the deep sea exhibit. "Always the same habits."

They stepped into the main hall. Light flooded the space through tall windows overlooking the ocean. The waves were just a few feet away, down the cliffs of the bay. Sprays of white and blue burst into the air as water broke against the rocks. A gray sky stretched far to the horizon where it met dark sea. A beach a little ways down the cliffs was largely empty, save for a few people milling about.

The aquarium had a cordoned outdoor section that sat atop the cliffs. Part of it was just visible through the windows. Low alabaster walls provided a foundation for a taller, black fence that enclosed the area. A woman stood at a corner of the space, staring through the slats of the fence at the ocean. Gray streaked through her brown hair. Her slight frame was unassuming, obscured mostly by a dark sweater.

"There," Irsa said and pointed to the woman. "She comes and stands out here for about an hour at a time, wanders the aquarium for another hour, and then leaves out past the city limits. I would have tailed her, but you forbade us to go further than three miles out."

Jian stared at the woman, seeing nothing remarkable about her. "What makes you think she's affiliated with the Gars?"

"Caught a glimpse of a brand on her wrist." Irsa folded her arms over her chest. "It's old and faded, but I know the packs out east are branded with a three-pronged arrow. Most of them are Gars now. They've got no reason to be out here either unless they're moving with your Ministry fae."

Jian glanced back at Carver. "You up for an interview, detective?"

Carver nodded. "At your lead."

"Hang back," Jian instructed Irsa. "I'll talk, but I want your ears."

Irsa stepped back. She was careful not to cross between him and Carver as she moved. Jian noted the tense way she regarded the other siren, keeping her eyes up and back straight. Perhaps this was some cultural issue that he wasn't aware of?

Before he could ask about it, Carver headed away. Jian hesitated before following after. Maybe it wasn't his business. There were many things he didn't understand about sirens, and Carver certainly didn't owe him an explanation.

A short set of stairs led up to a cavernous room. Life-size models of orcas were suspended from the ceiling. To one side was a large tank filled with kelp that rose over twenty feet. Brightly colored fish swam between the long stalks. Pale light streaked in warbling lines through the water. A pair of large, glass doors to the side of the room led to the enclosed outer area. There were only two people outside, both peering through binoculars over the ocean, and the Gar woman.

Jian headed for the doors. It didn't escape his notice how Carver kept more than a foot of distance between them as they walked. Something was wrong. Jian ignored the knot of anxiety in his gut. He needed to focus.

The air had a cold bite to it when he stepped through the doors. Ocean wind swept over his skin and into his coat, making his nerves burn. The vastness of water stretching out endlessly filled him with dread and awe in equal measure. Just a couple seconds in the ocean almost killed him. A full minute would have disintegrated his body.

The Gar leaned a shoulder against the bars of the enclosure. A cigarette burned between her lips. Strands of hair obscured her dark eyes. A sharp, silvery line cut across her cheek. Jian stepped closer and leaned his back against the gate, so he could look at her.

"Odd place to frequent," he remarked, prompting her to look toward him. "What's a wolf from the east doing on this coast?"

She took a drag from her cigarette and released the smoke through her nose. "Director Jian, I take it. Was wondering when you'd show up."

He held his hands out with a shrug. "Well, here I am."

She glanced back at Carver who stood a few paces away. "Tall-and-brooding over there set to kill me if I look at you weird?"

"Can never be too cautious." Jian stared over the ocean. "Not exactly in my element here."

She took another drag off her cigarette. "Guess not."

He narrowed his eyes, trying to decipher the flat expression she wore. "Well, you know who I am. Who are you?"

"Siprisa."

"And what are you doing here, Siprisa?"

She glanced back at Carver. "My pack got roped under Maeva a few months ago. I left when we started dying to some creature. Bitch pays good, but not that good. I don't fuck with monsters from the old times."

Her hand shook when she brought her cigarette to her lips and inhaled deeply. Smoke plumed from her lips on a sigh.

"Didn't think I could just walk into the High Court," she continued, "so I figured you'd find me eventually if I hung around long enough. Came to give you a warning—both of you."

Jian waved a hand toward Carver. "What kind of warning?" he asked when Carver got closer.

She stood straighter. "Maeva's getting impatient. She's been watching you and the male siren for a while. Don't really know how—above my pay grade—but I know that she's been considering launching a full-scale assault instead of trying to use subterfuge like she has been."

Carver scowled. The muscles of his jaw flexed under his skin.

"Why are you telling us this?" he asked. "What do you gain?"

"I want Maeva gone." Siprisa shrugged. "I certainly don't have the power to do that. Figure one of you might. Think of the warning as a show of good faith. I help you. Maybe you help me."

He narrowed his eyes suspiciously. "What do you want, other than Maeva out of power?"

"Immunity for my family. I tell you what she's planning, and my family gets to walk away from the whole thing."

Jian didn't need to consider the deal for long. It was more than fair.

"Consider it done," he said readily. "We can draft a contract back at the Court."

She nodded and took another drag off her cigarette. "Maeva has been moving the packs through the surrounding forest. Doesn't let them stay in one place for more than a couple days, but she's been hanging around the quarry a few miles out a lot."

The quarry was largely abandoned. There was just basalt and mud out there.

"And you don't know what they're after out there?" Jian asked.

Siprisa shook her head. "All of that is kept for Maeva's inner circle. All I know is that she's due to go back there in a week."

Jian sighed. At least it was more information than they'd had before.

"One other thing," she said. "The creature of the old times—she's very interested in it. Heard her talking to some guy about it over the phone a few times."

Jian resisted the urge to glance at Carver. "And what did she talk about?"

"Way beyond me. Something about sigils and Ancients and the old ways."

Maeva would know much more about that as a fae. Maybe she even knew what Carver was now.

"Detective," Jian said, "you're welcome to continue interviewing Siprisa. I need to make a phone call."

He went back through the doors. Irsa was waiting for him just inside. She walked beside him while he headed for the row of phones at the back of the room.

"Did you catch all that?" he asked.

She nodded. "I'll bring our Gar back to Court and get a written statement from her."

"Make sure you set up a surveillance detail for wherever you put her. I don't want her so much as coughing without us knowing about it. No communications in or out that aren't vetted." He shoved a hand through his hair tiredly. "What are the chances this is a trap?"

"Pretty high. You were already ambushed once at the cannery."

They came to the phones. Jian put a chip into the slot and dialed the Idylla direct line. Palus picked up after the second ring.

"Got something?" they answered.

Jian turned to lean on the dividers between phone stations. He stared out the glass to where Carver and Siprisa spoke.

"Gar seems to think Maeva's considering a full-scale assault," he reported. "We also have reason to believe that she wants something in the quarry outside the city. She's allegedly heading out there in a week."

Palus' sigh crackled through the receiver. "All right. Take—"

"Take Carver with me, yes. He's practically strapped to my back, Palus."

There was a soft chuckle. "Point taken. I'll stop nagging. Anything else to report?"

"Not yet. You'll get a full report later tonight." Jian put the phone back in its cradle.

Irsa glanced toward the doors and then back to Jian. "Strapped to your back, huh?" she murmured. "Never took you as the type to settle down."

He shook his head. "No, I'm not actually tied down. Palus just wants me to go everywhere with the detective."

The sound she made was halfway between a scoff and a laugh. "Whatever you say, sir."

She had never been particularly concerned with decorum, but outright dismissing him was odd for her. Was his relationship with Carver so obvious? Had she seen something in the deep sea exhibit? He thought they'd separated to a polite distance before she'd seen them, but maybe not.

"I shouldn't have said anything," Isra said when Jian didn't speak. "You're panicking."

He ran a hand down his face tiredly. "Am I so obvious?"

"Plain as gods-damn day, sir." She clasped his shoulder. "Permission to speak freely?"

"Can I stop you?"

She stepped away from him when Carver opened the doors with the Gar in tow. "Just let yourself be happy."

Jian didn't have an argument. It was sound advice. His stomach turned anyway as he stared at the man who'd held his attention for weeks.

Was he afraid to get attached? Or that he already was?

◊◊◊

It had been a very, very long time since Carver had produced the *mahtaib*—the claiming scent. But it was there all the same. Petrichor had hung heavy around him and clung to Jian while they were wrapped in each other at the aquarium. Irsa had obviously noticed it. As an unclaimed siren herself, she would have been sensitive to it, and she'd even gone out of her way to make sure she didn't put herself between him and Jian. He was grateful for that. The possessiveness building in him was harder to swallow in the presence of another siren.

"You've been more of a broody motherfucker than usual," Saoirse said as she moved her hand in a slicing motion. An arc of water at her fingertips followed her movements.

She went through various combat forms in Carver's living room. He followed her lead, as he had for the last week whenever he had time to spare with her. Falus had sanctioned visits with her every so often, so she could teach him how to manipulate water. The main stipulation was that she could only stay for an hour before going back to her safe house. And he wasn't allowed to know where she went or any specifics around her location.

She was much more practiced and confident with her forms. The difference between them was never more obvious than when he attempted to mirror her. She had a grace and fluidity with her movements that he just couldn't emulate. Water danced in thin tendrils around her, flowing easily with her. They weren't as cohesive on her left, and that might have been because she was still regrowing the eye on that side. Her eyepatch couldn't come off for another few weeks.

He mimicked her as she lifted both her hands, leaving a flat and wide arc of water in her wake. It was so smooth that it almost appeared as glass. His looked more like a ribbon in the air.

"I've just had a lot on my mind," he muttered.

She scoffed and extended one hand in front of her. The barrier of water dispersed before she touched it.

"Something happen with Jian?" she asked. "Was it physiological or emotional? Or both?"

He sometimes resented that he could keep nothing from her, between her empathic connection to him and her Inquisitor training to read people. But there was no one he trusted more. He only wanted some time to get his head sorted before he articulated why it was so jumbled.

"Drop it, Saoirse," he said flatly.

She sighed as she lowered her hand and brought the other up in a wide arc. The water at her fingertips thinned to a sharp blade.

"You know," she said, "it's fine if you're starting to catch feelings. We're creatures of devotion. And there are worse people you could hitch yourself to."

He grimaced. "I don't know what I'm feeling."

"Bullshit."

She planted her foot forward and swung her elbow out. The water around her sprayed out in a field of suspended droplets.

"I've seen the way you look at him," she insisted.

He mirrored her step back and willed the water to gather again into a single sphere. "And how's that?"

She laid a hand under her sphere of water, as if cradling it. "It reminds me of how you looked at Thomas when we first came to the

Republic."

His water lost its form as his heart skipped. Saoirse's hand shot toward it, and it stopped before it hit the floor.

"Gods, you're useless," she muttered and waved a hand toward the kitchen sink. The water streaked through the air and emptied into the basin.

He rubbed his forehead as a headache started to tug at the backs of his eyes. "Do you have a point, Saoirse? Or do you mean to wage psychological warfare on me?"

She clamped her hands around his face. "Meallán, I love you. You know I love you, yes?"

When he nodded minutely, she said, "You're dumb as a fucking rock if you think for a second that you're not falling for this man."

He averted his eyes. "And how would you know?"

"I know because I have eyes, dumbass. Well, I have one eye right now, but it can still see how hopeless you are." She squeezed his head between her hands. "No, you're not even falling. You are hurtling off the proverbial cliff—moving at terminal fucking velocity. Actually, it's not even proverbial. You literally jumped off a cliff for him and broke the terms of your asylum."

He straightened when she released his face.

"Listen, I'm not going to tell you what to do," she continued, voice gentler now. "I'll never understand what it is to be bonded to someone, but I know what it is to long for it. Damned if I let you throw it all away because you're too busy thinking your brain into knots."

A pang of guilt shot through him. His sister had lost the greatest love of her life because she was a khavira. And here he was with a second chance.

"Don't give me that look," she muttered. "No pity. I've made my peace."

He pressed his forehead to hers. "I think you're right that I'm dumb as rocks. I feel dumb as rocks."

She chuckled. "You are. You're also very, very smart. So use your brain for better things. You don't need to have all your feelings sorted out, just let them happen. Be brave, Meallán."

That was easier said than done, but it was sound advice.

"I'll do my best," he mumbled and pulled away to look down at her.

Before she could respond, a knock sounded at the front door. Her time was up. She patted his cheek before disappearing into the bedroom. He went to answer the door.

Jian stood at the threshold with two people in Peacekeeper blue fatigues flanking him. The gold of his eyes was oddly muted, just a thin band around his pupils. He didn't meet Carver's gaze, instead staring past him.

"I figured I'd join the Peacekeepers to get your sister," he said, "since I planned to come over anyway."

A knot of anxiety formed in Carver's gut as he smelled the faint petrichor on Jian. The *mahtaib* could cling for weeks. He stepped aside to allow Jian in and then headed toward his bedroom. Saoirse stepped out with a duffle bag over her shoulder.

"Don't break your bed," she whispered as she passed him. "I'll be back next week."

He narrowed his eyes at her as he waved two fingers at the kitchen sink. A thread of water pulled from the faucet and then shot through the air. It hit the side of her head, dousing her hair and the collar of her shirt.

She wiped at her face as she spun around. He didn't even see the water that suddenly drenched the back of his head. Cold rivulets fell down his back, soaking his shirt. He glanced back to see his window was open just a crack. All the rain droplets that had clung to the glass were gone. She stuck her tongue out at him when he returned his gaze to her.

He rolled his eyes and started with her to the door. "You're incorrigible," he muttered. "I won't miss you."

She flashed him a wry grin. "Yes, you will, you dick. Probably going to cry as soon as I drive away."

"My eyes will be bone dry."

"Liar. You—" She abruptly stopped as they neared the door, and her head snapped toward Jian.

Carver's stomach twisted when she sniffed the air, and he could guess what she smelled when she looked back at him. Her one eye was wide.

"*What did you do?*" she demanded in Aidheiran, presumably so Jian and the Peacekeepers wouldn't understand her. "*You were crying about how you don't know how you feel, but you laid claim to him!*"

Jian glanced between her and Carver. "Something wrong?"

"Not at all," Carver said with a pleading look toward his sister. "*It was an accident.*"

"*An accident!*" she echoed incredulously. "*My love, my life, my soul, I will flip you into the fucking ground. You don't lay claim by accident. Can you do other things now? You've got to be tethered to him, too. Fuck. Are you just cured? Is that possible? Should we be celebrating right now? I feel like we should be celebrating.*"

He ran a hand down his face, suddenly exhausted. "*I don't know what's happening to me. I'm not tethered to him. The claim just happened today accidentally, and yes, I don't know how to feel about it.*"

She blinked. "*You're not tethered, but you laid claim? Gods, you got some wild stuff going on with you.*"

"Yes, great. Thanks," he said in Imperial. "Goodbye, Saoirse. Message me when you get to the safe house."

She pulled him into a tight hug. "This conversation is far from over," she whispered against his cheek. "You better message me with details."

He shook his head. A mixture of exasperation and fondness welled in him.

The Peacekeepers led her out, leaving just Jian behind. He closed the door and shrugged out of his coat. There was an odd stiffness to his movements, as if he were uncomfortable. It didn't seem like physical discomfort.

Carver pulled his damp shirt off and tossed it over the back of the couch. "Sorry about my sister. Coffee?"

Jian followed him deeper into the apartment and laid the coat over the back of a dining table chair.

"Your sister doesn't seem to have a mode softer than loud," Jian remarked.

"Saoirse's always been a little…intense." Carver padded into the kitchen and pulled two mugs from a cabinet. "I still miss her loudness when she's not here."

Jian had the ghost of a smile. "Didn't you say something about having bone dry eyes?"

"Oh, hush. Bones are actually very wet."

Carver absently flicked his fingers toward the sink

Water streamed from the faucet and floated to the coffee maker. He opened the can of coffee grounds on the counter while the pot filled.

"You've gotten better at that," Jian remarked as he stepped closer. "Lessons with your sister paying off?"

The stream of water abruptly cut off when Carver waved a hand toward it.

"I think so," he said as he scooped coffee grounds into the filter basket. "She's a surprisingly good teacher actually, once you get past the swearing and teasing."

Jian's brows rose. "Is that not just all of her teaching?"

"Don't let her hear you say that." Carver set the coffee maker to brew and leaned a hip on the countertop. "I quite like you with all your limbs where they should be."

Jian just hummed tersely in reply as he lingered at the edges of the kitchen. His eyes didn't stay focused on one thing for long—an indication of nervousness.

"Are you all right?" Carver asked when the quiet stretched for several seconds.

Jian tensed briefly, before his shoulders slumped. "No, I don't think I am. Irsa was acting oddly at the aquarium, and then your sister just now seemed to sense something when she came close to me. And their reactions seem unusually...intense."

Carver's heart beat in his throat. "I guess it hasn't been subtle."

"What am I missing, detective?" Jian's eyes narrowed. "It's obviously siren-related, so is this cultural? Physiological? Irsa seemed certain that I had 'settled down' with you."

Gods, this was mortifying. Why did there have to be so many sirens around?

Carver took a deep breath and then another. It didn't help with his nerves, but it was better to get this over with. Jian had a right to know.

"They were acting strangely," Carver said haltingly as every part of him resisted confessing the truth, "because you have my claiming scent on you."

Jian blinked. "Claiming scent?"

"It's... Gods, help me." Carver ran a hand down his face. "*Mahtaib*, the claiming scent, is an additional oil produced on a siren's skin that clings to their partner. The smell of it tells other sirens that you're taken."

Silence followed the explanation. Jian slowly pressed his hands to his stomach and then stared at the floor. His jaw clenched and

270

unclenched a few times.

"How long has this been happening?" he asked after a moment.

Carver shoved his hands in his pockets to stop himself from fidgeting. The memory of gold eyes in the dark flitted through his mind.

"It's new," he said. "I first noticed it at the deep sea exhibit this morning."

Jian's brows rose. "Oh. That is new."

"It shouldn't even be possible," Carver said with a sigh. "Sirens can't lay claim before they've tethered to a partner."

"Tethered?"

"It's an empathic link between a siren and their partner. Not as powerful as a true bond, but the beginnings of it. It forms naturally when we're in love." Carver let out a long breath. "I don't know why I'm producing a claiming scent. I'm sorry it put you in an awkward position with Irsa. My body seems to be recalibrating how it works."

Jian didn't respond. He still stared at the floor. His hands were clasped together at his waist so tightly that the tendons were visible under his skin.

"Are you angry?" Carver asked as his stomach plummeted. "I'm really sorry. I can talk to Irsa about it if—"

"I'm not upset with you, detective." Jian's voice was flat. "You've done nothing wrong."

Thomas appeared in the kitchen, perched on a countertop. His eyes were trained on Jian.

"It sounds like something is wrong," he observed.

"Embarrassment?"

What did Jian have to be embarrassed about? It was Carver who couldn't control his strange physiological impulses. But there was something like embarrassment in the set of Jian's shoulders and how he curled into himself ever so slightly.

"What's going on?" Carver asked, keeping his voice gentle. "You may not be angry with me, but you don't feel good."

Jian released a long sigh. "I guess it'd be foolish to think I could hide anything from a being of connection and empathy."

Carver's ribs seemed stiff in his chest. "Did you want to hide something from me? It's fine if you do. You don't owe me your feelings."

Jian stared at a crack in the tile of the countertop as he smoothed a finger over it. He was quiet for a long moment, as if contemplating something, and when he did speak, his voice was soft.

"So other sirens can smell you on me." He picked at the crack with his fingernail. "How do you feel about that? Is it shameful? You didn't tell your sister."

Panic shot through Carver. He was going to ruin this before it ever really started. His sister had been right. He was dumb as rocks.

"No!" he blurted. "No, it's not shameful. I just knew that Saoirse would never let me hear the end of it."

Jian looked up at that. There was something almost wary in his gaze.

"Why?" he asked. "What's wrong with it?"

"There's nothing wrong with it. It's…" Carver took a breath in a futile attempt to steady his nerves. "To lay claim to someone is a very public declaration of commitment. It has great significance, but I shouldn't be doing it."

Jian averted his eyes again. "Ah, well, I suppose it would be disconcerting then to have something so important appear unintentionally. I'm sorry it's wasted on me."

Carver's heart twisted. He wasn't describing this well, and Jian didn't understand—couldn't understand without proper explanation.

Be brave, Meallán.

His sister's words rang in his head. He owed it to Jian to be brave, even if his throat felt dry and his heart wouldn't stop pounding.

"Nothing is wasted on you," he said as he laid a hand over Jian's on the counter. "You misunderstand what it means to be claimed."

Jian slowly lifted his eyes. "What does it mean then?"

The scent of petrichor bloomed in the air between them. Carver let all of the cloying, rapacious feelings he tried to ignore suffuse him. His hand curled around Jian's, holding tightly.

"It means," he murmured, "that I can't stand the thought of anyone else touching you."

He cupped Jian's cheek and ran his thumb over lips he had kissed raw many times before.

"It means I want you to think of me when I'm not there," he continued softly. "It means I want to keep you in my bed every night and wake up next to you every morning. It means I want the rest of the world to know who you belong to."

A shuddering breath left Jian as his eyes closed. His hand balled into a fist on the counter. Carver trailed his lips over Jian's cheek, feeling the heat there build.

"The evidence," he whispered, "of these selfish, possessive thoughts is on you, and if I had my way, I'd leave my scent over every inch of you—inside and out."

For a tense heartbeat, Jian didn't speak, didn't move, didn't seem to breathe even. And then he turned his head just enough to bring his lips to the corner of Carver's.

"I'm yours," he breathed.

The words were like fire in Carver's blood. It grew worse when he brought their lips together. It wasn't enough.

Jian nearly stumbled as he was pressed backward. Breath rushed out of him when his back hit a wall, but Carver didn't give him time to recover, crowding him. Blood rushed in Carver's ears. He was barely aware of his hands as they unbuttoned Jian's shirt. Every fiber of his being hummed with the need to touch and take—claim.

His.

He shoved his hand under the waistband of Jian's pants. Heated flesh strained against his fingers. Their kiss broke as Jian gasped. He bit his nails into Carver's shoulders, almost to the point of pain. Smoke escaped his lips as his head snapped back against the wall. Carver wrapped his fingers fully around Jian's cock and stroked slowly. Electric pulses thrummed between them, pleasure building into something delicious.

He balled a fist in Jian's hair and tugged. An expanse of neck opened to him, and he dragged his teeth along the heated skin. A groan escaped Jian. His breaths came harshly, and the rapid beat of his heart could be felt through his skin. Did he enjoy biting?

Carver's fangs ached as they elongated. He let the points trail down to Jian's shoulder and bit down just enough to hurt, but not break skin. A hand fisted in his hair and pushed. His fangs sank down, piercing flesh easily. The taste of blood, like molten copper, filled his mouth. Some part of him wanted to leave marks. Only sirens would be able to smell his claim, but everyone could see scars.

Jian arched back. Electricity shot from him and spread wildly. Carver bit harder as Jian's climax overwhelmed him. It hummed through his teeth and along his nerves, pulsing with the stuttered thrusts of Jian's hips.

Not enough. Not nearly enough.

Eventually, it ebbed. Blood dripped down Carver's chin when he released his bite. Deep punctures in Jian's shoulder welled with red. The claiming scent was stronger than it'd ever been. It clung to Jian.

"I'm sorry," Carver said and gingerly touched the skin he'd pierced. "I don't know what—"

Jian licked his own blood from Carver's lips. "Bed. Now."

Carver complied.

CHAPTER FOURTEEN

The quarry was nothing more than a mile-long fissure in the earth, lined with basalt and limestone. A smattering of trees surrounded it, but there was mostly flat land in all directions. The rain had died to a drizzle. Water from the previous night, however, crept along the bottom of the fissure and poured over the stratified walls. Thick, gray clouds moved quickly across the sky. Another storm was imminent.

Jian stared out at the bleak scenery from the passenger seat of Carver's auto. A pleasant ache in his shoulder lingered where the flesh had been punctured and torn repeatedly. Biting for demons was usually reserved for partners. It was one of the most intimate acts they could perform to demonstrate commitment. Jian figured tethering for sirens might be a cultural or emotional equivalent, but he'd yet to explain that. After all, it didn't mean to Carver what it meant to him.

Dull heat spread through him as he gingerly massaged the bruises in his shoulder. He was losing control. It'd been easy at first to just focus on Carver's pleasure. The demonic urges were satisfied with making his siren succumb to him with lips and tongue and teeth. And his drive to hunt had been remarkably quiet lately. It was as though it were stunned to silence whenever he met those blue eyes. His mind hushed under the dull roar of blood in his ears as his heart raced under just a touch, a look, a smile.

And Carver didn't need to be forceful at all. He was like the tides, persistent and patient in its pull. Just a finger at Jian's chin, and he moved where it led. A hand in his could pull him closer before he ever thought to resist. Gentle lips on his, drawing him in, stole his breath right from his lungs. He could do nothing to stop it.

He didn't want to stop it.

A dirt road led from the main highway to the quarry. Carver's automobile jerked sporadically over the uneven bumps as he pulled to one side of the road a few paces from the fissure. The hand he didn't have over the steering wheel was in Jian's. Something tingled through the contact. It was just a whisper of sensation, like fingertips on Jian's skin, but there didn't seem to be a source of it. The feeling disappeared as soon as he withdrew his hand. Maybe it was his imagination.

Another auto parked behind them. Irsa and Zhihao climbed out with handguns at the ready. Zhihao had a coat with a hood and gloves on to protect him from the rain. Jian grabbed the black umbrella under his seat before stepping out of the auto.

"Do we know what we're looking for?" Carver asked as he got out.

Jian opened the umbrella with a sigh. "Not really. Just anything that might indicate the presence of the Gars or Maeva's intentions here."

"I don't like this, *tahe*," his cousin commented. "Last time you confronted Maeva, she pushed you into the ocean."

"Well, we're a little far from the ocean now." Jian straightened. "Around me. Detective Carver will take point."

Irsa and Zhihao fell in step on either side of Jian without question. Carver dutifully led the front, eyes scanning the trees as he went. They came to the edge of the fissure. Mud squelched underfoot. Puddles obscured much of the ground, but Jian caught the shape of a large paw print in the earth.

"It's too narrow to be from a bear," Carver observed, "and the only other mammal that large out here are lycans."

They followed the tracks along the edge of the fissure until they abruptly stopped. He glanced at the water rushing at the bottom of the fissure. It would obscure any other tracks. There was little reason to jump in the fissure than to prevent imprints in the earth. The Gar that'd come this way hadn't wanted to be followed then.

"What did you expect to find, Meallán?"

Maeva's voice came from behind.

Jian turned with everyone else to see the fae standing at the edge of the fissure. She wore a long, black coat. Her hands were shoved into the pockets.

Carver came forward, putting himself between her and everyone else. His eyes were hard as they trained on her.

"Why are you out here?" he asked. "What could be of interest?"

She stared out over the sprawling forest. "The Ministry is getting annoyed with me. You should no longer have asylum, but the ICS keeps touting that you're dead. After all, Ernest Declan Carver is not

Meallán Carver. So why don't we make a deal?"

Jian tensed. "What deal could you possibly make with us? The Ministry wants him dead. I won't allow it."

"The Ministry just has to think he's dead. They did once when I killed Thomas."

Carver flinched at hearing his husband's name, and Jian barely stopped himself from taking his hand. Showing that kind of affection in front of Maeva seemed inappropriate.

"Saoirse is still an issue," she continued. "I will need to come back for her."

"No," Carver said firmly. "There is no deal if you threaten Saoirse."

She sighed. "Look, I'm trying to work with you. You got an idea to convince the Ministry that you're both dead? I guess I could take body parts back to them. Maybe an arm?"

Jian grimaced. "You're not taking limbs either. Why should we not just get rid of you and be done with this?"

"And what then?" She arched a dubious brow. "The Ministry is going to keep hunting them. I'm offering a way out."

"The ICS could do the same thing."

"They tried. They haven't been successful."

"And what makes you think you're any better?"

She didn't reply immediately, looking him over with narrowed eyes. "I don't know how you survived, Meallán. I know you're not like you were. What life do you think you could have really? Going to bond with Jian? Get married again? Is that actually possible for you?

No siren has ever been able to bond twice."

Jian's stomach dropped. It was a fear that he tried to ignore—that something physiological would happen and this tentative relationship they kept would crumble. They weren't stronger than biology.

"It doesn't need to be possible," Carver said stiffly. "No other race bonds. It's not necessary."

Maeva arched a brow. "Siren imperative, isn't it? As natural as breathing?"

"And what would you know about that? You're not a siren."

She tapped a finger against her hip. "Let me paint you a picture then."

A shadow fell over the ground beside them. Jian instinctually jumped away from it. Pain flared through his side. He rolled to his feet and held a hand to his ribs. Heat bloomed between his fingers, but he didn't dare look at the damage while a wolf prowled toward him, directly next to where he'd been. Irsa and Zhihao darted away from it. Carver immediately sank his fangs into the wolf's neck and ripped viciously.

More wolves emerged from the trees, dozens of them. Jian crouched down when the nearest him lunged for him. Claws sank into his shoulder as he collided with its chest and pushed it toward the edge of the fissure. Its weight took it forward, but the claws in him held fast as it tumbled over the side. He curled into himself as they plummeted.

The wolf broke the fall. It still hurt as he slammed shoulder-first into its ribcage. A yelp left it, cut off abruptly by the shattering of its bones. He struck his hand under its sternum, its flesh giving way. Heat rushed out of his arm. A bright glow burst within the wolf, silhouetting ribs and veins for a moment as his fire burned its innards.

His breaths came harshly when he removed his hand. Soot and coagulated blood coated it, bringing the pungent scent of burning flesh. The cracks cutting through his skin stung as more water fell over him. He needed to get out of the rain.

His head whipped up when he heard a shrill drone that cut through the air.

Irsa stood at the edge of the fissure. A wolf had clamped down on her arm. Blood sprayed around her as it gave a sharp jerk of its head, tearing flesh and splintering bone. The rain abruptly halted, drops held suspended in the air. Jian's breath left him in a thick, white plume as the temperature dropped steeply. Ice formed over the puddles on the ground rapidly. And then the rain droplets moved. They amassed together, coalescing into dozens of spears that froze into sharp points.

The ihret stepped into view at the lip of the fissure. Its skin was entirely black and tendrils of darkness writhed over its arms and legs. The sharp spines that emerged from its back resembled a siren's, but they were longer. An unnaturally wide mouth spread across its face, displaying rows of sharp fangs. It had a hand lifted toward the spears of ice. With a flick of long, delicate fingers, the spears flung forward.

The wolf collapsed as the points sank into its body. Blood sprayed out around it, and the crunch of its bones rang against the fissure walls. Irsa wrenched her arm free of the wolf's mouth. The ihret extended a hand down to Jian, and he jumped up to grab it. It pulled him up with ease, as if he weighed nothing.

"Sorry, director," Irsa said when he rushed closer to look at her shredded arm.

His brows furrowed. "You have nothing to apologize for. Can you run?"

When she nodded, he turned to move away.

Sharp pain pierced through his back, and then ice spread through his chest. It seemed to curl around his lungs and sear along the back of his ribs. He turned to see Irsa with an empty syringe in her hand.

"I do have something to apologize for," she said. "Ocean water. Little harder to get out of you like this."

Her skin lightened to a tawny color, and the blond curls on her head straightened and darkened to black. Maeva's green eyes stared at him. When had she replaced Irsa? Where was Irsa?

She disappeared from sight with a short salute. Zhihao rushed forward and caught Jian around the waist before he collapsed. They sank slowly to the ground. Rain sprinkled over them while ice continued to spread through Jian's chest. He gasped in breath futilely. Ocean water directly into the chest cavity could be fatal within a minute.

The ihret was starting to shrink back into a humanoid form. Irsa's figure appeared on the ground a few paces away. Her leg was bent at a wrong angle, but the water soaking into it was starting to force it into proper straightness as she crawled closer on her arms. Maeva must have expended immense power to pull off this mix of illusions.

But it had paid off for her.

"Here's the thing," she said as she reappeared on the other side of the fissure. "I think that Meallán is only clinging to life by a thread. And he's made you part of that thread. I'll just have to deal with your daughter later. I'm sure the Ministry doesn't want her around either."

Carver returned to the shape of a man, and the inky black coloring of his body started to fade. Zhihao's hands were fire-hot as he shoved them under Jian's shirt. It was futile. No amount of heat would fix an internal dose of water.

"Tick-tock, darling," Maeva said before vanishing.

Zhihao's arms shook. "He doesn't have much time. I... I can't do anything. I can't... It's in him."

Carver sank to his knees. Panic was clear in his eyes, but he closed them as he laid a gentle hand on Jian's chest. For a moment, nothing seemed to happen. And then that internal ice centralized to the place just under Carver's palm. Sharp pain preceded bloody water erupting from under Jian's clavicle and rising into the air.

He gasped in a breath and turned onto his side as involuntary fits of coughing took him. His ribs contracted harshly. A cool, damp forehead pressed to his temple. The rain was starting to cause cracks to emerge through Jian's skin, but he couldn't bring himself to care as Carver's breath passed over his cheek. Something tingled through the contact between them, getting stronger and stronger.

"I'm sorry," Carver whispered. "I should have known what she was doing. I'm sorry."

A burning kind of pain grew dimly in Jian's hand. The rain didn't seem as uncomfortable on him. In fact, it almost seemed pleasant. His coughing subsided as he focused on the new sensations. An inexplicable sense of connection to Carver filled him—like their bodies were just extensions of each other. One whole made of two forms.

Pain shot through his skull like a bullet. He flinched away from Carver, and the pain stopped almost immediately. That connection between them snapped. There was a moment where all sensation seemed to vanish, leaving only numbness. What had that been?

"Zhihao, Irsa," Carver said stiffly, "get Jian to the auto. I can keep them back for now. He needs to get to the hospital."

Jian's head throbbed. He was barely aware of the world moving around him as he was lifted. The blur of greenery around him made him dizzy. There was only one thought that lingered coherently in his mind.

Carver would help him.

◊◊◊

Carver had felt something stirring in him all day. It lurked in his skin, making it tight and restless. The urge to take Jian away and hide from the world had roiled in his chest. He dimly recognized the deep, protective instincts of a tethered siren growing in him. Seeing Jian in danger was difficult, even without physiology complicating things, and sometimes when he thought back on how Jian fell into the ocean, the air seemed harder to breathe.

But he hadn't anticipated this.

When Jian had been lying there, catching his breath after having ocean water removed from his chest, something warm had moved through where they touched. It'd grown the more Carver focused on it. Pain coursed through him, centralized on his chest. The sensations weren't his own. He hadn't tethered in so long that the experience—feeling someone else as himself—was almost foreign.

And then Jian had hissed and snapped his head away. The tether broke.

It broke.

It wasn't supposed to break.

Wolves emerged from further down the fissure and from the surrounding tree line. They encroached with fangs bared.

"Zhihao, Irsa, get Jian to the auto," Carver ordered as he stood. "I can keep them back for now. He needs to get to the hospital."

Irsa healed enough with the aid of the rain to help Zhihao carry Jian. Fatigue weighed heavy on Carver, but he swept his hands out. Massive walls of water rose up from the puddles in the ground. They blocked off a path leading back to the autos. Irsa and Zhihao virtually dragged Jian between them as they rushed down the path.

Wolves sprinted for them immediately, but spikes burst from the walls of water. They froze into spears of ice as they shot out. Some wolves jumped back before the spears could get them, but many more were too slow. Their blood decorated the ground as the ice burrowed into their limbs and chests and heads. They collapsed.

Carver's skin and scales blackened again as his form shifted. An extra joint grew in his hands. His bones shifted under his skin, reformatting into something larger. The ground got further away while his trunk elongated. A low drone burst from his chest, followed by sharp clicks so loud that multiple wolves dropped down and held their paws over their ears. Siren clicks were meant to travel several dozen miles through water. In air, they were deafening at close range.

Maeva's form appeared in front of him as Irsa and Zhihao disappeared past the tree line with Jian. The walls of water fell. Carver's limbs felt so heavy, but he forced himself to stay upright. This was exactly what the Professor had warned of. He wasn't at full strength. His recovery wasn't complete, and he couldn't take on this many Gars by himself.

But he could make sure Jian got away.

"I suppose this works just as well," Maeva said as she pulled a cigarette from inside her jacket. "All right, dear boy. I'll let your little demon love go. Didn't want to piss off his daughter that much anyway. Just be a doll and stand down, would you?"

Carver waited until he heard the rumble of an auto engine to fold his legs under him. His belly pressed to the ground as he lowered his head. He kept his gaze on Maeva while she pulled out a lighter from her jacket and lit the cigarette between her lips. She took a deep drag. Smoke emerged from her lips when she spoke again.

"Here's what's going to happen. You're going to shift back, and then we're going to use my auto-phone to call your sister. You'll have a pleasant chat with her that doesn't tip her off to your circumstances and keep her on the line while we triangulate her location. And if you don't, I'll kill you immediately and make a point to tell the Ministry they should make your demon boy their next hit."

286

Carver stared at her a moment before he let his form shrink. There weren't many options left for him, and he knew when he was cornered. His bones reformatted while he returned to a humanoid form. The black coloration of his flesh faded to the usual umber. His scales lightened to blue and gold. He got to his feet and pushed the rainwater from his eyes.

Maeva headed along the fissure. He followed. Wolves kept close, eyes trained on him while he walked. There wasn't much left in him. His nerves felt raw while he moved, and he wanted nothing more than to lie down and sleep. But he couldn't. Not yet.

Almost half a mile down the way was another strip of dirt road. A collection of black autos were parked on it. Maeva opened the passenger door of one and gestured toward the interior. Carver numbly slid into the seat and grabbed the phone built into the dashboard. He dialed the emergency line he'd been given for Saoirse. While it rang, a pair of wolves shifted back into women and headed for another auto. Maeva made a fist at them, and they nodded before climbing into their auto.

"Qarin," Saoirse answered after the third ring, using her call sign as always.

"Hey, *ahra*," Carver said evenly. "I just wanted to hear your voice."

She would find the show of overt affection from him unusual, especially because he knew better than to call for frivolous reasons. If he wanted to chat while she was in a safe house, he would have messaged her instead. And they never used endearments for anything other than teasing unless they were earnestly distressed.

Without missing a beat, she said, "You're cute. What's up? Jian dump you?"

His chest tightened. Thomas appeared in the driver's seat. He wore dark overalls with a red shirt—an outfit he hadn't had in life.

"It might not be what you think," he said haltingly, as if uncertain of his words. "You're different now."

Carver's eyes stung as he lifted his gaze to his husband. His ribs ached like they would collapse in on themselves at any moment. Maybe this situation was a ploy to get Saoirse's location, but that didn't mean he couldn't lean on her.

"I can't be with Jian," he rasped. "I think… I think I might be like you. I think I might be a khavira."

There was silence, and then she said, "Did you kill him?"

"He's alive and on his way to the hospital now."

"Oh, *albi*."

He bit the insides of his cheeks to keep from crying. His head dropped to the dashboard as he held the phone to his ear. Water dripped onto his knees, disappearing into his already soaked pants.

"Maybe it… It could be the Professor's power, or…" Saoirse trailed off, seemingly at a loss.

"Do the whys matter? I hurt him." He squeezed his eyes shut when his vision blurred. "The tether hurt him. It's not supposed to hurt. It's not supposed to break."

Thomas shivered as he said, "But we can't know if—"

"Don't." Carver took a shuddering breath. "Please stop."

Thomas was silent, and when Carver looked up, his husband was nowhere to be seen.

"What a pair we make," Saoirse mumbled. "Two khavira in one generation."

Carver ran a hand down his face. "I'm sorry. I didn't know who else to go to."

"You never need to apologize for needing me. I'm happy you called me actually, especially with your habit of suffering by yourself."

His chuckle was humorless. "I don't think I could suffer this myself. When I... When the tether broke, it felt like..."

He couldn't finish the sentence.

"It gets easier with time and distance." The breath she released crackled through the receiver. "When I put Iza in the hospital, it was like the earth had shattered beneath me."

"Yeah." He rested his head in his palm. "Yeah."

She was quiet for a moment. "I'm sorry. I almost feel like you have it worse than me honestly."

He rubbed his forehead. "How so?"

"You know what you're missing."

His eyes stung anew. "Gods, this is pathetic. You'd think I'd know how to handle loss by this point."

Her voice was so painfully soft when she whispered, "Loss isn't something you get used to, *albi*."

"I guess not." He glanced up at Maeva when she made a circular motion with her hand to wrap up. "Would you do me a favor and tell Jian I'm sorry? Tell him I wanted to keep our promise, but I don't think I can anymore."

She released a shaky breath as his meaning doubtlessly sank in. They'd kept their promise, their pact, to stay alive for each other so long—eighty years. And he probably wasn't going to survive this. She could. She still had a chance. He was making sure of it.

"I think he knows," she said, voice trembling. "He knows. I think he'd release you of your promise. I think he'd understand that you did your best."

A tear slipped from Carver's eye as he leaned back in his seat. She knew what he was talking about. This wasn't how he imagined saying goodbye, but he was glad he got the opportunity. That was more than either of them had hoped for in their lines of work.

"I love you, *ahra*," he murmured. "Thank you."

Her voice broke when she whispered, "I love you, too. *Keshata alshwa'atii, albi.*"

He set the phone in the cradle on the dashboard.

"If you somehow tipped her off in that conversation," Maeva said stiffly, "I will kill the demon. I'll make you watch me kill him."

"Why not just kill me now?" he grumbled.

Maeva reached over him to dial another number on the auto-phone. "Because you, *ihret ka-duul*, are not like you were."

The phone only rang once before someone picked up. The voice was faint through the receiver, but still audible.

"Gods, it's four in the morning, Mae," a man with an Imperial accent said. "What is so important?"

"Remember that siren I was telling you about?" She looked Carver over. "We've got him."

His limbs felt so heavy, and he couldn't keep his eyes open. Saoirse was a professional. She'd know what to do to save herself and Jian. Carver was the only one with little hope.

"I may not have to kill him," Maeva was saying. "Maybe just take an arm to appease the Ministry. Get me a plane back to the Imperium, and then we'll…"

Her voice faded as darkness fell over him.

CHAPTER FIFTEEN

The lights were loud. A dull ringing filled Jian's ears as fluorescents passed overhead, each one searing the backs of his eyes. There was a flurry of voices and faces. They blended into each other until he couldn't distinguish one person from another. Hands prodded him, finding tender parts and grabbing at his limbs to move them. Since being taken into the hospital, pressure had built in his head. He had enough presence of mind left to wonder if his skull would explode.

"Jian?" Damian's voice cut through the ringing. "Jian, can you hear me?"

As if coming up from water, Jian sucked in a breath. "Yes.".

Damian's head blocked out the fluorescents. His silver hair hung around his face. He wore glasses with multiple magnifying lenses on it. "What's your full name?"

"Jian Rong Tuan."

"What city are you in?"

"Vespera Bay."

"What year is it?"

"1912."

Damian pulled Jian's eyelid up and shone a light in it. He did the same with the other eye.

"How's your head feel?" he asked as he lowered his pen light.

Jian groaned. "Like it's trying to leave the rest of my body."

"Did you hit it earlier?"

"I don't remember hitting it." Sharp pain shot through his eye, as if a knife had sunk through it. "Fuck!"

Damian turned away and murmured something, presumably to someone else in the room. "We're going to give you some painkillers," he said after a moment, "but you can't go to sleep. Think you can manage that?"

Jian wanted nothing more than the sweet oblivion of sleep, but he grumbled, "I'll do my best."

Damian disappeared from view.

Dark shadows obscured the periphery of Jian's vision. His eyes ached when he looked around. He appeared to be in a hospital room. White tiled ceilings and white walls surrounded him. Machines were attached to his arms. Blood seeped from the partially healed bites and scratches in his skin. His clothes had been stripped away and replaced with blood-stained blankets. They were warm, but he still felt cold.

Someone in green scrubs pushed a syringe into an IV line. The pain in Jian's head eased almost immediately, and his eyes drooped. He bit his nails into his thigh in an attempt to stay awake.

Damian appeared again when Jian blinked.

"You've got some swelling around your brain," Damian explained. "There's no bleeding, but we want to monitor you for a little while until the swelling goes down."

Jian tried to sit up more, but pain shot through his shoulder and chest, swiftly ending his attempts to move.

"Easy," Damian said gently. "Give yourself a minute."

A nurse laid a mylar blanket over his electric ones. They were trying to get his body temperature up gradually. He must have been hypothermic.

"How long do I need to be awake?" he asked with a tired sigh.

"Until we're sure you're not going to get worse." Damian glanced at a machine with squiggly lines on it. "When did your head pain start?"

Jian tried to think back through the haze of memories. He'd been lying on the ground while water was pulled out of his chest. There'd been warmth, and then pain shooting between Jian's eyes.

"I was just lying there," he mumbled, "with Carver."

Damian's eyes narrowed. "Were you touching? Did he do anything?"

"I don't know. It was... I felt this...connection to him. But then there was pain."

Damian turned to someone. "I'll order dexamethasone. We'll treat this like meningitis without antibiotics."

Jian grimaced. "What's wrong with me?"

Damian wouldn't look at him. "The swelling is very treatable. You only need to stay awake until we're sure you'll respond to steroids. I'll be back, but I need to call Palus."

He headed out of the room.

Jian focused on breathing as his head throbbed. Few demons could claim to have survived not only falling in the ocean, but an injection of ocean water. If Carver had been just a few seconds slower, Jian doubted he would have lived. And where was Carver? Everything about the transport out of the quarry was blurry. Maybe he was bogged down in reports.

A nurse stepped in, interrupting Jian's thoughts.

"Excuse me, director," she said. "You have a phone call from your daughter."

She went to a phone attached to the wall in a corner of the room. He managed to move his least injured arm to grab it from her.

"Anh?" he answered.

"*A lo, Ba.*" Anh's voice, raspy and stiff like her mother's, was quiet through the receiver. "*So what's this Zhihao was telling me about you getting injected with ocean water? And this after falling in the ocean? You got a fetish?*"

She still preferred to speak Tieng Lac more than Tonghua. He couldn't blame her for wanting to abandon that half of her identity.

"*It was just a little dip,*" he said in Tieng Lac.

She chuckled. "*You're such a dick. I don't know why I bother worrying about you.*"

He smiled. The pain in his head was a little easier to ignore while she was talking.

"*Life would be boring if I didn't worry you,*" he teased. "*You should see the scars I got. Ocean water hurts like a bitch.*"

She groaned and then sighed. "*Do you have someone over there to look after you? If you don't, I'm going to deploy every agent I have in the area."*

His chest ached. *"Yeah, I have someone. He was the one who pulled me from the ocean and then also pulled the water out of me, so I think I can safely say he's reliable."*

"Oh?" Her tone was full of mirth. *"He's reliable, is he?"*

He shook his head at the obvious intrigue in her voice. *"Leave me alone."*

"Forgive your meddling daughter, but you don't exactly have many friends…or more than friends."

When he opened his mouth, she added, *"Not that it's my business."*

He chuckled until pain shot through his skull again, making him hiss.

"You dying?" Anh asked lightly, but there was a real note of worry in her voice.

He squeezed his eyes shut. *"Not yet."*

"I'll let you rest. It's four in the morning here anyway." Her breath crackled through the receiver. *"Call me again when you're feeling better. We're due to catch up."*

The sense that he was floating washed over him as he mumbled, *"Of course. I love you, monkey."*

"I love you, too, Ba."

Her voice sounded distant, and then it faded into silence.

The rush of falling ran through him, but there didn't seem to be ground for him to hit. Like sinking through the water.

"Jian."

He opened his eyes to see Damian standing over him again. The lights were off, leaving the room dim with the only light from the hallway.

"Sorry to rouse you," Damian said softly. "I just need to know if you've tethered with Carver."

Jian had trouble focusing his eyes. "No, I haven't."

Something like pain crossed Damian's face for just a moment, but it was difficult to determine in the dark.

"Get some rest," he murmured. "You're healing just fine."

Jian let his eyes slide closed as the floating sensation returned. He thought he heard Damian's voice again distantly, but it disappeared over the buzz in his ears.

◊◊◊

Saoirse was going to kill her brother before Maeva could do it. She set the phone back in its cradle on the wall. This townhouse had a tiny kitchen with white countertops and dark cabinets. The sepia walls were bare of any decoration. A window over the kitchen sink was covered with a curtain. The tiny table next to the kitchen was in what little space made a dining area. An archway beyond it led to the anteroom.

Saoirse took a deep breath against the tightness in her ribs and picked up the phone again. She dialed for Palus. It rang only once before their smooth voice came through the receiver.

"My agents have notified me about your brother," they reported. "Did he call you?"

She rubbed her intact eye. "Yeah, I'm assuming Maeva was using him to get my position. He knows I'd pick up on it."

"We'll move you to—"

"No, I'm staying. I don't know what threat Maeva made against my brother, but I'm not willing to gamble on her feeling charitable when she figures out my brother did tip me off."

Palus didn't respond immediately. "I could order you to leave. You're too valuable of an Inquisitor to risk."

"Well, then you'd need to consider this phone call my resignation, Superior Idylla."

They sighed loudly, making the connection crackle. "What do you want to do then?"

Saoirse propped her hip on a counter. "You should pull your Peacekeepers out, so that I don't need to worry about hurting them in the crossfire. Give me a handgun, two extra magazines, and fifteen minutes. I'll deal with them. You'll get a full report from me after everything's done."

"Very well. Peacekeepers have been notified to vacate. They'll leave you a handgun and two magazines. I'll await your call."

"One last thing, Palus." Her chest tightened as she stared at the floor. "I'm not sure how truthful he was being, but my brother mentioned he thought he was a khavira. Do you know Jian's state?"

There was a pause. "Damian suspected as much. He's taking care of Jian. It doesn't seem like the damage was severe. He anticipates a swift recovery."

The tightness in her chest grew worse, if only at the confirmation of Meallán's plight. No one should have had to endure this. Gods, it was so unfair. He'd gotten a second chance at something real and beautiful, and it was being stripped from him again.

"Understood," she said tightly. "You'll hear from me when it's done, sir."

Palus' voice was soft when they mumbled, "I'll await your call."

They hung up.

Saoirse put the phone back in the cradle and headed out into the anteroom. It was just a thin strip of russet tile flooring and sepia walls. The red front door was on one side, and stairs leading to the upper floor were on the other. A knock came just as she approached the door. When she opened it, a man in the blue fatigues of the Peacekeepers stood on the doorstep. He held out a handgun to her and two full magazines. She unstrapped the thigh holster on his leg without asking for permission and gave him a wink when he narrowed his eyes at her.

He turned to leave just as she closed the door. It was short work putting the thigh holster on, fitting the gun in it, and then slipping the magazines into the waistband of her pants. She went back into the kitchen to sip the tea she'd left on the table. It was jasmine. Her taste for it had developed because of her ex-fiancée who made tea for all occasions. Iza had brewed tea when she was celebrating or sad or worried or angry or just because she was bored. Saoirse had continued the tradition without knowing it, and even now when she did recognize it, she had no inclination to stop.

Her hands didn't shake when she pulled out her messenger and opened the chat with Iza. There were so many things that Saoirse didn't tell her former partner. The life of an Inquisitor was hard and dangerous, and Iza never knew how to stop fretting. Well, maybe that was one of many things that they shared in common.

I miss you, Saoirse typed out. *I might have to cancel visiting next month.*

Iza was supposed to be two hours into her shift at the lab, but her reply was immediate. *I miss you, too. Everything all right?*

Just a bit of work nonsense.

Maybe we can reschedule for the month after? I don't mind driving up to Balfour either.

Saoirse stared at the words with a heaviness in her chest. They'd maintained a friendship with the invention of the phone and messenger, but their in-person visits could never last longer than a handful of hours. Saoirse was too afraid the compulsion to tether would return. She couldn't do that to Iza again. It'd almost been fatal.

Maybe, she sent. *Things are a little hectic over here, but I'll let you know when I can.*

Iza's reply took a minute to come in. *Are you sure everything is fine?*

Saoirse couldn't lie to Iza, but she knew how to give half-truths. *I'll find out very soon how things will go. Don't worry. You know I can handle myself.*

All right. Think you can call me when you have a moment?

You'll be the first call I make when things quiet down.

Saoirse pocketed her messenger and waited. Minutes ticked by while she watched the front door. Her mug of tea had long emptied by the time she heard an auto approach and stop outside. A minute later, the door swung open. She grabbed the gun from her holster and fired three times. The man who'd opened the door dropped as his legs were torn through in a spray of blood and flesh.

Saoirse's ears rung from the shots, but wolves were more sensitive to sound. A woman behind the man immediately lifted her hands to her ears. Saoirse shot her twice in the chest and once in the neck.

Six bullets.

She changed out the magazine as she encroached on the anteroom. The woman dropped atop the man while they writhed in their agony. Saoirse fitted herself in the corner between the front door and the archway into the kitchen. Another man stepped in, looking automatically through the archway. It was only natural to look into the next room, but that meant he didn't see her soon enough when she emptied three bullets into his torso.

Her hearing was completely gone while she rounded through the doorway. There were two more people, a man and a woman, standing at the curb outside a gray auto. Rain streamed down over them. Saoirse waved a hand, and ribbons of water formed in the air. They wrapped around the pair's throats and squeezed hard enough to cause blood to well at their necks.

One of them reached for the gun at his hip. Saoirse let off another shot. Blood burst out of the hole that appeared in his hand. He dropped to his knees. She flicked her fingers out at him and the woman, and the water around their necks dragged them over the ground past her and into the townhouse. More water flowed from the rain toward her and amassed around her arms.

A man lying on the ground started jerking with the beginnings of his shift. She shot him through the head, and he stilled. Everyone else looked up at her. The two choking on water gasped in limited air. One of the women lying in the anteroom reached toward her hip. Saoirse shot her through the head as well.

Six bullets. She switched out her last magazine.

Water flowed over her hand as she pressed it to her ear and stretched her jaw. The ringing stopped, water healing the internal damage to her eardrum.

"Let's see," she murmured as she looked over the remaining three wolves still living. "Which one of you matters?"

She crouched down to the pair with her water vices around their necks and patted their pockets. They had messengers and pistols. Neither of them had conversations in their chat history that suggested strong leadership roles. She made a fist as she stood straight, and the water around their necks cut deep enough to sever their airways, carotids, and jugulars immediately. They choked briefly before going limp. Blood pooled under them.

The remaining wolf stared up at her with wide eyes while she went through his pockets. He also had a messenger and a pistol. His conversation history had orders from an unknown number to bring Saoirse's remaining eye back with him. That was promising.

She lifted the gun to his head, and he stared at the barrel.

"Can you hear yet?" she asked.

He nodded minutely.

"Fabulous." She grabbed his arm and dragged him into the kitchen, leaving a trail of blood on the floor as she went. "Don't try anything for a sec."

He stayed still when she released him. She went to the phone on the wall. Her gun trained on the Gar as she dialed for Palus. They picked up before the first ring completed.

"Is it done?" they asked.

She stared at the wolf on the floor and then the bodies in the anteroom. "I'm going to need clean up here. There's one still living. He's going to reassure Maeva that everything is fine here, and then take me to the wolf camp before she gets wise."

"Can I convince you to wait for back up?"

"If anyone else approaches the camp, Maeva is going to run away and take Carver with her. I'll call you from the auto-phone, and you can get my location from there to send reinforcements."

They took a moment to respond. "Fine. Don't die."

"Wilco, sir."

She hung up and grabbed the wolf on the floor.

He groaned and hissed when she dragged him outside to the auto. She had to use the aid of water to shove him into the passenger side since he was so heavy. Three bullet holes in his abdomen and chest leaked blood, and his eyes were starting to lose focus. If it were closer to evening, then his healing factor would have been better. He still wouldn't die from this much.

She holstered her gun at her thigh when she got into the driver's side. The key was in the ignition. Perhaps the Gars had hoped for a speedy fight and getaway. Water lifted off her and hovered in the air between them. It sharpened to a point as she started the engine. The man was stiff beside her. He stared at the water while it froze into a spear of ice levelled at his head.

"Call Maeva," she instructed. "Tell her you're coming back with my eye."

The man hesitated before taking the auto-phone and dialing. It rang once, and then Maeva's voice drifted faintly through the receiver.

"You have her?" she asked curtly.

"Yeah, I have her eye," he said, albeit a bit shakily. "We're on our way back."

"Good."

Maeva hung up without another word. What a bitch.

Saoirse dialed for Palus. It connected almost immediately, but they didn't speak.

"Directions," Saoirse ordered as she pulled away from the curb.

The man swallowed before complying. "Take a right up here."

She followed his instructions.

He led her to the northeast end of the city and then further out into the surrounding forest. The buildings transitioned into greenery. Redwood trees stood tall, and water coated the road. The amount of green here was dizzying at this time of year. Everything was always covered in a fine layer of moisture. The redwoods stood in vibrant contrast to the monotonous gray of the sky. They had almost fibrous bark, with threads of the russet wood shedding off them in clumps. There were few automobiles on the road out here. After enough time, Saoirse saw none.

The Gar eventually directed her to a turnout with a dirt road leading deeper into the trees. They were only able to get a short ways in before the road grew too narrow to continue by auto. Saoirse kept sharp points of ice trained on the man as they walked. She didn't want to waste bullets on him when she'd likely need it for getting her brother out.

Her boots squelched in the mud underfoot as she walked behind the man. The trees here were dense, prohibiting sight beyond a couple feet, but after a minute, they thinned. Large paw prints in the earth joined shoeprints. The man stopped in front of a line of trees.

"They're just beyond here," he said. "Please let me go."

She looked him over. He could alert his pack to her presence if she released him, and as a cultist who hunted mixed bloods for no other reason than their blood purity, he would likely kill innocents again. Gods only knew how many he had already. She had a responsibility to make sure that he couldn't hurt anyone again.

Her ice spears sunk into his neck, cutting off his cry before he could make any sound. Blood welled at his neck and streamed thickly down his chest as he dropped to the ground. It never felt good to kill and certainly not to kill in cold blood like this. But her willingness to do it was why she was an Inquisitor at all. She'd done worse than this before. She'd probably do worse again.

Her breath made a puff of white in the frigid air as she sighed. She pulled her gun from the thigh holster. Her hands didn't shake like they used to when she killed this way. They hadn't in a long time.

She had to end this.

The silver shores seemed dimmer than Carver last remembered. Water lapped at the sand, almost black for how dark it was. There was just a sliver of moon in the sky. Salwnsu sat at the edge of the water, with her legs crossed and back straight.

"What great suffering you endure," she murmured as he approached. "True cruelty."

He sat beside her and stared over the waves. "A couple months after Thomas died, I tried to kill myself. Took enough pills to down an elephant. Saoirse found me and got me help. There was a period of time where I resented her for it. And then she met Izabela. I'd never seen someone so capable of smoothing all of Saoirse's rough edges. They seemed perfect together."

"She didn't kill herself like so many khavira," Salwnsu said softly, "because she knew you'd follow her."

He took a shaky breath and let it out slowly. "I know."

They sat in silence for a long minute, just watching the waves come and go.

"Have you thought about what Thomas asked of you when he died?" Salwnsu said abruptly.

Carver glanced up at her. "I still can't remember what it was. Why?"

The stars in her skin seemed to shift as she sank her fingers in the sand below. "Matters of the heart are best understood when you have all the pieces."

He watched the silvery granules shift under her touch. "I'm going to die, aren't I?"

"Maybe. I would welcome you back readily, if so. My mother would be disappointed. She is fond of you."

He felt a little guilty that he'd be leaving the Professor behind. He felt even guiltier that his last act toward Jian was hurting him. But it was better this way. They couldn't have been together while Carver was a khavira. The compulsion to tether would always be there, and if he wasn't vigilant about keeping it restrained, he could easily tether again and kill Jian. And Carver wouldn't be able to stop the tether forever.

Thomas appeared beside him, wearing black robes that were unrecognizable. They enshrouded his form loosely. His curls hung over one side of his head.

"I shouldn't have bonded with you," he muttered. "I wouldn't have, if I'd known it would come to this."

Carver closed his eyes, feeling the sea air wash over him. The weight of his wedding band had never felt heavier.

"I refuse to resent our relationship," he said. "Even now."

Thomas didn't reply.

Carver's eyes opened to see an overcast sky. Rain streamed down. Damp grass was at his back, and redwood trees surrounded him. His eyes scanned around. He appeared to be lying at the edge of a wide clearing. Black tents were spread all through it, along with portable gas stoves and pots for cooking. Mud, clover, and grass covered the ground. Carcasses of animals hung from the trees at the edges. Men, women, and massive wolves wandered the camp.

He sat up, body stiff as he moved. The sound of clinking metal brought his eyes down. Black metal shackles surrounding his wrists. They attached to chains that connected to a large stake in the ground that was probably made to hold down wolves. The scent of the metal, like rot and iron, indicated it was decay metal. This much would inhibit his ability to manipulate water.

Breaking his hands to slip his binds would be simple enough, but he'd have a hard time fighting this many wolves. They'd just take him down. Saoirse had probably dealt with whoever had been sent to kill her, and when Maeva realized that her plan had fallen through, she'd move on and take him with her. There wasn't a great way out of this.

"Just taking a fucking nap."

His sister's voice made him tense. He forced himself not to look back at her. Water accumulated over the metal of his chains. It froze, leaving ice crystals on one link.

"What are you doing here?" he whispered, trying not to move his mouth too much in case someone was watching.

"You don't get to die for me," Saoirse muttered. "Just get ready to run. I have an auto nearby."

This was far too reminiscent of their young years when they'd been Inquisitors together. Saoirse had always been a better fighter than him. She was near silent while she moved behind him. The frozen chain link had water streaming over it in a circle. After a minute, it gave with a soft groan and snap. He didn't move yet, waiting for his sister's signal.

"On my mark," she whispered. "Rush into the trees with me and then stay close. We have to circumvent the clearing."

He tensed and slowly brought a foot under him.

"And…now."

He jumped to his feet and turned to sprint into the trees. She was at the tree line just a few paces away. Her form was coated in blood, which was less an unusual sight than it should have been. They ran into the forest just as the growls and snaps of wolves joined shouts. Carver stayed close to Saoirse as she led him between the trees, weaving through them and under low branches.

"You're insane," he muttered. "You shouldn't have come here."

She glanced at him over her shoulder. "A simple 'Thank you so much, Saoirse, for saving my sorry skin' would be nice."

He sighed. "I can't lose you."

"And I can lose you? Fuck off. We made a promise."

"You released me of my promise."

"I thought you were—"

A wolf burst through the trees in front of them. Water rushed up in a thin blade and cut through its head. Its cry was cut short. Saoirse cursed and ran past it, never breaking her stride. Carver leapt over the wolf to catch up with her.

"You don't get to die," she bit out. "You don't get to die just because you're like me. It's a hard life. It's painful. But I need you. I need my big brother, so you don't get to call it quits yet."

He stared at her back as his chest tightened. She wasn't the little girl he'd carried across the ocean anymore, and he wasn't the teenager who had figured out how to be a parent when theirs died. But they still needed each other. He'd made it this far for her. That was the pact. Either they lived or died together.

Wolves poured into the trees in front of them, cutting off their route. Carver grabbed Saoirse and yanked her to the side as a wolf lunged for her. They stumbled out into the clearing. It seemed everyone in the camp had shifted. There were a plethora of wolves in blacks and reds and grays throughout the clearing. They amassed at the edges, many of them sniffing—likely trying to follow scent.

Carver sprinted forward, pulling Saoirse with him. With his hands bound in decay metal, he wasn't much use. She pulled a gun from a holster at her hip and levelled it at a wolf charging toward them from one side. Her aim was as good as ever. The shot she let off echoed in the clearing, and blood burst through the wolf's skull. It collapsed to the ground.

They were near the center of the clearing when they saw more wolves on the other side, prowling closer. There was no path out. The Gars were on all sides. Saoirse doubtlessly didn't have enough bullets to take down all of them, and Carver had no energy left in him, even if he didn't have his hands bound.

Maeva's form appeared in front of them. "Just surrender," she muttered. "Look, I'll make it quick. We don't need to draw this out."

Carver's jaw clenched. Jian would never forgive him for dying here, and he couldn't face Saoirse on the shores like this.

The rain abruptly stopped, drops suspended in the air, and the ambient temperature dropped significantly. Carver's skin and scales blackened. His bones shifted under his flesh, growing longer and then cracking with additional joints. Sharp spines raised along his back and arms. The binds around his wrist groaned as his wrists grew beyond what they could contain. They snapped and fell to the ground.

"What the fuck?" Saoirse mumbled quietly.

A wolf lunged for him, perhaps thinking that he was more vulnerable in the middle of his conversion, but a maw with growing rows of fangs split open on his face. He caught the wolf's neck in his mouth and slammed it into the ground. Blood dripped down his jaw when he lifted his head.

"Stop him."

Carver glanced down. Maeva stood a few paces away from his sister.

"Listen, bitch," Saoirse said tiredly. "I honestly don't know what the fuck is happening right now, but that looks like an ihret. The fuck you want me to do about it?"

Maeva scowled, eyes growing cold. "I'm willing to let you both go, if you just stop now."

Saoirse scoffed. "So you can appear a couple years later to try again? No, I think it ends here, Maeva."

"There will always be another of me, always another person the Ministry calls on to kill you."

"Then we'll deal with them, too."

Carver didn't see Maeva move. In a moment, her hand was pressing through his shoulder, breaking bone and rending flesh. A hiss escaped him at the pain that burst through him, but then she was gone again. More illusions.

The other wolves swarmed. A low drone started soft in the air and then grew to a rumble like thunder in his chest. He rose to his full height as his skin and spines turned glossy black. The eyeless face of his form looked over the mass of wolves impassively. His hands, too long and with too many joints to be human, dug into the earth.

Blood burst up from the first line of wolves. Red rose into the air, joining the suspended rainwater. Spears of ice and frozen blood formed. They shot out wildly. More wolves were impaled or grazed as they sprinted toward him. Their blood joined the rain in the air.

Saoirse's hiss brought his head around. A wolf had black ichor oozing from its jaws—more of that poison that they'd brought to the cannery. It had clamped its teeth around her shoulder. She brought her gun to the underside of its head and fired a single shot. Blood sprayed out from it as it slumped to the ground. Its weight on her shoulder took her down with it.

Maeva's form appeared before Carver again as he crouched over his sister protectively.

"You're still outnumbered and outgunned," she said. "You can't win."

Carver stared out over the wolves. Maeva was right that they couldn't keep this up forever. He had to finish this.

A breath huffed out of him as he internally steeled himself. His body trembled while that sense he had for water extended out. It flowed through the air and saturated the ground and pulsed in the blood of the wolves around them. Most of blood was water—a little more intangible than purer sources, but present nonetheless.

All the wolves ground to a halt. Streams of red burst out through their eyes and mouths. Ribbons of blood rose up into the air. The scent of it was thick and metallic. A massive sphere of it formed in the middle of the clearing. The wolves started to drop as the sphere grew larger and larger.

"You can't do this."

Maeva's voice had an edge of panic to it as she appeared beside Saoirse. No illusions could stop this. She didn't even need to have her real position revealed for how far Carver's senses reached.

"We can," Saoirse said coldly. "Thomas was the forgiving one, and you killed him. Goodbye, Maeva. May the gods have mercy on you."

Maeva's shriek was cut short as her image disappeared. All through the clearing, the wolves whined and yelped before their howls quieted abruptly. And then they all stilled. There was no sound or movement. The mass of blood dropped. It spread over the grass in pools and soaked into the ground. Silence filled the clearing like a physical presence.

Carver slumped to one side. Fatigue weighed over him, crushing in its intensity. Slowly, his blackened scales lightened to blue and gold, and his skin turned its usual umber. His bones reformatted into the shape of a man once again. He drew strained and shallow breaths. Blood trickled from between his lips, and he shivered violently. He couldn't focus his eyes as Saoirse crouched over him.

"What's wrong?" she asked quickly.

Carver's eyes slid closed. The Professor had told him there was a price for using this kind of power before he was ready.

What was he going to pay?

CHAPTER SIXTEEN

Blankets were piled atop Jian to heal the cracks in his skin. There would be new scars just from how much water had coated him and gotten into his wounds. He stared at the white walls of his hospital room. At least one of the blankets on him was electric. He barely felt the heat of it. Numbness had settled under his skin, giving the world a touch of unreality to it. The feeling was familiar. He had spent most of his life in and out of hospitals. Getting patched up himself was never as bad as waiting to hear about someone else.

His head throbbed dully, but nowhere near what it had been. Everyone had been suspiciously quiet since he'd woken up. No one had told him where Carver was or what had happened with Maeva and the Gars. That set him on edge more than his own state. Something was wrong. What was it? Was it Carver or something else?

A knock came at his door before Saoirse stepped in. She was drenched and covered in blood. There was no indication of injury other than bloody teeth marks in her shirt that encompassed her shoulder. She didn't seem to have difficulty with that arm, so it had probably healed from water exposure already.

"Hey," she greeted as she came closer and sat at the edge of the bed. "I know I'm not who you want to see, but I hope I'm not too unwelcome a presence."

He sat straighter as he looked her over. "What happened to you?"

She glanced down at herself. "Well, funny story. My brother decided to be all noble and protect you after you were injected with water. Got himself captured, and I had to go fetch him."

Jian's heart dropped. "Where is he? Is he—?"

"Hold on. I'm getting there. I promise." She waited for him to settle back before continuing. "I'm going to say something that is very hard to hear in a second, and then I'm going to ask something impossible of you."

His blood felt icy in his veins as he muttered, "Just tell me."

She searched his eyes a moment, as if looking for any sign of hesitation, and then she drew in a deep breath. "My brother is a khavira."

He blinked. "What?"

"Did Damian talk to you at all about why you had swelling around your brain?"

"No, he..." Jian's ribs constricted. "I felt something. It was like a connection to your brother—there for a second. And then..."

He couldn't get the words out. His heart seemed to ache more and more with each beat until it was painful. The pieces were starting to come together in his mind. Everyone's avoidance of him and his mysterious head trauma made horrific, terrifying sense.

"He tried to tether you," Saoirse confirmed softly. "I don't know why or how, but it hurt you. You're lucky that you recovered this

316

quickly. When I tethered my partner, she was hospitalized for weeks."

A shaky breath left him as he clapped a hand over his mouth. His throat constricted. Saoirse lifted a hand, hesitated, and then continued on to cup his cheek. Her eyes shimmered as she pulled him closer. He went without resistance and pressed his face to her shoulder. The scent of blood was heavy on her. Demons weren't as tactile as sirens, but he leaned into her like it was all that could hold his fragile heart together.

His mind moved in too many directions, thoughts pulling toward disbelief repeatedly before harsh reality hit him again. If Carver was a khavira, then this was it, wasn't it? A tether formed naturally was what he said, and it would be lethal.

"He couldn't stop himself from tethering, could he?" Jian rasped. "I can't be near him."

Saoirse wrapped an arm around his shoulders and cradled the back of his head. "He could for a little while, but physiology will win eventually. It always does."

When he didn't reply, she whispered, "I'm so sorry."

His eyes stung, and a blood tear slid down his cheek before he could stop it. Demons couldn't cry water. He took several breaths to steady himself before pulling away. Saoirse lowered her hand to hold his in his lap.

"Where is he?" he asked. "Is he okay?"

She couldn't meet his eyes. "That's the other thing I meant to talk to you about. Carver is in danger of dying."

His heartbeat seemed stunted when it hit the back of his ribs. "And does that have anything to do with the impossible thing you need to ask me?"

"You can save him." She drew in a deep breath and let it out slowly. "There are some caveats."

His jaw set as he stared at her. "What kind of caveats?"

She squeezed his hand. "As Damian explained it to me, my brother hasn't fully come into his own where the Professor's influence is concerned. He expended a tremendous amount of energy when we were fighting the Gars and Maeva earlier, and it needs to be replenished quickly if he's going to make it through the night."

"Are... Are you asking me to sleep with him?" Jian narrowed his eyes. "I can't. By what you just told me, I can't be near him."

Her eyes were soft as she lifted them to his. "I'm afraid he doesn't have much of a choice. His body has rejected every consort we've called for him. It seems it only wants one person now."

His ribs froze. "You can't be serious."

"Normally this kind of attachment only happens with mated sirens, but he's not like most sirens. His physiology doesn't behave normally anymore." Her shoulders slumped as she lowered her gaze again. "I can't in good conscience ask you to do this. If he tethers, you could die. Honestly, just telling you this is against his wishes. He wants to just wither away and never put you at risk, and I certainly can't blame him for it."

Jian breathed through the tightness in his chest. He couldn't just let Carver die, but he wasn't going to force him either. That would have been heinous.

"How sure are you that I can do anything?" he mumbled. "My kind isn't known for healing. Maybe his body rejects me, too."

She smoothed her thumb over his hand. "My partner was a doctor. She would tell me that anyone is capable of great harm or healing. A scalpel can slice through flesh easily, but we made it for surgery — for healing. Take it from someone whose love was almost fatal, someone who has trained for over a century to be deadly in every regard, even people like us can bring good to the world sometimes."

He stared at their clasped hands. She did understand, didn't she? They were weapons. They were wielded to do harm and endure harm for the greater good. Healing and nurturing weren't their domain. But it had to be right now.

"He'll refuse me," Jian mumbled. "You know he will."

She wiped at his cheek before withdrawing her touch. "He's in three-fifty-two."

Jian stared blankly at her for a moment. This was so incredibly foolish, and still, he found himself climbing out of bed. He kept a blanket around his naked form while he moved on stiff legs out of the room and through the hospital. A couple of nurses gave him odd looks while he wandered the halls, but no one tried to stop him.

Room 352 was on the other side of the wing. The rooms here were larger, meant to hold patients long-term. Damian was standing outside the door when Jian shuffled toward him.

"She found you, did she?" he muttered with a sigh. "Can I convince you to turn back?"

Jian shook his head. "I doubt he'll agree to it, but I have to try."

Damian chewed his lip a moment before stepping aside. "I'll have an emergency team on standby. Just be careful."

Nothing about this was careful, but Jian appreciated the show of concern all the same.

He knocked on the door before he opened it. The room was larger than most, with a wide bed and a sofa on one wall. It had its own bathroom. A water pump rested by the bed, not currently attached, but the tubing emerging from the top could connect to the mattress. An end table sat on one side of the bed. Maybe the room was used specifically for sirens who needed to feed while they were hospitalized.

Carver lay in bed, turned on his side and curled in on himself. His skin was paler than normal, and he breathed shallower and faster than he should have. Blue curls were splayed messily over his pillow.

"I told her not to tell you," he said flatly. "Leave."

Jian crossed the room to sit at the side of the bed. "You don't have another option."

Carver stared at the wall. "Of course I do. I can die."

"Is death preferable to me?"

"That's not fair." Carver looked away from the wall then to meet Jian's gaze. "I could kill you. I almost did once. Nothing is worth risking that."

Jian lifted a hand. He hesitated briefly before cupping Carver's cheek.

"You're worth it," he whispered.

320

"Don't do this." Carver let out a shaky breath. "I'm a broken siren with no hope of recovery. My love is lethal."

Jian's heart sped away at the mention of love. They'd never spoken of love or romance, dancing around it like it was this delicate topic that could shatter them. But tethers didn't just appear out of nothing. Jian still didn't think he could handle hearing it said explicitly.

"I would have it anyway," he murmured.

There was a beat of silence. When Carver did speak, his voice was so soft that it was near inaudible. "I'm not worth your life."

"I get to decide that." Jian leaned closer until their foreheads met. "I trust you not to hurt me. Please let me heal you."

A shiver ran through Carver. He let Jian tip his chin up until their lips brushed. The scent of sea salt and petrichor bloomed through the air in an instant. It'd cling for a long time, Jian knew. His house was already coated in it, and when he went home, he was sure it would haunt him for however long it lasted. And then he'd miss it.

Jian felt hands at his shoulders, as if to push him away, but they didn't. Instead they gripped the blanket wrapped around him and pulled him closer. Their lips came together fully, and Jian let heat run through him. The cold from the rain that'd persisted his entire stay here seemed to vanish from his skin.

How strange that his heart could warm while it tore apart.

He pulled the blanket from himself and let it fall to the floor, knowing without a doubt that he would leave this room more broken than he had entered it. Cool skin warmed under his touch when he slid a hand under the bedsheets. Carver was already naked as well. A breath left him when Jian slid fingertips down a thigh and then steadily inched up.

It didn't take much for the cock at Jian's hand to harden. He wanted to draw this out, but that would have put more strain on Carver to control the tether. They had limited time. Better to be smart with it.

"What are you doing?" Carver asked when Jian pulled the drawer of the end table open.

As Jian had thought, there was a bottle of lube in the drawer. A room for sirens was bound to have amenities for them. He straddled Carver's hips as he coated his fingers. The sigh that left him when he slid them into himself seemed to fill the mostly silent room. His heartbeat was in his ears while he stretched his inner walls. When he found that bundle of nerves in him, Carver shivered, seeming to share in the pulse of pleasure it brought.

Jian didn't take as much time as he should have in stretching himself, but he couldn't find it in him to care. There was nothing that he wouldn't do for this infuriatingly kind siren. He'd even break his own heart.

When he finally removed his fingers, Jian saw some of the color returning to Carver's skin. The confirmation that his efforts were working made his cardinal fire heat with a deep-rooted instinct to provide. He'd always thought of his body as a tool, usually for death and destruction, but if it could be used to heal, then he was happy to be used.

He slicked Carver's cock with lube before straightening to rest his weight on his knees. His thighs shook as he lowered himself. Carver's eyes were fixed on him, lips parted slightly, as if in awe. Jian held the eye contact while he sank down. The hands at his thighs tightened, still weak but stronger than before.

Pain was familiar. Jian knew it intimately, and he wasn't surprised when he felt a slight burn inside him while he slowly took Carver deeper. He almost wanted it to hurt more. If it hurt, if it scarred, at least he could feel it after he left. His body carried the marks of torture and war, evidence of his survival, but today seemed a worthier scar to bear.

He stilled when Carver was completely buried inside him. The fullness alone threatened to undo him. His blood rushed in his ears. It was too much and not enough all at once, and he stayed frozen for several seconds while he adjusted to the intrusion.

He braced a hand on the bed as he lifted his hips and then brought them back down slowly. Smoke plumed from his lips. Shocks of pleasure burst from the base of his spine. Carver let out the softest gasp. His hands lifted to Jian's shoulders and gripped them.

The roll of Jian's hips grew faster as he found a rhythm. His breaths became harsher and then stuttered when he hit an angle that sent sparks from between his teeth. Carver's grip on his shoulders gained more and more strength until it could bruise. Jian hoped it would.

He took his own cock in his hand, feeling the familiar pressure of his orgasm building up his back. A firm hand took his jaw and pulled lightly. Jian went with it until their lips met. The kiss was softer than their others had been—almost reverent in its deliberateness. Jian was the one to break it when his breaths grew too fast and harsh.

He bit the pillow by Carver's head to muffle his cry. Pleasure shot through him, overpowering and nearly painful in its intensity. It pulsed in waves that seemed to have no end. His hips stuttered, unable to keep a consistent rhythm while his climax burned through him.

When he'd fallen in the ocean, there'd been a moment where he knew he wasn't going to come back up. The water had crept into him, submerged him entirely like it had a claim to him. This felt no different. He was drowning, and there was no coming up for air.

He'd hardly opened his jaw enough to release the pillow when arms wrapped around him. The world moved as he was turned and then gently laid onto his back. Carver hovered above, the blue in his eyes brighter than it had been a moment ago. Jian had only a second to appreciate that he'd helped before Carver snapped his hips forward.

Under normal circumstances, Jian would've been too sensitive to feel good after coming as hard as he had, but only euphoria rushed through him. His skin was alight with the desire for more. The scent of sea salt and petrichor was so thick that it made him dizzy. And when Carver started a leisurely pace, filling him again and again, he nearly bit through his lip to stifle his moans.

This wasn't like their previous times together. Jian had always maintained some of his natural proclivity to stay in control, but none of it empowered him now. He was helpless, caught in an undertow

324

too strong to even consider escape. It would have frightened him, if not for the person inspiring the feeling.

Carver was gentle. His arm hooked around Jian's waist, keeping them close as they moved together. As if by instinct, their lips found each other again. The kiss was so soft that Jian's chest ached with it. Why did it have to feel like this?

When he came a second time, his cry was muffled by the mouth on his. Carver's hips stuttered for only a moment before he bared his fangs and sank them into Jian's shoulder. The pain was lost under a wave of longing that accompanied the crests of pleasure between them. Warmth dripped from between Jian's legs. He found himself hurtling back to the edge of climax in an instant, bitten and claimed all at once.

A gentle hand guided his head to Carver's shoulder. It was almost like an invitation, and Jian was too far gone to think about his actions anymore. He let his fangs extend as he bit down into the flesh offered to him and held it like it was his only lifeline in open water.

Carver's thrusts grew faster and harder. He was getting stronger while Jian increasingly lost his ability to do much else than lay there and let the waves wash over him. It occurred to him dimly that he was being fed upon for everything he could give, and he'd gladly, perhaps stupidly, let himself be consumed, even as his heart seemed to rend itself in his chest with the knowledge that this would be the last time.

No one had told him that falling for someone would hurt so much when he hit the ground.

Carver knew he was a bastard. He'd never felt it quite so viscerally as when he looked at Jian beneath him. He was supposed to wither away and spare them both any more heartache. The compulsion to tether was a vicious thing, clawing at the inside of his skull, and still, he couldn't leave.

Jian released his bite and sank down on the bed. Blood smeared across his lips and glinted on his fangs. He looked up through half-lidded eyes. Smoke wafted from his parted lips with every stuttered breath. His hair splayed over the pillow like a black flower in bloom. Blood welled from the mess of bites in his shoulder, marking him the way he wanted—the way they both wanted.

Carver didn't know what a bite meant to a demon, but he knew that Jian had never bit him back in all the time they'd been together—until now.

"Please," Jian breathed on a moan. "Meallán, please."

Carver's name on those lips would surely haunt him for the rest of his life. He dragged his fangs up Jian's throat and hummed in satisfaction at the gasp it elicited. The next thrust of his hips had fingernails biting into his back, and he hoped it drew blood. Never had he wanted so badly to have the evidence of a moment etched into him, scarred in his skin where he could carry it long after it had passed.

When he brought his lips up to Jian's, they met readily. Sweet smoke and the metallic bite of blood settled on Carver's tongue. He barely restrained himself from attuning to the threads of the connection between them. It shrieked in the back of his brain, yearning to feel everything with his partner. That could never happen.

The way Carver angled his next thrust made them both cry out. They were close again—convergence. Bonded sirens experienced convergence, the simultaneous ebbs and rises of pleasure between partners, but it shouldn't have been possible between an unmated pair. Well, they had always defied logic.

The claiming scent, like fresh rain in summer, was thick in the room. It only grew as Carver's release built at the base of his spine. Jian panted against his lips. They clung to each other as their pleasure crested together.

Carver bit into Jian's shoulder again. The threads of the tether pulled at him with renewed force as he came, and when the warmth of Jian's climax rushed down his spine, it took all his willpower not to let himself connect. The absence of it made him shudder and ache, everything in him seeking the empathic presence of the man beneath him.

His hips stuttered to a halt as he buried himself in Jian. The world blurred. When he released his bite, he kept his face pressed against Jian's neck to hide the tears that spilled over.

It wasn't fair. He'd never dared to think he might have a second chance at love, and just when he thought it might be possible, that hope had been stolen from him. Part of him wished he'd just died with Thomas. At least then, he wouldn't have broken Jian's heart, too.

He just wanted to give him everything.

"Meallán?" Jian said, concern creeping into his voice.

Carver allowed his hand to slide up to find Jian's. Their fingers laced together automatically, and the tightness in Carver's chest grew until he struggled to breathe.

"*Santrizuka alshwa'atii*," he whispered into Jian's skin, needing to say it while he could get the words out.

Jian's hand tightened around his when they started moving again. It wasn't necessary to keep going. Carver had the energy he needed. Everything now was purely indulgence, but he just couldn't stop yet, couldn't bring himself to end this a moment early.

Time slid away as the minutes ticked by until Jian's movements grew slow. And then Carver enfolded his arms around him, held him closer than he had any right to while Jian drifted to sleep.

They had slept beside each other like this many nights before. But this wasn't normal. This wasn't what they did. Jian didn't submit. He controlled and pushed and tested. It was never supposed to be like this.

Carver carefully extricated himself, but couldn't muster the will to move very far, instead sitting on the bed's edge. He gently smoothed Jian's hair back, feeling the soft strands cling to his fingertips. After a feeding like this, most people would need at least a day of rest. Being a pureblood, Jian probably just needed a night's sleep. That didn't stop guilt from rising in Carver's throat.

The claiming scent grew stronger when Jian stirred and pressed closer to Carver. Even demons subconsciously recognized and craved touch from their partners, it seemed. Carver resented how his heart warmed at the knowledge.

He allowed himself to lean down until his forehead touched Jian's temple, feeling the extreme difference in heat that he'd come to seek. His eyes burned anew as he just breathed the same air.

The compulsion to connect was like fire behind his eyes. His head ached with how hard he'd worked to fend it off for so long. That it was still early in its development was likely the only reason he had made it this far.

He reluctantly stood and grabbed pants and a shirt from the stack of clothes on a chair by the door. The tendons behind his eyes throbbed while he dressed. His head seemed ready to split in half. The fluorescents in the hallway when he stepped out of the room didn't help the growing pain.

Damian sat on a bench just across the hall. The Professor stood beside him. They both held paper cups of coffee in their hands. Carver wasn't surprised to see the Professor, somehow aware of her like his own hand. He shut the door behind him as quietly as he could.

"What are you doing here?" he asked flatly.

She shrugged. "I can't be here for long, but I sensed that you did exactly what I warned you not to do and decided to check in."

His jaw set. "I want to go home."

Damian looked him over before speaking. "I see no reason to keep you here. How's Jian?"

"Asleep. He'll be fine."

"Good to hear it." Damian glanced up at his wife. "Do you have any other concerns?"

She sipped her coffee. "Many. Where'd you learn to control water like that, Carver?"

"Saoirse and...a woman who comes to me in dreams." Carver rubbed his aching eyes. "She calls herself Salwnsu. She refers to you as her mother."

The Professor's eyes were soft as she lowered her cup. "Sometimes the people I reclaim form a greater connection with their Ancient. Salwnsu, the Warden, is the Ancient of Devotion—mother of sirens."

Thomas appeared beside the Professor, making her jump. She looked him over.

"Is there no warning for this one?" she muttered.

"No," Thomas said with a glance at her. "I do as I please."

She sighed and waved a hand dismissively. "It doesn't matter. Carver, you're not a khavira."

He narrowed his eyes. "What do you mean I'm not? Tethering to Jian nearly killed him."

"Your changes manifest based on your personal understanding of yourself, and you weren't a khavira before. You wouldn't be now. There's something else happening."

Carver grimaced. She left for weeks and then returned just to poke at irrelevant things.

"Semantics," he muttered. "The outcome is the same. Tethering will kill him."

She glanced at Thomas. "It doesn't have to. You were mated once. That kind of bond doesn't just disappear."

Ringing filled Carver's head as he saw his husband's lips move without sound. The Professor abruptly stepped between them and placed a hand at Carver's forehead. The ringing stopped.

"You need to figure out what he told you," she said. "It wasn't said in this world."

He rubbed his head. "I know."

"Knowing hasn't helped." She smoothed a hand over his hair. "Go home, Carver. Think on it. Maybe stop ruminating on how terrible you feel for just a moment."

Easier said than done, but he couldn't resist a direct order from her.

His legs were stiff as he made his way out of the hospital.

CHAPTER SEVENTEEN

There was no energy in Jian's body. He wasn't accustomed to feeling this weak, and it might have alarmed him if he didn't know exactly why he was like this. Given that he woke up alone, he must have been successful. That was enough of a comfort to soften the deep sorrow that cut through his chest at feeling the cold space beside him. He'd slept alone for years before without thinking much of it, but now he wondered how he was going to tolerate it for the foreseeable future.

The room was dim. Evidently, someone had turned the lights off for him. He lay in the cold silence, unable to do much more than breathe and turn over. His limbs were heavy and useless. That'd probably be true for awhile.

He wasn't sure how long passed before he heard a soft knock at the door. Light streamed in briefly as a feminine figure stepped in, silhouetted by the illumination from the hallway outside. Her steps were near silent as she approached him and sat on the edge of the bed.

"Sorry to intrude."

Saoirse's voice was smooth like her brother's, and her intact eye, even in the dark, looked near identical to the blue of his. She'd changed into clean clothes since he'd last seen her.

"What are you doing here, Saoirse?" he asked, voice hoarse.

She pushed her dreads from her face as she released a breath. "The Inquisitors want me back now that Maeva's dead, but I didn't want to leave before thanking you properly. You saved my brother, in more ways than one. I owe you a great debt for that."

His chest tightened. "You don't owe me anything. I only did as I wanted."

"You wanted my brother. That's no small feat."

His chuckle was more a huff. "Easiest thing I've ever done."

"Now you're just bragging." She gave a smile when he chuckled properly. "How are you feeling?"

He ran a hand down his face, but even that felt like a great effort. "Thoroughly drained. Bringing a siren back from the brink of death takes quite a bit, as it so happens."

"You should be back to normal after some more rest." Her touch was gentle on his leg through the bedsheets. "That's not what I meant though. How are you feeling really?"

He had no idea how to answer that. How did he describe how just thinking about returning to his empty house filled him with equal parts dread and sorrow? Or that he'd miss how his body ached now? That he'd put off cleaning his bedsheets to keep the scent of petrichor in them a little longer?

"Bad," he mumbled after a beat. "I feel bad."

She nodded and squeezed his leg. "You know, when I nearly killed my partner, we didn't have phones or messengers yet. I'm thankful for that honestly. I probably would have been too tempted to reach out to her and just made it harder to let her go—for her to let me go, too."

He liked to think he'd have the self-control to leave things alone with Carver until the feelings settled. Or maybe they'd just never talk. Jian knew himself well enough to know that he would probably always be a conversation away from falling all over again.

"Have you talked to her since?" he asked.

Her gaze lowered. "We check in every so often. She's married now to a great man who makes her happy."

Part of him felt ill at the idea that he might move on with another while Carver was eternally alone. It seemed cruel.

"Don't let your relationship with Meallán dictate how you live your life," Saoirse cautioned, as if reading his thoughts. "Our lives are too long to spend them stuck in a moment, and I know my brother wouldn't want you pining over him forever."

Jian stared at the pillow beneath him. "I wouldn't. It just seems like insult to injury."

"He'll be all right. Time may not heal all wounds, but it lessens them." She smoothed his hair back from his face. "Thank you for loving my brother. For whatever it's worth, you're part of our little family now. Anything you need, I'll provide. You need only ask."

It was oddly affectionate for her, and he knew that she meant every word, solemn as a vow. A future where she might have been his sister-in-law flitted through his mind and disappeared like a dream half-remembered.

"Thank you, Saoirse," he rasped, throat suddenly tight.

She pressed her lips to his temple before standing. "I'll check in when I get to the north. Try to get some rest, yeah?"

He nodded minutely.

When she turned to leave, a hazy memory of whispered words bubbled up in his mind.

"Wait," he said.

She stopped to look back at him.

"What does...?" He paused as he tried to remember the words. "Santri... Alsh... Alshwa..."

"*Santrizuka alshwa'atii?*" she supplied.

He nodded. "Your brother said it earlier, but didn't translate."

Her gaze was almost pained, as she peered down at him. "It's usually said during bonding vows. There's no direct translation, but it roughly means 'Wait for me on the shores.' We live life alongside our mate and return to the silver shores together in death."

Jian's heart twisted in his chest. "I see. Thank you."

"Anything you need."

She continued out, shutting the door softly after herself.

◊◊◊

The apartment was quiet. Carver lay face down on his couch while Mouna kneaded his back. She hit a tender spot every so often where Jian had clawed a little too deeply, and then he'd feel especially miserable for a while until the numbness returned. It was truly pathetic. He hadn't been this distraught over someone since Thomas, and he still had ultimately married him.

Thomas appeared on the edge of the coffee table, sitting on it with his legs crossed. His curls were pulled back tightly, and he wore a red hoodie.

"We need to talk, Meallán," he said firmly.

Carver took a breath and let it out on a long sigh. "Can I not just wallow in my misery for a minute?"

"It's been two hours."

"Then surely you can wait a minute more."

Thomas flicked his nose, making him jump. Mouna chirped in protest at the sudden movement. Her claws lightly grazed his back as she kneaded him with new vigor.

"What did I tell you on the shores, Meallán?" Thomas asked, voice hard.

Carver groaned and squeezed his eyes shut, so he wouldn't have to look at his husband anymore. "I don't know. Every time I try to remember, it's like all sound vanishes from the memory."

Thomas' exhale was sharp and short. "May I try something?"

"Be my guest."

There was a light touch at Carver's cheek, and then warmth spread through the contact. He had the odd sense of falling. The thrill of it tightened around his stomach for a minute before it abruptly turned into sharp pain that bloomed through his side. His skin ached with claw marks that bled steadily.

He couldn't tell what was his own pain or Thomas'.

His eyes opened to a riverbank. Densely packed birch trees

surrounded him as he lay on damp earth. Sunlight streamed through the thick, green canopy. Water flowed by at his feet, but the amount of decay metal in him prevented him from healing with it. Saoirse heaved sobs beside him as she cradled a broken arm to her chest. Thomas appeared between the trees. His form was blurred as his tie to this world faded rapidly. Blood covered his body where bite marks sank into him. His arm had been torn off entirely. He was going to die, and Meallán was going to go with him.

"I'm sorry," Saoirse rasped as she crawled toward her brother. "I tried. I'm so sorry."

The earth below was starting to shift. His fingers sank into sand when he curled them. It glittered silver. He didn't have much time.

A gentle hand, calloused from years of smithing, cradled his cheek. He found the strength to look up into the brown eyes he'd woken up to every morning for thirty-five years. Thomas' mouth moved, but no sound came out.

The sands were creeping up around them, and Meallán wasn't sure if the water lapping at his legs was from the river or the dark sea. As if from a distance, his husband's voice reached his ears.

Break the bond.

The words were like ice through Meallán. He sank his fingers into the sand, wanting nothing more than to fall into it. He was so tired.

You can't leave her like this.

Thomas' voice was louder, more urgent. He'd always been the stronger of them.

"I can't," Meallán rasped. "I can't."

Try.

It was too much to ask. He was supposed to die with his mate, and there was no breaking a bond. He might as well have ripped himself in half.

Let me go.

Saoirse curled into him, as if to give him the only comfort she could while he left to the silver shores. Tears stung his eyes as he withdrew his mind from his husband's. Every part of him protested it, but he kept pulling away. The sands disappeared from under him as his nerves seemed to tear from his body. Ripping flesh off his own bones would have been easier. He was losing his sense of Thomas, unable to feel him more and more.

And then he felt nothing at all.

Saoirse sniffled into his shoulder. He weakly turned to wrap an arm around her waist and pull her to him. Every touch and movement brought the sensation of needles into his skin, but he ignored it and held her close. His breaths were ragged as he slowly lost feeling throughout his body. The sands didn't return for him. He almost wished they would, as he was certain he wasn't meant to be alive.

He opened his eyes to his living room. Mouna was still on his back, seemingly asleep. His head ached as he slowly pushed himself up. She jumped off him with a mewl of complaint. He sat upright and ran his hands over his face.

Breaking a bond was unheard of, and he couldn't be sure if he'd been successful or if Thomas had died part way through the process.

Either way, that probably explained how Carver had lived as long as he had.

Thomas stood in the kitchen, staring out the window over the sink. His posture was stiff while Carver came up to him.

"You didn't break the bond, not entirely," Thomas murmured. "If you had, I wouldn't be here."

Carver leaned on the countertop as his head throbbed. "You're not here."

Thomas glanced at him over a shoulder. "You know what I mean. This construct has been taking up space in your mind, and I don't belong here."

A knot formed in Carver's chest. "You have always belonged with me."

"Not now." Thomas turned and lifted his hands to cradle Carver's face. "I died, Meallán. I died a long time ago."

Carver's ribs constricted until he had trouble breathing. "I know."

Something of a smile touched Thomas's lips. "You can't tether to someone when you're already bonded. You have to let me go."

The truth of the words sat oddly in Carver's chest. He hadn't imagined life beyond his marriage, beyond bonding, but here he was anyway with a second chance. And it still hurt.

Carver hesitated before he pulled his wedding band off and set it on a counter. There was no pain that accompanied the loss of it. Thomas stood on his toes to bring their foreheads together. The touch was almost there, but not quite.

"You've wasted enough time," he murmured. "You deserve to

actually live."

Carver closed his eyes as he leaned closer. The lips at his were just a memory of what once was.

"I love you."

Thomas' voice was barely above a whisper.

Almost forty years of marriage, of a shared life and existence, and then a century of whatever this was—it seemed like too much to let go. But Carver had to, didn't he? For so long, this piece that inhabited his mind had existed like a phantom limb. It felt what was no longer there, and it belonged to a man who had died on the bank of that river outside their home. There was nothing to let go really. It'd been gone for over a hundred years.

Carver let the vestiges of his sense for his husband dissipate. It faded more and more, like sand slipping between his fingers, until there was nothing left. His kitchen was empty when he opened his eyes. For the first time in a long time, he felt truly alone. There was only himself in his thoughts and in his senses.

He rushed for his front door.

"What— Oof!"

Saoirse stumbled back when he collided with her on his doorstep. He managed to catch her around the waist, keeping her from falling. She peered up at him with a crease forming between her brows.

"You in a rush?" she asked. "I was just coming to let you know I'm leaving."

He held her tightly to him. If not for her, he really would have died with Thomas, and then she probably would have killed herself after discovering she was a khavira. They were alive now because of Thomas and his final wish. They were alive because she wasn't willing to give up when Carver was. They were alive because she loved him.

He owed her everything.

"I need to renew our promise," he said into the top of her head.

She pressed her cheek to his shoulder. "Worried about killing yourself again?"

"No, worried about you." He tightened his hold around her. "Don't leave me alone in this world."

She leaned into him. "I wouldn't. I promise."

He held her for a moment longer and then pulled away enough to meet her gaze. "Do you need a ride to the train station? Or are you good to go by yourself?"

She narrowed her intact eye. "I'm fine. Why? Where are you running off to?"

"The hospital."

Her brows rose. "Trying to kill him after all?"

He shook his head. "I don't think I'm a khavira, but I need to know for sure."

Shock crossed her face for a moment before it settled into something softer.

"Well, I guess it's good you'll be at the hospital," she said and jerked her head to the side. "Go on. He's waiting for you."

He kissed her forehead before hurrying past her to where his auto was parked.

Thunder had started to rumble on his way to the hospital. Light flashed through the dark clouds in the sky and disappeared again with a dull roar. The storm was getting closer as he sped through the city streets. He parked terribly when he finally got to the hospital, not caring to spend more time to fix it. Rain clung to him while he rushed through the grids of autos to the front doors.

The staff at the front desk hadn't changed shift yet since he'd left. They gave him odd looks as he turned straight to the stairs from the lobby. The Professor appeared beside him as he came to the second-floor landing. Her eyes narrowed at him, and he could almost sense her wariness.

"You sort something out for yourself?" she asked while she strode beside him.

He glanced at her. "I don't know. Maybe. I hope so."

They came to the third-floor landing, and he stared down the white halls with the weight of uncertainty pressing on his ribs.

"If this doesn't work," he said haltingly, "if I hurt him, is there anything you can do for him?"

Her gaze was soft. "Damian and I would do everything in our power to see him safe."

A different kind of fear crept up his throat as he made his feet move forward. He had no idea if he could tether safely and just proposing the idea seemed insane. If he was wrong, then Jian risked brain damage or worse. He'd survived the first attempt unscathed, but that didn't mean he would a second time.

But Carver kept going, moving through the halls until he found a door with 352 embossed on it. There was no response when he knocked, and he pushed it open anyway.

The room was dim. Only the windows on one wall provided illumination. Lightning flashed beyond it a moment before thunder rumbled through the floor. The scent of sea salt and petrichor was still thick in the air. Jian lay in the lone bed in the room. He was curled in on himself with the sheets up to his neck. A slight tremor ran through him.

Carver's heart dropped when he saw red streaks down Jian's cheeks.

"Meallán?" Jian murmured when he lifted his eyes.

Carver closed the door behind him and came close enough to crouch at the bedside. He carefully wiped at the blood tears on Jian's face. If he had his way, he'd never make him cry again.

"I'm sorry," he whispered. "I've hurt you."

Jian released a shuddering breath. "Why are you here? Isn't proximity difficult?"

The compulsion to tether was strong, but Carver swallowed it down. His finger traced over the half-healed bite marks he'd left in Jian's shoulder. He bore a matching one now.

"May I try tethering again?" he asked softly.

Jian went statue still. Thunder rumbled through the room again, but he didn't so much as flinch at it.

"What changed?" he murmured, voice barely above a whisper.

Carver glanced at the pale line around his finger. "I don't think I ever really lost my bond to Thomas, and I couldn't tether while bonded. But it… I think it's gone now."

Jian's brows furrowed. "That prevented you from moving on?"

"I hope so." Carver ran a thumb over where his ring once was. "He's been lingering in me, but I can't feel him anymore. There's just me."

A long silence stretched between them, save for the patter of rain outside. And then Jian laid a hand over the one at his shoulder. Light flashed behind him, silhouetting him for a second before thunder reverberated in the air.

"I trust you," he whispered. "You can try tethering again."

Carver leaned closer until he could press their foreheads together. His senses stretched out tentatively. At first, there was just an odd sensation of warmth, and then an ache built in his shoulder. There was a slight sting to it, like an open wound exposed to air. Fatigue was leaden in his limbs. The feelings didn't belong to him.

A gasp left Jian, but no pain touched him. The pulses of his surprise mixed with the sharp beginnings of panic. He gripped Carver's shoulder. A twinge ran through the bite wound there, and Jian sucked a breath through his teeth as he withdrew his touch, probably feeling the sting in his own skin. The tether hummed between them. It was strong, letting Carver sense Jian as easily as himself. And then something warm as sunlight bloomed where they touched.

"It worked," Carver breathed, not quite believing it.

Jian drew in a deep breath and let it out slowly. "Please tell me this means I can keep you. My heart can't take much more today."

Carver answered by closing the distance between their lips. The blood of a demon's tears was metallic in the kiss, but beyond it was a sweet smoke that he would have happily tasted for the remainder of his life. His heart beat against his sternum as a startled, almost manic laugh slipped from his chest. Warmth slid down his cheeks.

"I love you," he rasped against Jian's lips. "I love you, and I'm yours."

Jian was tense for a beat, and then his eyes squeezed shut as fresh tears fell from them.

"I'd wait for you on the shores, Meallán," he murmured.

It was almost a vow — a promise unto death. Someone else had promised Carver that once, and it'd been true, even if only for a moment. The words now unknotted the persistent dread that had followed him since he'd glimpsed the silver shores.

He would walk them again one day, but it wouldn't be alone.

ABOUT THE AUTHOR

V.T. Hoang did what all good, Vietnamese sons do and went to school to be a doctor, studying pre-med until he realized that he would rather do anything else, and he decided instead to take his biochemistry knowledge to the lab rather than medicine. That was expensive, though, so he was an editor of genre fiction for several years in order to pay the bills. Now, he writes his own stories.

As a transgender man of color, he seeks to add more stories with people like him to the world because he didn't have any growing up.

CONTENT WARNINGS

- Mentions of suicidal ideation and attempted suicide

- Mentions of past sexual assault

- Non-graphic depiction of attempted past sexual assault

- Minor depictions of psychosis and altered mental state

- Graphic depictions of violence

- Mentions of past torture and abuse

- Mentions and minor depictions of past intimate partner violence

- Mentions of structural racism and exploitation of a disenfranchised indigenous group

- Minor body horror

Made in the USA
Las Vegas, NV
26 August 2024

93745249R00208